UNDER THE AMBER WAVE

a Black Sun Novel

Shawn Brooks

Ninja Nomad Press

GET A FREE BOOK

Sign up for my newsletter below to get this Japanese cannibal ghost story.

For ebook readers, click this link: https://dl.bookfunnel.com/hlaez dpu8g

For print readers, go to my website here, and the sign-up form is the first thing you'll see: https://www.shawnbrookswrites.com/

SMALL BEGINNINGS

The sea was an open grave. Welcoming to all, discriminating of none. Beneath the violent waves, below the churning waters, how many souls had lost their way?

Upon the gray horizon, stretching past Mako's sight, there was no past and there was no future. There was only one moment, only a hideous and persistent now. What the present held for her, she didn't know. Yet she couldn't shake the ice that had filled her stomach, weighing her to the deck, paralyzed by fear.

She looked out into the endless expanse of water as the boat sped across it. Mist sprayed over the gunwale each time the vessel slammed into the sea. She could feel the salt clinging to her cheeks and her hair curling in the humidity. Her clothes were wet, but her throat was dry. She sat on a bench with a back support in front of the captain's chair. Strapped in a seatbelt.

Mako looked down at her enlarged stomach and gently placed her hands over the life inside.

The child, boy or girl, was also buried in the depths of her body. Just like the earth beneath the sea. Just like her future, in the horrible now.

Her heart told her to protect the child, to give it the future she could never have. She would have done it. Would've given everything for the baby. Yet, looking out at the infinite sea in front of her, she doubted that she'd see anything else ever again. Nothing would exist past this, not for her, anyway.

"Ryotaro," she said, her voice barely above a whisper, barely above a whimper.

He stared straight ahead from his position in the captain's seat under the canopy, hands gripping the wheel tightly. A smoldering nub of a cigarette hung loosely from his lips. His eyes were red. He hadn't shaved in days. His very aura gave off the air of a madman.

Mako cleared her throat. "Ryotaro."

His eyes met hers, and she winced at the intensity of the gaze.

"What?" he shouted over the chainsaw roar of the motor.

"Where are we going? You told me it would only be a few minutes, and it's been at least an hour, hasn't it?"

She remembered him telling her he had a special surprise for her. Some beach strip he wanted to take her to. Mako was never one for the outdoors but couldn't say no to Ryotaro. He was smiling when he pleaded with her to get on the boat, and when he smiled, no one could resist. The sun was shining. A warm wind blew through her shoulder-length hair. She was undeniably happy.

For the briefest moment, she thought he was going to finally leave his wife for her.

That was then; this is now. Here, in the middle of an uncaring sea, things like the past didn't matter. Clouds covered the sky, and the intense wind lashed her face. Happiness was not to be found here. All she could feel was despair.

Ryotaro hadn't said a word since they boarded the boat. Didn't look at her. Didn't even pretend to smile.

Mako glanced around. Five fishing poles were tied to the side. Sliding across the deck were a bucket for gutting fish and a steel rod for killing them. It hadn't been cleaned out in a while, by the looks of it. She gazed behind Ryotaro at the shoreline. The mountains surrounding the harbor were quickly shrinking to foothills. Soon, they would be mere smudges staining the canvas of the sky.

"Don't worry about it," Ryotaro said. He took his mad eyes off hers and gazed back at the sea. She felt some relief in this.

"My mother is going to worry about me."

He didn't reply.

The wind picked up and scattered her hair. Ryotaro piloted the vessel faster. The boat bounced off the water, and with each crash against the surface, she swallowed her breath.

"If this is about the baby, I won't tell anyone it's yours!" she cried into the wind, though she doubted her voice reached his ears because of the increased roar of the boat. Even if they had, they couldn't reach *him*. "I swear, your wife will never know. I'll keep it a secret."

Nothing. No movement on his face. No attempt to hear her words. His knuckles were white against the steering wheel. He bit through the rest of the cigarette, and it fell to the deck.

Mako knew that sleeping with a married man could have its consequences. But she never imagined this. This boat ride into infinity.

Ryotaro killed the engine. The sudden stop pushed Mako's body forward. The ragged seatbelt snapped. She covered her stomach with her arms. She smacked her head against the railing in front of her. Lightning crackled through her brain. She didn't feel pain—not yet—but she felt something thick and wet trickle down her face.

The boat rocked from side to side in the still water. The wind had also vanished. There was hardly a sound to be heard. The sudden change from speed and rest was unsettling.

She stood on shaking legs and wiped the blood off her face with the sleeve of her light blue blouse. Something she chose specifically for what she thought would be a fun day at the beach with the man she once, if not loved, had at least hoped would be her way out of the small town she was trapped in.

Her eyes scanned the environment. Mostly open water. The shoreline too distant for comfort.

To her left, there was a small island. There was hardly a beach to speak of: rock walls shot straight out of the sea on all sides of it. Atop the ridge, a few dead trees curled up towards the sky, their branches beckoning would-be travelers to crash upon the rocks like a siren. The island was the color of ash, with a few tar-black rocks spread throughout. No sandy beaches here. Only the hard and uncaring surface of some scorched alien piece of land that looked like it didn't belong on Earth.

"Take me home now!"

She stepped forward and kicked something. Looked down and saw the steel rod, coated in a dull red by the blood of countless fish. She picked it up.

With the weapon raised above her head, she repeated her demand.

Ryotaro got up. Mako's head only came up to his neck. His arms were twice the size of hers. Years of wrestling tuna out of the ocean chiseled him into an imposing man. He walked over to her.

"No!" Mako brought the rod down. Ryotaro stepped back. She flew forward and fell on the deck.

"It didn't have to be like this," he finally said as he took the rod out of her hand. "Sit down."

She got off the deck and sat back by the bow of the boat. "Please don't hurt my baby. *Our* baby!" She was choking back the sobs. Trying to sound firm. She didn't even convince herself.

Ryotaro struck the side of the boat with the rod. The sharp clang resonated in Mako's bones. Her hands shook as she pressed them over her stomach, tighter now. Anything, any act, to protect what was inside.

As long as he doesn't touch the baby.

Her mind raced through her options. Fighting back was meaningless. But she could always target his ego.

"You're nothing, know that?" Mako let out in a voice that did not feel like her own. It felt loud and firm. Almost strong. "Couldn't make it as a fisherman, couldn't make it as a husband, father, or even as a fucking man."

He looked down at his hands. Mako saw his lips quiver. Was he crying? Did he feel something akin to remorse?

"You don't understand; I have to do this," he said. Refusing to look her in the eyes.

Ryotaro lifted the metal rod and took a step forward. A flash of light reflected off the metal. They both covered their eyes against the intense glare.

Ryotaro dropped the rod and backed up, looking stunned.

Mako felt something warm coming from behind her. Despite not wanting to take her eyes off the man who meant her harm, she turned around. Dark clouds still covered the sun. But something glowed in the water.

A pink and golden light radiated from the water between the boat and the island. A reflection? Of what, the sun somehow? It warmed her skin, but something inside her chilled. No, it wasn't either of those colors. It was softer and at the same time brighter than they were. It was beautiful. It was terrifying. "Amber" was the word that came to her mind.

Mako's eyes widened, and her pupils dilated as she stared into the light. Her hands clutched her belly—her child — tightly. All warmth left her veins.

A shadow formed in the light.

"The ocean is an open grave," she said.

A sound of shoes scraping quickly against the wooden deck.

A tight grip around her neck.

Closing in tighter.

She couldn't breathe.

Then all was dark.

ONE

This is the end.

Junichiro chewed on those words in his mind as he held the coffee mug to his face. The warmth of the cup had died eons ago, but he felt some comfort in gripping it. Like it was the handrail on a bus about to crash into a cement barrier. It couldn't save him, but he could pretend that it would.

Sunlight bled into the apartment through its single window, from which he had a magnificent view of the next-door office building's dull white walls. His own walls were nothing to be proud of. Bulging yellow wallpaper, decades-old stains of unidentifiable origins, and maybe even the early signs of black mold spilling out over the ceiling near the air vents. He meant to take care of it all last spring, and he would someday, just not now. There were too many other important things to do.

It was muggy. Tokyo's summer was just kicking off, and the tidal wave of humidity poured into his home. His AC unit was ancient and regularly called it quits, like it did this morning. Not even 9 a.m. and he was already basting in his own sweat.

Fucking perfect.

In front of him, scattered about a dining room table that could seat exactly one, but, in fact, sat his family of three, was the source of his woes. Torn open envelopes. Letters with red warnings highlighted on their faces. The one nearest him:

DUE TO THE FAILURE OF MORTGAGE PAYMENTS, AND THE REPEATED FAILURES TO RESPOND TO NOTICES, SATOSHI-LIMITED HAS FILED SUIT. IF YOU WISH TO CONTEST THIS CLAIM, YOU MUST...

"Good morning," Haruka said as she glided past him, holding a basket of laundry. Her dyed auburn hair reflected the little daylight that stole its way into the dim room.

The coffee mug came down hard on top of those red letters of doom, almost spilling out the tepid caffeine across them.

Junichiro, *Juni* to all his friends, was once a man in love, if rumors were true. Wildly so. But the years passed and kids changed everything. He barely registered her presence in the kitchen.

"Hey, is everything okay?"

She put the basket down on the sink counter and came over to him.

"What? Oh, yeah. Good morning."

Haruka stared at the collection of papers under the mug. Juni knew she wasn't an idiot and had probably already guessed what was going on. But he couldn't show them to her, not yet. There was still time to fix this. There had to be.

Juni stood and plastered on the best smile he could force. "Hey, we should all head to the countryside this weekend. It would be good for you to get out of this apartment. Mayu needs a city break too. Maybe we could hit up a farm and play with some goats or chickens or something. You know, she really needs new friends."

Juni laughed at his own joke.

Haruka smiled, but her eyes weren't in it. She still cast them down at the buried secrets beneath the cold coffee.

"Juni, is there something you need to say to me?"

"What? Of course not."

"Juni," she said, with a new gravity weighing down her voice.

"You've been acting like I'm hiding an affair or something lately." His face flushed red. His voice rose.

"I'm not accusing, but you're obviously—"

"Papa!"

The high-pitched voice echoed off the walls of the room.

Juni smiled and called out, "Is the monster awake?"

"Maybe, no, yes," came the voice from the back rooms of the apartment.

As Haruka looked towards the sound, Juni slipped the letters from under the mug and into his pockets. He could always throw them away later. He got up, went into the hallway, and entered the first room on the left. A red stuffed dragon hit him in the face. He caught it, roared, and tackled the little girl who threw it at him.

"Mai-Mai, don't you dare throw dragons at me ever again." Juni lifted the girl and pretended to eat her tummy. She squirmed and screamed with delight. The sound of her giggles eroded the anxiety that had been growing in his mind all morning.

At least for a moment.

When he put his daughter back down and saw her run back to fetch her dragon, Keke the Wonderful, her trustworthy companion that went everywhere she did — the worry flooded his mind again. Seeing her innocent face pained him all the more considering what he had discovered.

Reminded him of what he could lose.

"Okay, missy, time to get ready for school," Haruka said from the hallway.

Mayu pouted and hugged Keke the Wonderful so hard that had it been alive, it surely wouldn't have been any longer. Just like her pet goldfish a year back, but he didn't like to recall that particularly ugly episode. Not an easy task consoling a five-year-old child and explaining why taking a fish for a walk was a bad idea.

Juni ruffled Mayu's long black hair. "Come on, baby, do as Mama says and you'll get ice cream after you come home."

Haruka stared at Juni with the intensity of the sun. Mayu screamed and laughed and ran out of the room, Keke the Wonderful in tow, the dragon's face slamming into the wall as the girl sprinted wildly away.

"Juni, we've talked about this; you can't keep giving her these bribes."

"Well, if I did that, I'd have to stop spoiling you too." He smiled and kissed her left cheek. She pushed him away. Her face tried to show anger, but she couldn't repress the smile that finally broke through.

If Juni was skilled in nothing else, it was in making people smile. Sure, he was shit with money and even worse as a husband, but Haruka forgave him every time he flashed that dynamite smile at her. If only he could call upon that magic now to do battle with Satoshi-Limited.

"What time will you be home for dinner?" Haruka asked.

"Ah, I probably have to put in some overtime tonight, so maybe around eight." And by overtime he meant "dealing with the problem on the kitchen table."

It wasn't even his fault, really. All he ever wanted to do was give his family the best life. A better home. Give Mayu a happy future. So what if he tried to do it his way? Why punish him for trying to do right by them?

True, the loans he took out on the house far outstripped his income. But with a teacher's salary, what else could he do? His side-gig also ate up his spare cash, for now at least.

One day it'll pay back.

Has to.

Haruka slipped out of Mayu's room, and Juni stood there alone. The neon-pink curtains and the mountain of stuffed animals swallowing up the bed made him smile. Evidence that his little girl was happy.

For now.

He had to go to work, but his mind was on what he had to do afterward.

I have to fix this.

Ka-chuck, ka-chuck, ka-chuck.

Steel balls fired out of the passage and landed in the tray with ferocity, as if fired from a machine gun.

Hot fluorescent lights of many colors seared Juni's eyes. He didn't even blink. Didn't even care. This required focus.

Electric beeps and jingles almost drowned out the sound of the large man seated next to him, breathing so heavily through his cigarette smoke. Juni, for a moment, wondered if he'd pass out then and there.

Ka-chuck, ka-chuck, ka-chuck.

The pachinko balls fell down, smacked into the gold pins, and missed the catcher.

"Shit," he said under his breath. The heavy smoker glanced over at him and nodded in solidarity.

Juni had two thousand yen worth of pachinko balls on his card tonight. The black hole of empty promises had already swallowed much of what he had. But he shoved the card into the reader one last time. He made ten thousand just last week. He knew he could do it again, just one more time, just one more chance.

The card went in. A cartoon of a maid in a skimpy outfit played on the screen, cheering him on as he pulled the knob. The balls fired away.

Ka-chuck, ka-chuck, ka-chuck.

Every single ball missed the target. The card was now empty. As was his mind.

Juni leaned back in the hard plastic seat and cracked his back. He rubbed his eyes and put his forehead against the machine. The man next to him said nothing, but he could feel eyes of understanding, maybe even empathy, resting on him. Eyes that said, "Yeah, buddy, I get it, you lost, and you'll probably lose tomorrow again, but what can we do? Someday we will win, right?"

Juni had been coming here for months now after work. And the sick thing was that he didn't even like gambling back then. But put a needle in a man's arm for long enough and he'll love anything you shoot up his veins.

The bank's letter crowded his already stretched mind. Juni needed cash fast, and he needed it by last Tuesday.

Maybe I can ask Nakamura for an advance on my salary?

He laughed. Had anything so daring been attempted in Japan before? He couldn't even imagine his elderly boss lifting a single arthritic finger to help him.

Juni got out of his seat, nodded at the smoking man, now lost in his own world of bright lights and empty dreams, and walked down the aisle to the bathroom. The husk of a human being filled almost every single seat. Most of them were men in their forties on up, though a few women of the same age range could be seen here and there. Aside from the young worker girls carrying pachinko balls in trays, all while balancing on high heels and maneuvering in mini-skirts, Juni was the youngest person there.

Fucking great, he thought to himself. *Exactly where I thought I'd be in my thirties.*

The future awaiting Juni, found in those wrinkled faces, those heavy purple bags under their eyes, and those unwashed clothes, lit a fire under his ass, and he sped until he got to the bathroom. Another second spent looking at what he could become was too much for him.

He peed, washed his hands, and stood half bent over the sink, staring at himself in the murky mirror, stained by some unknown gray substance. He used to think of himself as handsome, and maybe he still was, somewhere under the weariness masking his face. Whenever he told people he taught high school science for a living, without fail they all made the same remark: "No way! You look like you should coach baseball or soccer."

He took it as a compliment then. But he had no interest in sports. Or science, for that matter.

Juni laughed as he stared into his eyes. "Then why the fuck are you teaching it, huh? Why the fuck are you doing any of this shit?"

A dirty and cramped apartment. A wife he no longer loved but pretended to. A job he hated. It was all a joke. His whole life was smeared the same way this mirror was, shat on by missed opportunities.

He stood up straight, tightened the tie around his neck, and left the bathroom. The stark contrast between the dark toilet and the supernova of the pachinko parlor almost made him gag.

"Yes!" came a gruff voice that sounded like it had been sandpapered down. An alarm and a siren went off. It was the smoking man; he was smiling and clapping his hands above his head.

Lucky bastard.

Juni nearly jogged his way out of the room and came out on the sidewalk. The parlor may have been a sensory overload, but at least it was air-conditioned. The June air in Tokyo, even at night, wrapped him like a warm and wet blanket.

He turned to the right and began walking. Not too many people out, five or six others with him on the sidewalk. A young couple, the girl wearing some cosplay bunny outfit; the boy wearing baggy jeans, his hairstyle blond and more expensive than anything Juni had ever doled out for a haircut. A man holding a briefcase, his face staring off into oblivion. Another man, Juni's age, wearing track pants comically contrasted with his expensive-looking leather shoes and sunglasses. He was leaning back against the wall of a building, arms crossed, observing the crowd.

This detail lodged itself in his brain. It was already 9 p.m., so what the hell was he wearing sunglasses for? Juni passed the man and kept on walking. He heard the scuffling of shoes on the pavement behind him. The man with the briefcase stopped walking and parked his ass on a bench at a bus stop.

The clack of the sunglasses-man's shoes was steadily keeping pace behind him. Juni was walking home in a neighborhood that didn't see a lot of foot traffic. There were streetlights on here, but he knew once he turned down the last street to his apartment, there'd be none.

Juni stopped and turned around. The man in sunglasses also stopped.

"Do you need something?" Juni asked.

The man smiled but said nothing.

Juni tried to stare him down, but the man just stood there. Unwavering.

"Just... stop it, okay?"

Juni moved on, and the man continued to follow.

The couple in front of Juni stopped. The girl was crying and shoved a smartphone into the boy's face. He couldn't look her in the eye.

Somebody's learning about infidelity at a young age.

Juni wanted to stop with them, maybe give the boy some life advice, and let the sunglasses-man pass. But there was no socially acceptable way to do that, so he kept on walking. Soon, the cries of both the girl and the boy became distant. But the clack of the shoes did not change pace or rhythm. The footsteps didn't care about being noticed.

Juni turned around again and took a step towards the man.

"If you keep following me, you'll regret it."

Aside from smiling, the man made no other move and said nothing. He didn't flinch at Juni's attempt at intimidation. Juni would not throw the first punch and get arrested.

"Fuck. Off."

Juni turned left onto a small street only residents should be on. No shops or anything else that could attract a visitor. The clacking footsteps followed. Juni took the next right turn, intentionally going the wrong way. He could always double back later. The steps followed.

The clacking was much closer now. If he turned around, he might even brush up against the man. Where could he go?

Go straight home and I could lose this guy behind the security gate to the building, but then he would know where I live or could push himself inside the gate when I opened it.

Or keep walking in a dark neighborhood and just hope that he goes away? Walk to a police box? Too far. Guess a fight it is.

Juni spun on his heels, his fists balled up, ready to go.

The man had his hands in his pockets, and he was smiling; the glint of a few silver teeth flashed in the dim streetlight. Juni could see his own reflection in the man's sunglasses and hated how stupid he looked with his fists clenched at his sides.

"What do you want?" Juni asked.

The man half-walked, half-slouched his way forward. Juni held his ground. The man came within a few inches of his face and put his hand on Juni's left shoulder. Juni could smell the acrid beer and nicotine on his breath.

He spoke with humor-filled familiarity, "Mr. Hatayama, my boss, is a very patient man, but you've pushed him too far. He's very upset with you."

Oh fuck.

"I'm sorry. Please tell Aido-sama I'll have his mon—"

The man punched Juni in the stomach.

"Oh, I know you will, because you have to, because we know where you live. We know which school your daughter goes to. We know every fucking move you make. So yes, you will have the money by...?"

The man was holding on to his shirt. Juni was bent forward, recovering from the blow. He thought for half a second about decking the guy right between those stupid sunglasses. Maybe he'd get lucky and break them, and his eyes would get stabbed by the shards.

No, that was useless. There was no fighting this.

"By next week. Monday. I promise."

The man let go of Juni's shirt and took a step back. The yellow streetlight shrouded the man's black clothes, giving him a murky and ill-defined look, made all the more sinister because of his sunglasses, as if a demon from an alternate dimension were standing there.

"Four days? And you'll have it all?"

"Yes, yes, I will. But don't you fucking come near my home—"

A slap across his face. The stinging pain blinded Juni to the man's next movement. A fist smashing into his right eye.

"Oh my God, what happened?" Haruka said, staring at him in horror.

"Nothing, I just got hit with a tennis ball at club."

She almost said something else. The words were halfway out of her mouth, but she cut them off. "Oh, that's awful. Let me get you some ice."

Seeing Juni's eye swollen, speckled with blood, was nearly the tipping point for her. Haruka had kept her mouth shut for so long, she almost forgot why. She grabbed some ice out of the freezer and wrapped it in a hand towel.

"Daddy, you okay?" Mayu said as she came walking down the hallway, rubbing the sleep out of her eyes, dangling Keke the Wonderful in tow.

That's why.

The pained expression on Juni's face ripped Haruka's heart as well. He bent down and kissed Mayu's forehead.

"Yeah, I'm okay, honey, just had an accident at work."

"Accident? Then Keke can fix it." She smushed the dragon onto her father's face and made a kissy sound. The action must have stung Juni's black eye, but he didn't wince or push the toy away.

"Ah, thank you, Mai-Mai, I think I'm all better now." She laughed and skipped away towards the kitchen with renewed energy, the source of which none of the adults could hope to fathom. He looked at Haruka, guilt painted over the bruised eye, grabbed the ice from her hands, and went to the bedroom.

Juni loved Mayu; she knew that, and that was the only thing keeping them together. She knew the finances were fucked. She knew her husband was unraveling at the seams. But she said nothing. She hated herself for that, but she couldn't find the strength to do anything about it.

She never could.

Worst-case scenario? Divorce him and move back in with Mom.

Not ideal, but there was an escape route out of this mess. She hated to think about what that would do to Mayu, and for that reason only, she held on.

Haruka went into the kitchen and saw Mayu sipping out of an orange juice container she'd pilfered from the fridge.

"Hey, you know you're not supposed to do that."

"Daddy lets me."

For fuck's sake.

"Well, I'm not Daddy." She took the juice from Mayu and put it back in the fridge. Tears welled in Mayu's eyes, but Haruka closed herself off to them. "Off to bed now." She watched as her daughter complied, thankfully not erupting into a fit this time.

She looked down the hall at the closed bedroom door. Yeah, right, no help coming from there. Haruka finished doing the dishes; she had paused when Juni got home.

A black eye? What is he, sixteen?

She pulled out the trash bag, tied it, and set it by the front door for early-morning drop-off. She went through the to-do list for tomorrow: make Mayu's lunch, iron Juni's shirt, take Mayu to school.

The list became opaque and dragged her mind down into weariness.

The apartment was silent. She went over to the window without a view. The neighbor's wall. The small alleyway down below. Lovely sights.

This was life. The same routine day in and day out.

And this is what you gave up the job at the hospital for.

She felt like crying. Or drowning the tears in a half-bottle of wine. Or of waking Juni up and giving him a matching set of black eyes.

Instead of doing any of those things, she pulled out the piece of paper she'd gotten from the trash that morning and hidden behind the toaster. It was crumpled and had a circle of coffee stains on its center.

"Satoshi-Limited," she said in a whisper. So these were the last words her once-happy family would hear before everything was taken from them. And it wasn't just the bank, was it? Her husband's black eye spelled out something else; he must have gotten in with loan sharks too.

Before going to bed, Haruka quietly packed a small suitcase while her husband snored. She filled it with enough clothes and toiletries for her and her daughter to live off for a few days.

Just in case.

There was no room for Juni's things.

TWO

"Come on, guys, take this seriously."

Dead pigs lay out on steel plates. Their insides opened for all the world to see. Teenage boys poked the organs with metal tools and screeched like wild boars; the girls screamed and wished to God for it all to end.

Juni moved from table to table, trying to focus the mob on the task at hand.

"This looks like your wife, Mr. Hatayama," said a boy with spiky red hair. Ryusuke, captain of the soccer club and son of privilege, was leaning back in his seat as if he didn't have a spinal cord while holding up the pig in front of his face.

"Mr. Sakai, you can make out with the dead pig on your own time," Juni said.

Laughter erupted and Ryusuke dropped the animal onto the plate with a sickly *thump* sound. He used his thumb to lift his nose at Juni.

Oh, the joys of the job, he thought.

He moved on to a table of six girls, all of whom were on their phones posing with their fingers in peace signs and recording themselves. Juni saw panda ears on one girl's head in her camera frame. "Ms. Ito, could we please focus on the very real animal in front of us and not on making videos where you pretend to be one?"

She clicked her tongue and gave off a scoff that said, "Back off, lower-class scum."

Please God, don't let Mayu grow like this.

Juni grabbed the girl's phone and put it in his pocket.

"Give it back!" she yelled.

Juni ignored her and moved to the next student, hands out, demanding the phone. The kids protested and moaned, but no one resisted, not with force at least.

"You will all get your precious little phones back at the end of the day. I'm sure all the Tiks and all the Toks will be there when you come back."

Juni stood at the front of the classroom, unloading the phones onto a table, laughing at his own joke. Most of the students stared blankly back at him as if he were an alien life form. He didn't mind much; he didn't need them to laugh back. As long as he could amuse himself from time to time, that was enough. His mind was always on another planet from the moment he entered Saga Science Junior and Senior High School every morning. It was the only way to survive.

But small mercies are sometimes given out to the undeserving. Ami, his favorite student, burst out laughing. The boys seated on either side of her gave a disgusted look and slightly leaned away from her. Ami's face, beneath her bowl-cut bangs, lit up with joy.

And so did Juni's. Students like Ami were as rare as finding diamonds at the beach. Even so, he appreciated her response. It was in the rare moments like this when he halfway thought he liked his job.

But then the other half comes into play.

"Sir, honestly, do we even need to be learning any of this? And from you? My dad says you're a dropout from Tokyo University, so what kind of role model are you supposed to be?" The polar opposite of Ami, Ryusuke, the boy who just couldn't let things go. For two long years, Juni had suffered this kid in his homeroom, wishing he'd either hurry and graduate already or just drop out.

"And what happened to your face? Did you get into a fight?" came a voice from another corner of the room.

"Yeah, it looks like you tried to put on eyeshadow."

A shit-eating grin appeared on Ryusuke's face, too similar to Juni's own plastic smile, annoying him to no end.

Juni smiled and refused to respond. He might not stop the flood of emotion if he let it out, and that feeling scared him. He had to keep control.

He was doing great, too. The insults bounced off his armor-plated ego. Aside from the rare mutations like Ryusuke, he'd never had a class that didn't love him by the end of the year. He just needed time to work on them.

This would not be forthcoming.

As Juni turned his back to the students to write out the weekend's homework assignment on the board, time slowed down. The first thing he noticed was the gasp. It might have come from Ami; he wasn't sure. In what could only have taken two seconds, he felt minutes move by in morose fashion, the torture of those moments amplified by the humidity in the room, until he felt the wet and rubbery thud against his back. It didn't hurt him at all, but it took the breath out of him. He knew what had just happened. With horror, sadness, and dismay, he looked down and saw the fetal pig by his feet. Ryusuke's hyena laugh pierced the stunned silence in the room.

Nobody else laughed.

On any normal day, Juni would have let it slide. He would have shot back at the kid with an indefatigable smile and let it go. But like an elephant walking across thin ice, the pressure of the last few days was too much.

He snapped.

Juni took the ruler from the chalkboard and marched over to Ryusuke's desk. The kid looked up at him with arms crossed and defiance burning in his eyes. "What? I didn't do—"

Juni struck the ruler on Ryusuke's desk, nearly breaking it in two. The boy jumped and nearly fell out of his chair.

"You little shit, you think your daddy knows a fucking thing about success? Role models? Your dad's been fucking whores behind mommy's back for at least a year now. How do I know? He brags about it during PTA drinking nights." The kid's face dropped, and Juni could see the insecurity that lived inside those eyes. He didn't give a shit. He was going in for the kill. Juni grabbed Ryusuke by the necktie and pulled him close. "You want to fuck around with someone, I don't care anymore, fuck this job, you can meet me outside if you think you're so big." Juni let go and dropped the ruler on the ground.

He walked back to the front of the room, smiling. His rage had found an outlet. Turning around, he caught sight of Ami's once-lively face, lips now downcast, eyes wet, skin pale. Juni's own face mirrored hers at that moment. She couldn't bear to look at him descending into this stupid rage.

Oh shit.

The once-dead classroom came alive with the insect buzz of gossip. Friends texted each other from devices Juni missed during his purge; others leaned into the ears of their neighbors; Ryusuke had completely melted into his chair, face now sun-fire red, tears on the verge of spilling out over his face.

I guess I'm done.

"Hatayama-san, in my office, now." Principal Nakamura didn't wait for Juni to respond and instead slammed the door to the classroom shut.

He was alone in the science lab, cleaning up the leftover trays from the dissections.

He had never done anything like this before. Sure, not all the kids liked him, but enough did. And he was always reliable. Always got his grades in on time. Worked well with the parents. Never missed a single duty doled out by the Principal. Would it be fair to fire him for one misstep?

Everything is falling apart at once. May as well get it over with.

Yet a secret part of him reveled in what happened. He hated his job, and this might be the way out of it. Out of the slave-like club system of unpaid overtime teaching boys tennis. Out of the mandatory drinking parties with most other teachers either twice his age or half of it.

Mayu's face brought him back to reality. It would be nice to fuck off out of this place and never look back. But what would happen to *her* if he did? He didn't care about himself in this moment, but he couldn't abandon her. Whatever he had to promise his boss, however low he had to bow his face to that dusty carpet, he'd do it. He'd lick her shoes to keep this job.

He went out of the room and walked down the hall to the Principal's office at the end. Baseball trophies lined the hallway; the teams had won the newest ones over six years ago. A placard of the school's charter hung outside Principal Nakamura's door. A long-winded speech about the values of discipline and honesty in making a bright and industrious Japan. Dust covered the worn glass frame. The hall lights flickered. The bathroom he had just passed smelled of bleach and ammonia. The entire corridor gave off a slight green hue that made him sick to his soul.

He knocked on the door. A muffled bark shot back, one which he assumed meant, "Come in and be berated."

Nakamura was sitting behind her desk, looking like a child playing as an adult because of her diminutive stature. The carpet in the room was a faded lime green from the 70s, spotted with decades, if not a full fifty years, of tea and coffee stains. A stuffed deer was in the corner adjacent to her desk, its lifeless eyes observing the comings and goings of generations of the school's fine leadership wallowing behind that same desk.

"Sit."

Juni closed the door behind him and sat down on a tattered chair covered in aged felt.

"Do you know why you are here?"

"If it's about what happened in class today, I'm sorry; it wasn't like me. It won't happen again, I promise."

Nakamura raised her stenciled-on eyebrows. If she had been younger—much younger—the act would have wrinkled her forehead. As things were, it was difficult to tell if her face was showing any emotion at all.

"What are you talking about? I've heard nothing. Never mind. It's about this letter that came today."

She took out a manila-colored envelope, already opened, and placed it on the desk.

Juni's heart raced, and his throat tightened. Had the bill collectors been contacting his employer directly? Was it the sunglasses-man? He figured he had to be connected to the shady loan he took from the pachinko parlor. His instincts screamed yakuza or some other low-level gang involvement, but he took it anyway. It was the only way he'd been able to pay for groceries and utilities these past six months. Had they been harassing his boss? No matter what, he couldn't lose his job on top of everything else that was happening. No matter how much he hated it.

"Do you know what this is?" Nakamura asked.

Juni took a deep but silent breath, smiled, and said, "I have no idea."

Nakamura studied him through her ancient eyes, half-closed because of exhaustion or the lack of musculature in her face.

"We can't be getting your personal mail here, especially of this nature, Hatayama-san."

"Well, can I see what it is? I'm sure this is a misunderstanding."

She held on to the envelope. "Misunderstanding? Hatayama-san, legal affairs of this nature should be sent to your home, not to our school."

Juni felt a lift of scorn and pride. "If it's a legal matter, then why did you open it?" His voice teetered on the edge of a shout. The dam to his rage had already cracked an hour ago; he felt the water pour through the cracks even quicker now. It would take only a nudge to set him off again.

Nakamura's already sour face soured even more and became down-right acidic. "Because, Hatayama-san, it was addressed to me."

What? All the scenarios of loan sharks, of thugs in striped running pants and black-and-gold jackets, came to his mind. Had they been pressuring his boss behind his back, to what? To humiliate him? To scare him?

She slid the envelope over the glossy film covering the wooden desk. He grabbed it and took out the letter inside. White noise filled his head as he tried to regain his thoughts and read what was in front of him.

Images of losing his job then and there, of losing his home, of losing his family, blocked out the words on the page as he unfolded it. He closed his eyes, took in another deep breath, and began reading the notice.

MR. HATAYAMA, YOU HAVE BEEN SUMMONED TO APPEAR...

Summoned? Shit. He went on, skimming through the letter.

...ON SATURDAY JUNE 8TH, 9 AM, 2024, AT THE OFFICE OF...

The white noise started screaming inside his brain.

...TO DISCUSS THE LAST WILL AND TESTAMENT OF HATAYAMA RYOTARO...

Wait, what is this? He read on, a sudden feeling of weightlessness overtook him, so great he felt his body float up into the stratosphere.

...WHO PASSED AWAY ON THE EVENING OF TUESDAY MAY 28TH, 2024...

He was reading about the news of his father's death. Apparently, just a week ago. The first time he had heard about it.

...THE FUNERAL HAS ALREADY BEEN CONDUCTED AS PER THE REQUEST OF MR. HATAYAMA'S ESTATE. YOU ARE REQUESTED TO ATTEND THE READING OF THE WILL IN MUTSU CITY, AOMORI PREFECTURE, ON THE AFORE-MENTIONED DATE...

Not his debts, not him losing his job, but the passing of the old man.

Tears ran down his face, and his hands shook as he read the letter.

Nakamura's face softened, almost as if she was about to offer her condolences.

"Hatayama-san, if you need a moment in private?"

"Could I? If it's not too much trouble for you?"

Nakamura lifted herself out of the seat and walked past him. She gently placed her hand on his shoulder for a moment and kept on walking out of the room.

Upon hearing the door shut, Juni clutched the letter to his chest and looked up at the moldy ceiling.

With tears pouring down his face, he smiled wider than he had ever done in his life. He had to fight to suppress the fit of laughter that rose in his throat.

"Thank you, God."

THREE

"Why are you so happy?" Haruka asked him, her eyes wet with tears.

"Because this is the answer we've been waiting for," Juni replied. The oppressive burden of the morning had evaporated into nothing. His violent outburst against Ryusuke was a distant memory.

He was so happy, he could see himself jumping up on the table, which just the morning before had been filled with red-stamped papers of death, and dance without an ounce of shame. Haruka stared at him with curiosity when he came home. He was almost skipping as he walked.

They had just finished dinner, and Mayu was asleep when Juni told his wife that his father was dead. She didn't take the news well. Family was family or some shit like that.

"Juni, I'm confused. Your father is dead and you're sitting there smiling? Come on, even I'm sad about this, and I only met the man once. He was your father. And why are you just hearing about this now? You find out through a letter not even addressed to you?"

"You know, my Dad and I, we never talked. I have no one else, no other family, Haruka. Mom is dead. No aunts, or uncles, or cousins. It makes sense that no one told me because there is no one. The lawyer probably just found out where I worked through Dad's will or something."

"Then why was the letter sent to Nakamura-sensei personally?"

"Dad hated me. And the feeling is fucking mutual. Was mutual? Anyway, he probably set this up to cause trouble for us. He always liked to embarrass me somehow. But the thing is, honey, we are out of trouble now. Things are finally going to get better."

He took Haruka's hands in his and pulled her close. She resisted and took her hands back. Her downcast eyes clashed with his feverish outburst. He knew he needed to explain things to her right now, on the spot.

"Honey, I haven't been able to pay the mortgage for six months."

She held her gaze down at her hands, her fingers interlocked tightly over one another.

"I know."

Juni's eyes widened, and his face dropped. "How?" His voice rose more sharply than he had intended.

"You're not exactly as smooth as you think you are. I've seen the notices in the trash from time to time. And the way you try to hide your feelings and pretend everything is okay is obvious. I've been waiting for you to bring it up with me."

Juni leaned back in his chair with his hands behind his head. "Alright, everything's on the table, then. We were days away from losing the apartment. The bank started the foreclosure process, but it's not a done deal yet. Dad was loaded. I'm the only remaining family, and I'm sure he had no friends. I'm getting it all, honey—his whole estate. My boss already gave me a week to take care of things. You should have seen Nakamura's face. I didn't think she could look more like a prune."

Juni laughed. In fact, he had been suppressing his laughter ever since he had gotten home from work. Now he let it out with near-maniacal abandon. Haruka didn't react. She stayed plastic in her expressions.

"Juni, banks don't send people to punch debtors in the face. There's more you're not telling me."

"My eye? Like I said, that was an accident at work. That doesn't matter. All we have to focus on is paying back the bank, I promise."

Haruka smiled, but not in the way of a loved one sharing a moment of happiness. Her eyes were miles away. She looked like a patient at an old folks' home, smiling at the wall, remembering times long past.

Juni failed to notice or care about her aloofness and continued, "I'll leave tomorrow, attend the hearing the next day, and come home right away. The meeting with the lawyer is in Mutsu City, so I don't even need to go all the way home to Tanosawa. The funeral has already happened. I can't imagine anyone actually setting one up, but if it happened, no one told me about it, and I'm fine with that. I go for the hearing, get the money, and then I can pay off the debts and we can even move out of this shitty apartment, and get something bigger and nicer. Get Mayu into a good school. I can quit my job and-"

"Juni, stop. You don't know what your dad left you. And since when did our life here become so 'shitty' that you want to change it? This is the first I've heard of any of this."

"First off, I'm getting everything. I know it. Secondly, of course, I don't mean my life with you and Mayu. I mean," he looked around the room and waved his hands in wide circles, "this cramped shithole. The train that keeps us up at night. The weird wetness in the air that never leaves no matter how much we crank the AC. You want a better life, don't you?"

"I get what you're saying. And I hope you get what you think you will from your father. But never, not once, did I think our life was so terrible. Was it really so bad with us?"

"Of course you didn't; you don't know what it's like to have something better and have to move down in life. I mean, us together is great; it's just this," he gestured once again around the room.

Juni knew he had crossed a line here. Haruka came from humbler beginnings than he did. He'd resolved never to bring it up to her, never to make her feel like she was lower class, but here he was, breaking that promise.

Haruka let out a sound from her throat that bordered on a sob, maybe even a shout, but she choked it out by keeping her mouth closed tight.

Regaining composure, she said, "You're so worried about being like your father that you'll end up just like him. And to get your mind off the money, I'll get a part-time job, and we can always move to a cheaper place until we get back on our feet. And don't forget us, or you'll end up losing more than this 'shitty' apartment."

She got up and left the room.

He watched her until she disappeared into the hallway. He looked at the letter once more. All he had to do was go back to Aomori Prefecture tomorrow, spend the night at a hotel in town, and then take care of all the legal matters the following day. He couldn't suppress the smile that had taken hold of him.

Only one line of the summons bothered him, one he hadn't been able to read in Nakamura's office due to his excitement.

...YOU WILL RECEIVE FURTHER INSTRUCTIONS ABOUT THE TERMS AND CONDITIONS OF THE WILL BY THE MORNING OF JUNE 7TH, 2024, AT YOUR PLACE OF RESIDENCE...

So Dad knew his address and where to send the letter. The only reason Juni could think of for why he sent it to his boss was exactly what he told

Haruka: to humiliate him. One final stab at Juni's ego before the old man lost all ability to influence events.

The weird waiting around for second instructions? Also on par with what Juni expected out of his Dad. He was confident he'd get the money, all of it. Well, maybe some of it will go back into Dad's estate, but there's so much that even half of it would be more than enough.

Juni walked over to the cabinets above the kitchen sink. On the top shelf, too high for Haruka to reach without a stepladder, from behind a bag of old British tea bags, he pulled out a bottle of Yamazaki Whiskey.

Two ice cubes from the freezer, a dash of carbonated water, swirled together, he took the drink to the tiny living room. No chairs or sofas to sit on, so he plopped down on the tatami mat in front of the laptop-sized TV resting on top of a rickety coffee table.

He turned it on and flipped through the channels with the remote.

Late-night variety shows with celebrities famous for nothing more than inventing some dumb catchphrase.

Change.

An interview with an old farmer about how the recent heat has destroyed his oranges.

Next.

A news report about an incoming typhoon, set to hit Tohoku on June 9th.

Thank God I'll be out of there before that happens.

Turn off.

Juni downed some of the whiskey and looked at the wall behind the TV. Some of Mayu's artwork was taped over the fading wallpaper. Most of it was of Keke the Wonderful, Mayu riding her like some dragon warrior princess. One was of the family, with a big pink heart drawn around the three of them, with purple butterflies shooting out of the heart like comets.

He imagined framing them properly and hanging them on wide walls. Not walls that bubbled in the humidity and sweat obscured brown stains from the upstairs apartment. Clean walls. Sturdy and thick ones. Ones that could properly block out the fighting couple next door and the horns honking below. Four of them supporting a massive home in the country. A castle for him and his daughter.

For a moment, he felt hot shame for not including Haruka in the fantasy. When he tried to jam her image into the castle of dragon princesses, something just felt off. Juni thought about her last words before she went to bed: "You're worried about being like your father."

Of course I am. The man was a monster. But if I get that money, I can get us out of here, babe. I can build a life that means something.

He smiled and downed the rest of the whiskey.

FOUR

Juni rolled over in bed and failed to find his wife beside him. Her spot was already cold. He was so used to being the first one up for years that this new reality startled him.

Birds sang their songs of morning greeting. Juni could smell fresh coffee being made. Now that he had a week off from work, he could just stay in bed. A childlike giddiness took hold of him like he was playing hooky from school and pretending to be sick.

He rolled forward and sat up. He'd have to get ready, though, big day ahead. Juni looked at the bedside clock, 8:35. The letter should arrive soon. Then, he'd have to buy a shinkansen ticket to Aomori, pick up the rental car already reserved at the station—already purchased through taking on even more credit card debt—and drive the three hours to Mutsu City, check into the hotel, and take care of business the next morning.

Home.

A place he swore never to go back to. But if it was for one day, he could stomach it. He wouldn't even need to go back to his home village. Just hit the one city of any significance on the peninsula and bounce. In and out. Attend a legal meeting, sleep through most of it, and then go back to the train station as soon as possible.

Juni got out of bed, dressed, and went to the kitchen. Haruka was cramming a bento box into Mayu's oversized backpack. He glimpsed Anpan-man faces made from seaweed, spread over rice balls, all designed and crafted by his wife.

Mayu shouted, "Daddy! Are you sick? Your eye looks gross."

"No, baby, just got a day off today. Lucky me. And my eye is just taking a break today too." He walked over to her and knocked his fist on her backpack. "Not taking Keke today?"

"She hasn't taken her to school for over a year now, Juni," Haruka said—nearly snapped—while zipping up the backpack.

"Ah, that's so mean. They don't let dragons at school anymore?"

"Don't be silly, Daddy. Dragons can't come to school. They'd eat up the teachers."

"Ah, good point." He grabbed the coffee left for him on the counter and sat down on the floor in front of Mayu. "Mai-Mai, if there are any teachers you don't like, I can come by later and bring Keke, so she can eat them. It'll be a secret between you and me."

Mayu smiled, licked her palm, and wiped it across Juni's face.

"Oh, is that how you show me love now? So rude."

"You're leaving tonight?"

"Yeah, I have to go home for just a few days to take care of something, okay? But I'll be right back."

"But this is home."

Yes, yes, it is.

"Alright, off we go," Haruka said. Her usual cheeriness had recovered since her last comment. Or at least it appeared that way. "Juni, there's some mail for you on the table."

She ushered Mayu out to the front door. Juni followed with the coffee mug in hand.

"You guys be careful out there. Love you, Mai-Mai, and I'll see you in a few days."

"Love you, Daddy!" Mayu screamed as she flew down the stairwell, Haruka on her heels. Then, Mayu about-faced and flew back up to the door. "Forgot to give you this, Daddy." She pulled out a piece of paper and threw it at him in a crumpled ball. Giggling, she ran back down to her mother. They disappeared down to the ground floor and out of the building.

Juni bent down and picked up the paper. It was a picture drawn in crayon. Mayu was riding Keke, who looked more like a giant red dolphin than a dragon. Mayu had a crown on her head and was shooting pink laser beams out of her eyes.

"Thank you, baby."

He shut the door and went back to the kitchen. On the table was a manila envelope, the exact kind that Nakamura had given him yesterday. He set Mayu's picture down and grabbed the mail, sat down at the table, and opened the envelope. He took out the letter, skipped the perfunctory greetings, and got to the good stuff:

THE MEETING WITH THE LAWYER OF YOUR FATHER'S ESTATE—ONE MR. OKADA—WILL TAKE PLACE TOMORROW MORNING AT 9 A.M. SHARP IN THE TOWN HALL LOCATED AT OMINATO SQUARE. FAILURE TO BE PRESENT WILL NULLIFY THE TERMS OF THE WILL. ONE OTHER STIPULATION IS THAT YOU MUST TAKE UP RESIDENCE IN THE DOMICILE OF THE DECEASED, LOCATED IN TANOSAWA VILLAGE, FOR ONE WEEK—THAT IS SEVEN NIGHTS STARTING FROM JUNE 7TH—AS PER THE REQUEST OF THE DECEASED. FAILURE TO DO SO WILL NULLIFY THE TERMS OF AGREEMENT...

Juni put the letter down on the table. His goal had been to stay one night in Mutsu, a three-hour drive south of Tanosawa, and take care of the affairs there.

This ruined everything.

Now he had to go back. Home. And stay at his father's house.

He stood up and walked over to the window. An elderly man was picking up plastic bottles in the alley below.

Juni hadn't been home in nineteen years. On the day he left, he remembers slamming the door shut to his father's house, getting in that taxi, and never looking back.

He never said goodbye to his friends. Never even properly broke up with the girl, Nanako, that he had been dating. He fled as if his life depended on it.

And in a way, it did.

A memory came back to him. One that he had time and again buried under the weight of work, marriage, kid, and alcohol. Now it proved it wasn't dead, but was very much alive. It was poking its decomposed fingers through the soil of his mind. Reaching for the light of day.

A memory of his feet kicking under the water. His arms grasping at the underside of a boat. Being pulled under. Screaming for his Dad to pay attention to what was happening. Being met with silence.

He hadn't thought about this in years, fuck it if he was going to start now. Juni felt a sudden rush of ice in his veins. It felt like the shadows of his past were clawing at him, tugging at his shirt, pulling him down into a dark grave.

The memory came back in full against his will.

"Come on and swim," Juni's father growled at him as the violent waves rocked the boat. Juni looked down into the water. He had to lift himself over the gunwale to see it; he was so small.

"Dad, I can't."

Dad took a long drag of his cigarette and then threw it into the water. He came near and grabbed Juni's collar. The smell of alcohol on his breath smothered Juni. He felt like he could get drunk just from breathing it in.

"Do not make me say it again. In the fucking water. You need to learn to be a man. Swim!"

And with that, Juni was flying through the air. The last thing he saw before his body hit the ocean was his father's face. He was smiling.

Splash.

Juni gasped but let in too much water as he did so. He resurfaced and did his best to cough it out but swallowed way too much instead.

He struggled in the water, but soon stopped. To his surprise, he could float if he just calmed down. Still gasping for breath, Juni focused on his rapid heartbeat. That helped. He lay on his back, floating. He wanted to say, "Look at me, Dad, I'm doing it." But he thought better of it: that display of emotion was sure to set off the old man even more. Just swim with a straight face and maybe he'll praise you then. Maybe even accept you.

Dad looked at him from the boat. He wasn't smiling anymore. He scowled and grimaced. Looked disappointed. Behind Juni was Tajima Island. He was so near that he could have swum over had he wanted to, which he definitely did not. Something about the rock faces of the cliffs scared him. Maybe it was the way they towered over him.

Uncaring.

Unfeeling.

Just then, something tugged at Juni's feet. His head went under the water for just a moment before it resurfaced. His father smiled again.

"Dad, I want to come back in."

Again, something pulled him under the water. This time he stayed submerged for a few seconds, unable to free himself from whatever had latched onto his ankles. Then it let go, and Juni came back out of the water. He thrashed his arms about and swam towards the boat. When he reached it, his hands clawed at the side of the hull. He tried to scramble his way back into the boat, but the side was too big, the wood too slippery, and his arms too short.

"Dad, please." He said in between gasps as seawater rushed into his mouth and he felt his body drift towards the underside of the boat as if he was being sucked in.

Juni looked down, towards his feet. He could see nothing but the dark blue of the water, nearly black. At any moment his feet might be pulled under again by some unseen creature. Terror and panic seized him.

His father kept on smiling and staring down at him, not moving. Juni thought he could almost see anticipation in the man's eyes.

A sudden burst of force from under Juni. As if he had found footing on solid ground and jumped off it. Or as if something pushed him up. Juni was lifted towards the rail of the boat, his father holding his hands. Dad looked terrified. At first, Juni thought it was because of almost losing his only son in the water.

"Why not?!" His father yelled out at no one. He pulled Juni fully back into the boat and dropped him. He turned back to the sea, ignoring his son.

"What am I supposed to do with him!?"

No one answered his father that afternoon, save for the solitary cry of a gull and the lapping of the waves against the boat.

Juni never understood what his father had meant that day when he said, "Why not?" He had assumed it was just the alcohol. The feeling Juni had when he was nearly drowned under the water that day when he was only ten years old was more than fear. More than horror.

He felt *called* by something. Like something *wanted* him. It was clear that it wasn't Dad.

"Fucking ridiculous," he muttered while watching the old man down in the alley finish purging the streets of plastic scrap.

It was dumb, he felt, to fear something that happened so long ago. He got his feet tangled in some seaweed; that was all. There was nothing to be afraid of.

And the reward if he went home? Beyond anything he could have hoped for.

But the weight of that memory would not let him go. He would never have admitted it to anyone, but this single event buried itself so deep into his subconscious that even had his home life been a paradise, he still would have left all the same.

Juni went to the secret stash on the top shelf.

He grabbed the whiskey and poured himself a breakfast shot into his coffee. He downed it in seconds. One more mug of coffee, one more shot of whiskey.

Juni got up and grabbed his laptop from the living room table. He fired it up and typed into Google, "Tanosawa, Aomori." A Wikipedia page popped up first. Probably nothing but the population size ten years ago.

He scrolled down.

A few results for towns of the same name but in different regions.

Halfway down the page, some news from five years ago. "Biggest Catch of Tuna in Years! Pulls in Millions." Of course, he found his father's fishing company mentioned in the opening line.

He almost closed the screen but had an idea. A morbid one. He typed, "Deaths at Sea in Aomori." A few stories came up, but none looked notable. Just the same old yarn about drunk fishermen getting lost during a storm. One thing he noticed, though, was that in the past two months, there were five missing-person cases like this. None of them at sea, though. And none of them deaths, but rather missing-person articles. None near Tanosawa, though. But the fact that they were in the same prefecture did nothing to abate his unease.

Come on, stop.

He held onto the coffee mug, much the same as he had just a few days ago, holding on for dear life. His was about to crash headfirst into one of two cement walls.

Do nothing and face the wrath of debt. The wrath of his wife. The abandoning of his daughter. He was convinced Haruka would divorce him and take Mayu away should everything go to shit.

Or go home and face the trauma of the past.

For one week.

I can do this.

He poured himself a third mug.

FIVE

I can't believe I'm doing this, Juni thought as he drove the rental car through Mutsu City.

A small town. But it was the largest one for hundreds of miles here at the edge of the peninsula, an axe-shaped body of land jutting out towards Siberia, sandwiched between the Pacific Ocean to one side, North Korea and Russia not too far off to the other. Hardly anyone was out walking the streets. Traffic was minimal. The whole town looked like it had its heyday decades ago. Old bars and restaurants were still operational but rundown. It was a town frozen in time. Bleeding out its young. There were a few new businesses here and there. Fuck, it even had a McDonald's.

But Juni knew this was the most civilization he was about to see for the next few days. He drove out of Mutsu and further north up the peninsula. Towns became villages. Sparse groves of trees became deep forests. No one was outside. Human population became a rarity the further north that he drove.

Soon, the sea came into view. A stretch of water separating Aomori from Hokkaido, though the latter was out of sight. It gave him the sense of being at the edge of the world. The sea to the right of the road, its waves rising up like white-edged knives. Tall mountains to the left, jagged and steep, rose into the clouds. People lived only on the narrow flat part between the water and the mountain. In the winter, snow would cut off every road in and out of the area. Thank God he came in the summer.

Almost three hours after he had left Mutsu, and thirty minutes since he had seen any other settlement, he finally arrived at the village of Tanosawa.

Juni drove down the hill that led into the harbor and the surrounding community.

The place consisted of just a few hundred buildings at sea level, not too far from the ocean itself. Most of the houses were built right next to each other. No one had a yard. Most of these buildings were old; some were even built out of tin. Population maybe a thousand.

A few homes were built into the hills that Juni currently drove by, situated high above the lower part of the village. There was a flat ledge that the wealthy had constructed decades ago—Juni and his friends used to call it the Table Top. A gated community whose residents rarely, if ever, visited down below. The well-off could afford to raise their domiciles far above the deadly sea.

Concrete barriers rose out of the waves, minimal protection against high tides and the rare tsunami. Juni remembered typhoons and swells that had spilled out into the streets of the village. He was safe from it all: his father's home was up in the base of the mountains that overlooked the village, above even the well-to-do homes of the Table Top.

At the far end of the village, a large rock formation jutted out of the sea, near the shoreline. It looked like a giant had stacked five boulders together and then smashed them down into one another. A wooden bridge connected the stone tower to the hillside above the shore.

Seagulls flocked around the area. Juni could see white splotches from their shit painted across the rocks. As he drove down the hill to Tanosawa, an island to his right came into view. It was far away, nothing more than a speck, with dark storm clouds hovering over it. A deep thunder reverberated over what had to be raging waters out there. Over the village itself, the sky was ashtray-gray.

Juni looked away from the island, from the place his father had tossed him in all those years ago.

You're doing this for Mai-Mai, remember that.

Over text, thankfully not in person, Haruka had been furious that Juni would be gone for a week. She was a stay-at-home mom, so Juni had assumed her routine wouldn't change much at all. Grave miscalculation. He'd make it up to her when he got home with his father's estate backing him, he was sure of it.

Juni's white kei car entered the village proper. There was exactly one streetlight and no stop signs. A few people were out, all of them elderly, with faces downcast and focused on whatever task they were doing. They shuffled about as if dead.

One woman, perhaps in her eighties, was cleaning a fishing net while she sat on a bench in front of her home. He saw a man, back bent forward, hands clasped behind him, strolling the street in front. Juni slowed down to a stop to let him cross.

No young people, not even in their thirties, out at all. Didn't surprise Juni too much; even when he lived here, the youth had to travel to nearby towns to go to school. The young left Tanosawa like blood from a traumatic injury. No jobs, no future prospects, not even a single convenience store in sight. Aside from Tanaka's, a general store run by the family of the same name out of their living room, there were no shops.

The man crossed the street, and Juni sped up. He didn't want to be seen or recognized by anyone. He wanted his presence to go unnoticed, in and out. No need to get caught up in having to talk to people he really didn't want to have anything to do with.

Despite its remote location, all the streets were narrow. Not what one would usually expect out in the countryside. But the sea and the mountains left little room to build. The homes near the ocean were old. Some even had sheet metal welded to their sides. A trick some people employed to keep the humidity from rotting out their walls.

There was no beach to speak of, only a thin stretch of gravel that abruptly ended in the water. No rich-folk summer villas here. Those were up in the hills, surrounding the village in a semicircle. Juni looked out the window and saw them, a dozen homes on Table Top, like gargoyles watching over the village. Their owners must have come from money at some point in time, yet none of the homes had been refurbished in decades.

Even the wealthy in Tanosawa lived a rustic and meager existence.

These thoughts disgusted Juni. They were among the primary reasons he left in the first place. No matter what, he would not end up in some fucking tin can, fishing for the rest of his life.

He left the village and turned onto a narrow road that led up into the mountains near the tower of rocks rising out of the sea. This road took him away from the Table Top, onto a different set of hills on the far side of the settlement. The village below disappeared behind the trees as he hit the switchbacks. There were five of them, sharp, near-90-degree turns that threatened to turn Juni's stomach all over the rental.

As the car climbed, he caught glimpses of Tanosawa Elementary School in the distance. He was sure students didn't attend anymore, but the building still stood. It was also set on a hill above the village, the same one his dad's house was built on. Amagase Dam separated the two buildings. Juni couldn't see it through the trees, but the dam was a massive project carved out of the hill. It created a makeshift valley between his father's house and the school.

The turns stopped, and a massive house appeared. It was modern, as far as modern went in a place like this. The outer walls were dark gray. Half of the home's bulk was suspended over a hill, supported by cement beams, with a large wooden deck hovering over the drop. That side of the home was a glass wall looking out at the sea. The body of the house looked like two cinder blocks stacked diagonally over each other.

The designer ought to be shot.

Above and beyond the home was a mountain peak with a ledge that opened up to the sea. On that ledge, Umibozu Shrine. Juni could see it hadn't changed in all these years. White paper tied to the posts of the shrine, fluttered in the wind. Its red-orange paint caught the sunlight, making it look like a small fire.

Beyond the patio, though he still couldn't see it now, was Amagase Dam. Rivers of rain would run down the mountains in a storm and collect in the man-made lake down at Amagase. He used to hike down to the dam from his father's place with his friends, break in and swim.

He drove through the open gate and parked in front of a fountain with a small naked cherub pissing out water. He got out of the car. Walking by the fountain, he saw it wasn't an angel like he had assumed. The figure at the center was a cross between a fish and a man, its bulbous head, filled with serrated teeth, spewing out water into the fountain.

That's new. First thing I'm doing when I get the money is selling this house, maybe even demolishing this fountain first.

Juni's memories of the place filled him with too much sadness for him to want to hold on to it even if it had a killer view. As he walked up to the front door, someone called out his name from around the corner.

Juni turned around and saw an older man in his seventies, back bent by decades of farm work. He was wearing a loose-fitting yellow collared shirt with navy blue stripes, tucked into khaki pants too big for him. Atop wispy gray strands of hair, he wore a black bowler cap.

"Haruto! Good to see you."

The man bowed and smiled. "Junichiro, it's been ages." He raised his hands to his mouth and let out a dry and raspy cough. "Your father's lawyer called and told me you'd be staying here. I wanted to make sure you got here all right and had everything you needed. I let myself in and left some food in the fridge for you. Oh my, what happened to your eye?"

Juni thanked the man for the food but dodged his last question. He was tiring of having to talk about it.

"How's the wife?" Juni asked.

Haruto stopped smiling. "Been gone seven years now."

Shit. Never ask the elderly about their spouses, you idiot.

"I'm sorry, I shouldn't have asked," Juni remembered Haruto and his wife Asuka as the constant fixtures of the neighborhood. They lived on a small ranch just down the road from his father's house. Juni's father had always relied on Haruto to watch over things when the family wasn't around, fix up the place, any odd job that needed to be done.

"Don't worry about it. How long are you staying?"

"For a week, maybe. The lawyer says I have to. Weird, right? Not that I want to leave quickly, it's just, you know—"

Haruto stared off into the *hiba* forest surrounding the home. "Hmm."

Juni waited for the next word. Even half a syllable would've been nice. Haruto seemed to slip into a state of dementia that Juni was ill-equipped to deal with. Finally, the old man let out a cough. He cleared his voice and said, "I think it's best if you leave tomorrow night. Right after the reading of the will."

Juni tightened his lips and furrowed his brow. "Wish I could. Can I ask why you're so eager to get rid of me?" He added a laugh at the end, just to soften the situation.

"Nothing, nothing important. Just," his eyes glazed over and his mind seemed far away once more, "if you stay that long, only go where you have to."

The fuck does that mean?

"Sure," Juni said.

"The shoreline. It's been acting up lately. That's all; no need for an accident is all." Haruto bowed once more and walked back towards his home around the corner, muttering to himself.

At least he didn't say, "Sorry for your loss."

Juni watched him leave and heard a sudden explosion of clucks from what had to be a dozen or so chickens. Even the bleating of a few sheep and goats. Haruto always had some animals around, good for him. Juni remembered he even had a horse when Juni was younger. He tried riding it once, but Dad told him a story about his dog getting its head kicked off by that horse years before Juni was born.

Add fear of horses up there with fear of water. Thanks, Dad.

Dad had let Haruto use some of his land from the sprawling backyard for his mini-farm. Juni always wondered at this. Dad wasn't the kind of guy to have friends, be nice, or even smile. So why was he always so kind to Haruto?

Juni opened the front door and entered. The ceiling was high, no second floor, though there was space for one. Odd angles of the two-block structure made him dizzy looking up. The home was an open plan, with the kitchen, dining room, and living room all in one area. The floor was gray stone, the walls impeccable, and the fireplace at the far end of the living room was the size of Juni's rental car.

Hanging over it was a deer's head, an *Ezo* buck with a crown of ivory antlers, eyes glassy and black. Many paintings hung on three of the walls. Various scenes of hyper-masculine men dressed as samurai, riding out into stormy weather. In some paintings, the men wrestled great fish and whales. In others, dark shapes, like giant men, rose out of the waves. Juni tried not to look at them as he walked through the room. They were priceless, as far as he knew. And as far as he cared, they could burn.

To Juni's right, the fourth wall in the room was entirely glass. He could see the ocean clearly. The sunset poured in, washing everything with its warmth in an orange glow. He couldn't help but compare this all with his hole-in-the-wall apartment back in Tokyo. No train shaking the walls here. No next-door neighbors fighting and keeping Mayu up all night. Though he held no fondness for his father's home, he couldn't deny that it was worlds beyond what he currently had.

Juni threw his backpack onto a nearby sofa and sat down. He kicked his feet up on the coffee table and looked out at the view. Almost perfect, except for the sea. Replace it with a forest or mountains or even a fucking set of high rises, anything but the never-ending expanse of water.

Juni refused to sleep in his old room. He was only going to be here for the shortest time possible. Fuck if he was going to spend an entire week here, he'd find a way out of it. Sleeping in his old room, supposing it still had a bed in it, would admit he was staying.

He got up and grabbed a banana from the fridge. He saw it was stocked up with fruit: apples, oranges and bananas. In the freezer were several packs of frozen rice wrapped in plastic sheets.

Juni finished eating and took a shower. Dried off. Walked over to the sofa in his underwear and sat down.

The sun was nearly gone, and a silver sheen colored the sea.

Juni's eyes grew heavy as he stared out at the water. Haruto's cryptic words about only going where he had to rang in his brain. He set the alarm on his phone for 4:30. As his mind slipped between consciousness and dreams, an image took hold in his mind. A little boy clinging to the bottom of a wooden boat, feet thrashing in black water, something pulling him under.

Then all was darkness.

Despite it being cooler in Tanosawa than in Tokyo, the house was still full of heavy humidity. The glass wall had no curtains. The view it showed was of deep night layered over the hill that led down to the ocean. The moon cast a wavy light across the still water. He couldn't hear the waves; the home wasn't that close. Yet he imagined its sound.

Melodic. Soothing. Dominating.

The slight pattering of rain on the roof came in.

In the dim moonlight that filled the room, Juni stared up at the ceiling. A fan whirled slowly. The hum of the machine nearly lulled him back to sleep despite the heat. Off in the distance, somewhere outside and down the hill, he heard something. Like the shrill cry of a hawk. The mountains were full of them. Even monkeys came down right into the middle of the village. In the daylight. The only thing he could think of that could make that sound at night was a fox. Sometimes they did sound like a screaming woman. He ignored it and turned over onto his side.

He was facing the darkest corner of the cavernous room. The swish of the fan took over his thoughts, and his eyes closed. Once more the scream came. Was it closer now? Juni sat up and looked out of the window wall. He suddenly felt vulnerable. Anything could be staring at him from outside, and he would never know. Until it was too late. Still, he refused to sleep in his old room, or God forbid, his father's, even if they had curtains.

He thought about moving the sofa so it wouldn't face the window.

Fear gripped him in front of that wall of darkness. Yet he wouldn't admit it and move rooms or move the impromptu bed. *Childish fears*, he told himself. And he was a grown-ass man. He lay back down.

His blood went cold, and he bolted upright.

There in the corner to the left of the window wall, a shape. A shoulder, legs, a head. A protruding stomach. Juni jumped off the sofa, ran over to the wall, and flipped on the lights.

Nothing there.

I'm fucking losing it.

He turned towards the window wall. With the lights on, all he could see was a reflection of the room. In the corner where he thought he saw the shape, something in the reflecting image moved.

He turned around.

Nothing.

Juni sat back down on the sofa.

The lights stayed on all night.

SIX

Floating in the dark. Feet dangling over the abyss. Hands clawing at the side of a boat. Can't find traction. Lungs taking in dark water. Gasping for air. Pulled under the waves.

Juni was in the Void. His father's boat was above him. A silver halo of light surrounding it. His father smiled down at him from the surface, eyes blazing red. Then it was all gone. Total darkness. Light non-existent. Something moved in front of him.

Behind. Above. Below. All around.

He was pulled further down into the depths. Towards the Dark within the dark. The thing that writhed at the ocean's depths. The thing that was calling his name.

All his past, present, and future, melded into one moment. A moment of absolute terror.

Then a blinding, golden light.

Warmth. Love. Acceptance.

A woman's scream.

Pleading. Begging.

The cry of a baby. Hysterical in its frustration and fear.

Then.

Nothing but the Void.

"No!"

Juni woke on the living room floor, underwear twisted around his thighs, his right cheek numb from the odd position he must have fallen asleep in. More sunlight poured in through the window wall. His throat was like sandpaper. His mind, a Rubik's cube bent out of shape.

His phone's alarm was blaring. One of the back-up times he set, just in case.

He looked at his watch, 5:43 a.m. Mutsu was a three-hour drive away.

Fuck, the lawyer!

The office was stuffy. A slight smell of mildew and rotten eggs seemed to be soaked into the sick-green chair Juni sat in. Across from him was a short man in a suit, seated behind a desk so large, it made him look like a child. The man's few strands of obviously dyed black hair were greased over his prominent forehead. Spectacles smaller than his eyes rested precariously on his pug-nose.

Juni wore white shorts and a ruffled light-blue T-shirt, a shell necklace, and his short hair stuck out in multiple directions. He must have looked like a college student on vacation in Hawaii. The lawyer behind the desk, Mr. Okada, seemed to look down on Juni for showing up so casually and unkempt. Mr. Okada refused to start the reading of the last will and testament of Juni's father until exactly 9 a.m. It was 8:59, and Juni was about to snap under the oppressive heat in the office and the stare of the little man across from him.

The clock struck nine.

Like an automaton, Mr. Okada sprang into action. "On this day of the 8th of June, 2024, we all convene here" — Juni looked around sarcastically; they were the only two in the room — "to read the will of Hatayama Ryotaro and to dispense with his final wishes. I, Okada Makoto, will be reading the contents herein exactly as the deceased intended."

Juni tuned the man out for the next ten minutes. Mr. Okada droned on and on about which laws applied and which extenuating circumstances would render the will null and void. He watched the clock on the wall, counting the seconds. The desire to murder the short, greasy-haired man mounted inside him.

"The prefectural authority of Aomori has issued me, Okada Makoto, with the task of issuing—"

Oh dear God, make it stop.

"Concerning my estate and all funds, investments, and savings attenuated to it—"

Juni sat up straight. He cleared his mind of the fog.

"—I hereby bequeath it unto my long-time friend, Tachibana Sakura, for her to divide its value and assets as she sees fit."

Juni's heart fell into his stomach.

"And to my son, Hatayama Junichiro—"

Juni was on the edge of the chair, his ass hardly touching it.

"—absolutely nothing."

A ringing filled Juni's head. He felt lightheaded, and his body swayed.

"If he wishes to acquire wealth as did his father, he must—"

"Hold on! Stop. What do you mean, 'nothing'?"

"Mr. Hatayama, 'I' do not mean anything. I am reading exactly what your father wished me to."

"I know, but... sorry, but what the hell? I'm his only son, so how can he give everything away? And I've never even heard of this Sakura."

Juni spoke quickly, his voice shaking, tears welling up in his eyes.

"May I continue, Mr. Hatayama?" Juni nodded. "If he wishes to acquire wealth as did his father, he must take my journal and follow the instructions therein." Mr. Okada took a black leather-bound journal out of his briefcase and put it on the table. "Thus concludes the final will and testament of Hatayama Ryotaro. Do you have any questions?"

"Do I have any questions?" Juni stood up, kicking the chair away from him. "What does he mean? Read his journal? Is this a sick joke? And Sakura isn't even here; doesn't that nullify what she gets? It would have for me!"

Mr. Okada cleared his throat, shuffled the papers in front of him, and said, "Mr. Hatayama, I assure you, I have done my due diligence. Mrs. Tachibana is not under the same terms and conditions as you are. It is unfortunate if this is not to your liking, but this is what your father wanted."

Juni sat at the kitchen bar in his father's home. His knees shook in irritation as he looked over the journal. It was a normal enough-looking thing, the size of an average notebook. It had writing only on the first page. The rest were blank.

Dear Junichiro,

If you're reading this, then I'm dead. Lucky you. You're asking yourself, "Why didn't daddy leave me anything?"

Boohoo.

I know I was hard on you when you were a kid. I don't regret shit.

I was training you. Making you a man. Preparing you like a warrior.

Because I want to pass on my legacy to you, son. You weren't my first choice. Fuck, you weren't my last one, either.

But blood is blood, and there is no way around it.

I've tried, but there it is, we're stuck together, family and all.

I'm not giving you my estate. What I'm offering you is greater than that.

If you do what I say, exactly what I say, you'll come to understand everything.

Sound crazy? Because it is. But it's real, son. It's all fucking real.

Do what I say, and you will have the riches you came out here to get. Or you could walk away now. And never know what I left for you.

Your choice.

Your instructions:

1. *Go down to the shoreline. Any spot is fine as long as it's in Tanosawa, it HAS TO BE in Tanosawa. I know you're a pussy about water and all so don't worry you don't have to get in, just stand by the shore.*

2. *Toss something valuable into the sea. Anything is fine, start small. Your watch, your wallet, a picture of your wife. The trick is, it has to be VALUABLE to you.*

3. *Lastly. Say these words, "From what is mine to you, so that what is yours will become mine."*

Then you'll understand.

Love you, son,

Hatayama Ryotaro

Juni picked up the journal and hurled it at the face of the mounted deer on the wall. It watched impassively as the pages bounced off its nose and fell to the ground.

"Fuck!"

Juni paced around the living room, his hands grabbing at his hair, nearly tearing out small patches.

What do I do? Dad is just playing some sick post-mortem joke on me. I used all my money to come here. I have just enough to get back home, and then what?

Juni passed the painting of the samurai riding the waves to conquer a whale. He grabbed it by the sides and unhooked it from its holder. The stoic face of the warrior, the obvious symbolism his father derived from it, go and be a man—take shit and conquer. Fury boiled on Juni's face.

He brought the painting up and then forcibly down on his knee, breaking the backboard. He did it a few more times until the painting bowed out of the frame. Dropping it, Juni tore the painting out and ripped it apart as best he could, given the material's strength. He chucked the mangled pieces into the fireplace.

He moved to another painting, one of a drunk man leaving an izakaya with two women on his shoulders. Brought it down on the knee. Tore it out of the frame. Tossed it into the fireplace.

One by one, he moved through his father's collection, destroying what he could.

When he came to the one with the large shadow rising out of the sea, he stopped. The white eyes of the figure froze him in place. Ever since he was a child, he avoided this one in particular. Something about it creeped him out. Maybe it was the dead eyes, lacking focus so you didn't know where they were looking, bright and penetrating. Or it could have been the size of the thing, some giant ghost of the sea that could come out and grab him from out of his bed.

He left this one alone.

Juni found a stick lighter on top of the fireplace mantel. He bent down, lit the paintings, and watched as the fire consumed them, sending up noxious fumes into the chimney. It was hot as hell in the house before he started the fire, and he didn't care how much hotter he was going to make it.

He stormed to his father's liquor cabinet. Still well-stocked and full, could always count on Dad to make sure of that.

He grabbed what he could and drank himself into oblivion.

SEVEN

Weeping. Mournful wails. A foxlike cry.

Juni opened his eyes to a dark room. To the darkness of the night beyond the window wall.

The space behind his eyeballs pounded and throbbed. A fault line ran through his brain. His stomach wanted to come up and say, "Hello, world, nice to meet you."

An entire bottle of whiskey lay on its side on the coffee table, a trail of liquid coalescing around it.

The sound of crying.

A muffled male voice, "This isn't what I want."

Juni got up from the sofa and nearly hurled. He put his hands on his knees for balance until the pain in his head subsided enough for him to move.

Distressed wailing.

Where is that coming from?

Unsure if he was dreaming or completely trashed, Juni turned on the light. He focused his hearing. The crying was coming from somewhere outside the house.

It took him a minute before he could stand, and when he did, he went over to the front door and opened it. The sound of crickets assaulted his ears, but at least there was a cool breeze flowing.

The crying was coming from Haruto's home around the corner, separated from Dad's by tall blackberry bushes. He went back inside and put on sweatpants and a hoodie. Juni exited the house and left the front door open. He stumbled down the driveway and turned right.

He could hear it more clearly now. It was Haruto. And he wasn't just crying; he was lamenting, borderline shrieking in despair.

Juni walked down the road for less than a minute and turned into Haruto's small drive.

A light was on in the old man's window. A single flickering orange light, probably from a lantern, danced in front of the dirty glass. A clatter of aluminum cans on a hard surface erupted from within the house. Juni walked over to the front door and knocked.

"Hey, you okay?"

Sadness and rage combined to make an awful sound. Another crash from inside, the sound of more cans tumbling down, and at least one glass bottle shattering. Juni opened the door and walked in. Haruto had sprawled out on the floor. His pants soaked through and powerfully reeked of urine. He turned and looked over at Juni. It was evident the man had been crying, maybe for hours. He was piss drunk as well.

Join the club.

"Shit, Haruto, you're still doing this?" Juni bent down and helped him to his feet. He nearly fell over with the man, himself being far too drunk to be somebody's rock and anchor.

"I'm sorry, I just, I'm so sorry." Haruto's knees shook as he grasped onto the wall for stability.

"It's okay, come here." Juni put Haruto's arms over his shoulders and walked him to the bathroom. There were no other lights on in the place save for the lantern by the window in the kitchen. Juni flipped the light switch on the wall, and nothing happened.

Figures.

Juni opened the bathroom door: no light inside, but he could see the outline of a grimy toilet and a small bathtub. He helped Haruto out of his clothes. He turned on the shower—water lukewarm – and led the tanned and shriveled man to it. Juni left the room to let Haruto do what he needed to do, but didn't walk too far away, just in case something happened.

Juni squatted in the hall outside the bathroom. He momentarily forgot his own nausea and headaches as he helped Haruto into the tub, but they came back with fury just now. He put his face in his hands and breathed deeply.

Looking up, he couldn't see much around him in the tiny home. But he could smell the sweat and the booze and the vague mustiness of the elderly around him. In the cramped, dirty, and small home, so different from his father's, Juni saw a potential future for himself and his family. Most likely it would be him alone, though, just like Haruto was now.

And who would come by and help me if I piss my pants?

In his drunken stupor, he could swear he saw himself sitting alone in the darkness, wetting himself on the floor in some government-subsidized home in some forgotten corner of Tokyo where the elderly die alone in apartment blocks and aren't discovered for weeks, months even.

At least Haruto had his wife and his kids around him for most of his life. Only at the end did he fall into aged poverty and neglect. Juni's future could be just like Haruto's with a head start of a good forty years.

I'm not letting that happen.

"I'm so sorry," Haruto said from within the bathroom.

"It's okay, Haruto, don't worry about it."

Juni soon realized the man wasn't talking to him. Haruto was whispering now, "Please don't do this. Leave him alone. It's ours to bear; we did it. Don't pull him in." More wailing erupted from the tub.

Juni opened the door and saw Haruto outside of the tub, lying face first on the floor, naked, his face pressed up against the drain.

Juni helped Haruto into some dry clothes and, when he was sure the man wouldn't hurt himself, he went back home.

It was 3 a.m. and Juni was wide awake. He scrolled through his phone on the sofa until he couldn't take the boredom anymore. He went outside onto the patio. The stars were out, uninterrupted by clouds. The moon wasn't nearly as bright as last night; a blanket of shadow hid the sea. Juni's father was an asshole, but he knew how to relax. A sauna was built on the side of the house, accessed via the patio. Juni went inside, opened the wood fire stove under the rocks, filled it with wood from the pile leaning against the structure, and lit it. He went inside, grabbed some potato chips he had picked up while in Mutsu, and poured himself some water. As the sauna took half an hour to heat, he sat on the patio's only chair, looking out into the darkness.

When it was ready, he went inside, poured some water over the rocks, and sat in the steam, letting the heat sap him of the restless energy that was keeping him awake.

Haruto's condition disturbed him. Talking to "the man in the drain," he told Juni. He was drunk and probably senile. Still, the inhuman wailing he did while communing with shadows in the drain didn't sit right with Juni. But it wasn't his concern. He felt bad leaving the man to his fate, but what could be done?

Juni leaned back and stared at the wooden ceiling. Black stains across the surface. He cringed, thinking it might be mold. It must have been the steam clouding his vision, but it looked like the stains were spreading. Juni got up and left the sauna.

Tomorrow, I'm going home. No point in staying if Dad didn't leave me anything, is there?

EIGHT

The sky was obsidian. It glistened like a fragment of volcanic rock. Juni was floating in the middle of the ocean, its waters reflecting the sky above, black as death. There he was, suspended, only able to see black wave upon black wave.

Something pulled him under the water. He struggled. Kicked out at whatever had grabbed onto him, but it was useless. He looked down and saw something in the dark depths. A shadow moved within shadow. Something massive and titanic.

Then, a warm yellow light burned from below. Illuminated what was hidden.

Juni opened his eyes and found that he was still in his father's house. Sweat drenched him. Daylight poured in from the window wall. Juni's head still hurt, but not as much as the previous night.

The sunlight warmed his face. Was almost a welcome intruder to the dream he had just woken from. Juni got up, opened the sliding glass door, and went out onto the balcony. The cicadas screamed out their mating song into the air now blurry with the heat wave that was enveloping the area.

The sun burned above the sea. The roofs of the village below reflected the glare of daylight.

He went back inside, took a shower, made coffee, and got dressed. Looked into the fridge and took some tiny, fresh-caught fish and frozen rice. He heated the food up in the microwave, sat at the kitchen bar, and flipped through his phone, mindlessly checking Instagram for camping lifestyle pictures. Something about the fantasy of leaving the world behind, living out of a tent, maybe just him and a golden retriever, appealed to him. He didn't know the first thing about cooking over a fire or even how to pitch a tent, but a man could dream.

What am I even doing today? There's no reason to stay. If Dad would not give me anything anyway, it doesn't matter if I just go back home today. Does it even matter if I just burn this place down?

Messages popped onto his screen from Haruka. He knew he should text his wife, but that was a reality he wasn't willing to face. Not yet.

If this is the end of my life, may as well enjoy it.

Juni pulled his car into the onsen parking lot. He got out and went inside. The place was dark, barely lit by some unseen bulbs behind the front counter. The wooden walls were worn down, with holes and cracks everywhere. A smiling man with a large wart on his forehead stood at the reception desk, sipping a beer.

"Morning."

"Good morning," Juni said. "Do you have towels?"

"Yep. An extra hundred yen."

Juni winced. Any price hike, no matter how small, hurt.

Then why are you here?

One last moment of peace before all hell breaks loose.

Juni paid the money, went into the men's changing area, and undressed. He walked into the bath. There was one other man, elderly and asleep on the floor next to some steaming water. Juni washed himself and dipped his body into the hot bath. The heat pulled his mind away from his anxiety. With his father's sauna, and now the hot spring, he was feeling unduly luxurious. May as well, if this was his last chance. His mind drifted to Aido-sama's thug. He promised the money by Monday. It was Sunday now. Instead of devising a plan, Juni just let the hot water take the fear away. He knew he'd have to act soon, but that could wait until later this afternoon. *If there's even anything that can be done.*

The baths were geothermal, so the sulfuric smell was commonplace enough. The smell of rotten eggs thickened. But this was something stronger than he was used to.

The water rippled and rose to his neck. Someone joined the bath, and Juni opened his eyes. The man was staring at him with a leery smile.

"Can I help you?"

"What?" said the man.

Great.

The man leaned back against the side of the bath, exposing the dragon and koi fish tattoos on his chest.

Juni didn't care about this intimidation tactic. Life was already over, wasn't it?

"Look, man, I don't want a problem, but if you do—"

"What?" The man laughed, exposing a gap-filled smile. "Juni, yeah?"

"Yep, that's me. Sorry, but I don't-"

"Don't recognize me? Tamura Shun."

Shit fuck.

"Oh, hey. How's life been?"

"Fucking fantastic. What's a piece of shit like you doing back?"

"Hey, I'm just going to leave."

Juni got up to leave, and Shun matched his movements. Juni never expected to run into the bully that made his life hell back when he was sixteen. Lucky for him, Shun dropped out and spared him two more years of torment. He thought the guy would be dead already or locked up, but no, here he was, standing inches away from Juni on what would probably turn out to be the worst day of his life.

Shun came uncomfortably close, given that both men were nude. Juni looked over at the old man as if help could come from that corner.

"Hey remember when I fucked your sister?"

"I don't have a sister. Can you let me pass, please?"

Shun looked honestly confused for a moment. "You calling me a liar? Well, one thing I remember is that your dad is dead, yeah? No one to cover your ass anymore."

Juni sighed. "Man, are we still talking about shit from almost twenty years ago? I'm over it. Apparently, you're not. Is life so boring here? Never achieved anything? That's why you're still messing with people? I bet the old guy who runs this place is too scared to say no to you because of your tats, yeah? Waste of a human being."

"Look who grew some balls while he was gone." Shun feigned grabbing Juni *down there* but pulled his hand back and laughed. "I ain't no queer. But you still are, aren't ya?"

Juni was done. If he had to push this guy out of his way, he'd do it. If Shun threw the first punch, maybe he could sue him and get something out of it?

Not a bad idea, actually.

Juni imagined him as a fetal pig on a metal dish, with the metal utensils sticking out of the organs, ready for dissection. The same rage that boiled in his gut when he almost beat Ryusuke fired up in him.

Shun was about to put his hands on Juni's shoulders, as he had done many times long ago when Juni didn't fight back. Times were different now. Before Shun could touch him, Juni slapped him in the face.

The man looked shocked, as if this sort of shit simply did not happen to him.

The old man woke up and said, "Keep it down!" and then rolled over and went back to sleep.

"You're dead," Shun said as he pushed Juni up against the tiled wall. Juni pushed against his forearms, but Shun was too strong. Juni swung his arms, trying to connect his fist with Shun's face, but he couldn't reach. The hard edge he was pressed up against dug into his spine.

Shun fixed his mad eyes on his own. Until they darted upwards, at something on the ceiling. Juni saw his expression soften and his eyebrows rise. Was that fear in his eyes?

"No," Shun said as he released Juni. He backed out of the water, nearly tripping on the top step. He turned and ran out of the bathing area.

Juni coughed and rubbed his neck. The old man snored.

What the hell?

Juni turned and looked up at the ceiling. Nothing but a damp surface. The area near the corner was dark, but nothing out of the ordinary. Something fell into the water. Juni at first assumed it was just condensation. Until it happened again. Whatever was falling was black and thick. It sizzled as it touched the water. It spread out from the dark corner of the ceiling near a faded painting of the sunrise over the sea. As Juni squinted to see what it was, the shadow moved as if alive. Juni took a step back, nearly backing into the old man asleep on the floor. He looked again, no movement.

The stain on the ceiling, deep and black, reminded Juni of the mold seeping through the walls of his apartment. Of the mark in the sauna.

Juni put his keys on the counter and sat down on the sofa.

Maybe I should just pack and leave?

As for what he saw at the bathhouse, he didn't know. A trick of the light? Stress-induced hallucination? Whatever it was, it scared Shun off as well, not something that Juni wanted to dwell on.

A message popped up on his screen. From Haruka, asking if she could call. He rang her up.

"Hey, Haruka, how's Mai-Mai?"

"She's been a little terror, Juni! If everything is finished out there, I need you to come back home."

"What do you mean?"

"Just, is it possible to come back?"

"I don't know; things are kinda complicated with the will at the moment."

"Did you even check the weather, Juni?"

"What do you mean?"

"A typhoon is coming tomorrow. I've been checking to keep an eye out for you, and by this time tomorrow, a huge storm will hit you, and then you're stuck for longer, and I just can't anymore with Mayu-"

"What can't you?" Juni's voice came off more stern than he would have liked.

Haruka was silent for a moment. "She's been having bad dreams since you left, okay? She just needs her Daddy around."

Juni remembered his dream. Being pulled down into an infinite nothingness. But it wasn't quite nothing, was it? There was a *something* down there.

Haruka continued, "She told me just this morning that she's afraid she'll be with Grandpa and she doesn't want to. Come home. Please. I'm begging you."

Juni was stunned into silence. His blood ran cold despite the heat. But it couldn't be more than a coincidence, father and daughter both having bad dreams at the same time. Nothing to worry about. "Just tell her Daddy is coming home soon, and that he loves her. He also loves his wife very much and will take her out to eat anywhere she wants to go when I come back."

"There's... one more thing."

"Yeah?"

"Somebody came to the apartment last night." She sighed heavily. "It was almost midnight, so I didn't open the door, but I saw him through the keyhole, some gangster-looking guy in a tracksuit, wearing sunglasses. He asked if you were home. I said yes, but you were taking a bath. He just smiled at the keyhole, said he'd be back again soon and left."

"Do not talk to that guy again. He's bad news."

"Juni, who was he? Are we safe here?"

"It's just... yes, I know him. I took a loan from his boss a few months ago, and he's trying to collect. He's not a good guy. Can you stay at your mom's until I get back?"

Silence on the line. In those moments of hearing her breathing, Juni knew that a suppressed fury tinged with fear shook his wife's face.

"Understood," she said.

"Good. I'm sorry, babe, I'm going to make this right."

She hung up.

A part of Juni told him to go home. Go home and hug his little girl and keep the monsters out of the house. Both nightmares and gangsters. Maybe even repair his fractured marriage.

Another part told him that without money, it was useless. He was useless. The man would just come knocking again, maybe even worse. There was always going to be a man like him, like Shun, waiting for him. Unless he did something about it.

He put the phone down and looked at his father's journal on the floor by the deer's head. He went over. Picked it up. Read over the three instructions written on the only page with any writing on it.

He grabbed his keys and got in the car.

NINE

Juni stood outside his car in the parking lot of Tanosawa Harbor. The lot itself had only five parking spots, with only two of them occupied. One by Juni's rental, the other by a dirty—maybe once white, now fully caked in mud—kei truck with fishing gear in the bed.

Juni approached the dock. A few boats were tethered to it. All of them were small, private fishing boats. One was blinged out with an imperial Japanese flag, red streamers, and a float of a pufferfish attached to an antenna on the cockpit.

Damn, people are serious about their fishing here.

His father's ships didn't operate in Tanosawa, the waters weren't rich enough, and the ports were too small. All of his trawlers were in nearby towns like Oma, a good hour's drive away and an hour nearer actual civilization.

The splashing of the waves under the dock unnerved him. Ever since he was ten years old, Juni had not gone in the water. Not just the ocean. Lakes. Rivers. Even pools were a no-go. The shower and the bath were all he could stomach.

It wasn't the water itself that scared him. It was the unknown space under his feet as he dangled above the abyss.

As he started walking down the dock, his legs became noodles, his breathing intense, and his head light.

He wanted to do it right now, go no further down the dock, but he was afraid of being seen by someone. What he was about to do was ridiculous. He forced himself to walk to the midpoint of the pier. When he got there, he kept his eyes up and on the sky.

He passed a man working on the gaudy boat tied to a post. He felt the man's eyes on him, but kept on walking.

Taking a deep breath, he looked down. Gentle waves fell against the wooden poles of the dock. Barnacles and other shelled creatures clung to their surface. The foul stench of fish made him gag.

He took out his wallet. He opened the change flap and took out a five hundred yen coin.

Am I really doing this?

But where else could he go, and what else could he do? This was most definitely foolish. Idiotic. A fever dream of stupidity. But if there was even a fraction of a percent of the smallest chance, he had to take it.

Was this really so different from pachinko?

The journal was in his left hand. Juni looked over his shoulder to make sure no one was there. Satisfied, he read from the journal: "From what is mine to you, so that what is yours will become mine."

He flicked the coin into the sea.

Juni wasn't sure what he was expecting to happen. A spark of lightning? Shifting of the earth? A fuzzy feeling deep down inside?

What happened was... nothing.

The coin sank out of sight.

He waited for something. Some sign that this bullshit magic had worked. The only things he noticed were the cry of a seagull and the dinging of a bell somewhere out in the water.

Waves of embarrassment washed over him.

He closed the journal.

"Fucking useless," he said as he threw the notebook into the water.

A voice, like someone had a towel wrapped around their face, came to him. He couldn't make out the words. It was more of an incoherent groan than actual speech. But it was loud. And it came from under the wooden boards of the dock.

Juni walked, nearly jogged, back down the dock. He must be hearing things, amped up by the very weird week he'd been having. There was no voice from under the dock, or more accurately, from the water. He imagined that voice back at Haruto's house, and in his stress, he conjured it up again.

Right?

"Hatayama, is that you?" came a gruff voice that sounded like it had been run through a blender.

Juni flinched as he heard it, unprepared for the very real and very human words greeting him. The image of a naked Shun flashed before his mind. Not again.

It was the man with the boat. He was sitting on a wooden post in the parking lot now, smoking a cigarette, next to the beat-up and filthy white kei truck.

"Yeah, it's me. Who are... no fucking way. Shota?"

"The one and only," Shota said, grinning so hard his cig almost fell out of his mouth. He got up and slapped Juni on the shoulder. "What the hell are you doing here?"

"My dad died, so I had to take care of some legal shit."

"And you didn't even think to call." Shota's face was cast-iron indifference as he spoke.

"I'm sorry, it's not personal—"

Shota's face exploded into a fiery grin. "Just fucking with you, I don't care. But sucks about your dad, I worked for him a few years back, did you know that? Independent now," he nodded at his boat. The very one with the imperial flag and the pufferfish. "Didn't know he died. But that's really not sad news for you, is it?"

Shota knew what he was talking about. Out of all the bad memories that crowded Juni's mind when it came to Tanosawa, his friendship with Shota Sakagawa was one of the few bright spots. He wasn't a star student or an ideal role model or anything, but he let Juni stay over at his place when things got rough with Dad. If Shota was ever around at the house when Dad went into a rage, it was he who shut the old man up.

Built like a water silo, thick-chested, broad linebacker shoulders, and an ugly brick face, Shota was a hero to Juni back in high school, but he hadn't thought of the guy in almost two decades.

"Yeah, you know what it was like. But still, family is family, and I gotta take care of things. So, you're fishing? Like as a job?"

"Captain fucking obvious over here, you see my boat."

"Married?"

"Three times. Didn't suit me much. Free as the open sea now. You?"

"Yeah, married. Got a little girl, too. You got any kids?"

Shota flicked his stub of a smoke into the water. "You're blessed, man. Kids are the only real treasure, ya know?" He took another cigarette out of his shirt pocket and lit it. Juni noted his dodging of the question. "How long you here for?"

That depends on whether a potentially existing magical water fairy grants my wish or not. Maybe try a different sentence.

"Until tomorrow, I think."

"Get a drink with me tonight. At the Sea Breeze. Drinks on me. I've gotta go run an errand now."

"That place is still standing? I thought the mold would have eaten through the walls ten years ago."

"Who says it hasn't? It's one of the many charms of the place. So, you down?"

"I don't know, man; I was thinking about leaving tonight."

"Got work tomorrow?"

"Well, no, but—"

"Then why not? I'll call Keisuke too and have him drop by. We'd love to sit down with you, man."

Keisuke, there's another name he hadn't thought of in years. In school it was always the three of them; Shota getting into trouble, Juni watching on, and Keisuke trying his best to keep them all on the straight and narrow.

"Sure, what time?"

"I'll meet you there at nine. What happened to your eye, by the way?"

TEN

Juni stood in front of Tanosawa's only drinking establishment: the Sea Breeze.

The place had been in business as far back as he could remember. The owners, Mr. and Mrs. Sato, seemed old to Juni even back then, almost twenty years ago. He was a minor the last time he had visited the joint. In Tanosawa, the bar didn't care how old you were. Single moms got wasted at the counter while their kids scribbled crayon on the walls.

The door to the place brandished the treasures of the sea as if they were armor-plating. Starfish, conch shells, and a fishing net, all draped over the entrance haphazardly, and probably done so more than half a century ago. The small sign, hung directly above the cluttered door, said "Sea Breeze" — in English — once upon a time in yellow letters against a blue backdrop. Time, and sea salt in the air, had since worn down the sign to where the only two letters visible were the "S" and the "z." The yellow was a creamy piss-white and the blue was more gray by now.

Not that it mattered. Only locals came here, and they didn't need a sign to know what it was. The village's only easy access to alcohol and cheap nuts. A haven for dead dreams and lonely winter nights.

Juni opened the door and stepped in.

Mrs. Sato was behind the counter, looking exactly the same as Juni remembered. Sure, there were more wrinkles by now, and she was slightly more hunched over, but she held the same confident don't-give-a-fuck attitude in her stare. Mr. Sato wasn't beside her, as he usually was.

Don't mess up like you did with Haruto. Never ask the elderly how their partners are doing.

The bar was big enough to hold about ten people. Five at the counter, with one table in the room's corner. A grizzled man who could have been fifty or twenty because of the hard life of the sea sat in the far left corner of the bar, morose and staring down at his drink.

Looks like Mr. Ando.

Given that he and Shota used to steal the guy's beer, kept in crates in his backyard like a barbarian, he was in no rush to talk to him.

At the table in the corner, Shota sat with his feet kicked up on a chair, with two empty glasses in front of him, a third almost empty one in his hands.

"Oh my, is that Junichiro?" Mrs. Sato asked.

"Yep, it's me."

Mr. Ando turned a bloodshot eye over to him.

"Haven't changed one bit," Mrs. Sato said.

Same goes for you, almost. "It's good to see you."

"Sorry to hear about your father, dear. Your drinks are on me tonight."

Juni tried to say no, but Mrs Sato was having none of that. She passed him a draft beer and shooed him away to the corner. He pulled out a chair and sat down. A glass of whiskey on the rocks was waiting for him.

"Shota, starting early without me? It *just* turned nine."

He and Juni clinked their glasses together and did a quick shot. "Never too early to start drinking."

Nothing changes in this town.

Juni sipped at the beer and then put it to the side to grow warm and forgotten.

In a low voice, Juni asked, "Is Mr. Sato... you know?"

"Dunno, he was here last week." He turned to face Mrs. Sato. "Hey, your husband died?"

Juni's back was to the bar, but he could feel the discomfort on Mrs. Sato's face as the silence stretched. She said, "No, you piece of garbage. But he didn't come home last night, and I'm worried, okay? Thanks for bringing it up."

"You're welcome," Shota replied and turned back to Juni. He was never one to read the room. Juni thought, more than once, that he might be on the spectrum.

"So, how'd your dad die?"

Juni was going through waves of culture shock here. "Umm, I think it was a stroke."

"Better than cancer, I suppose."

"Yeah."

Moments of silence as Juni sipped his whiskey while Shota ordered another highball.

"Sorry if that was rude; people keep telling me I don't handle things like this well," Shota said.

"Things like normal human interactions?" Juni smiled.

"Fuck you," Shota punched his arm with the impact of a silverback gorilla.

Just like old times.

"Anyway, you said you were married before, but single now. Dating anyone?"

Shota leaned back in his chair and let out a whistle. "Ain't that the story of my life? Seeing this girl down in Aomori City on weekends. I wanna make it work and start a family. But knowing me, I'll fuck it up soon."

"Yeah, you probably will," Juni said with a grin.

Shota exploded in a hearty laugh and punched Juni's shoulder.

Still smiling, but rubbing his arm, trying not to let out a cry of pain, Juni said, "But seriously, don't worry about it. Kids aren't all they're cracked up to be."

Shota's unbroken stare prompted him to continue. "I mean, I love my girl, of course I do. But there's a lot of freedom you give up when you have a kid. And get married, but you know that."

"Freedom? To do what? Travel the world?"

"Never left Japan," he said with a pang of regret. "But that's what I mean. Whatever you want to do; travel, fish, screw around, you can't when you have kids. They hold you back from your dreams."

"So what dream is your lovely little girl holding you back from?"

"Dude, you make it sound bad when you say it back to me. That's not what I mean. But have you ever just felt like you were meant for more than what you're doing right now? Like, your life is supposed to mean something."

"If I had a kid, that would mean that my life means something."

"Yeah, some people might be happy enough with that. But if you're not doing what you're supposed to be doing, achieving dreams and shit, then you can't even take care of your family, can you? What good is it having all these mushy feelings of love and romance if I can't feed my kid, right? The way I see it is, and this is my dream: get wealthy first, make a name for myself, and then all that feel-good stuff can come after."

The jangling of a bell as the door opened.

"Keisuke, is that you?" Juni asked, more than a slight hint of confusion laced in his voice.

The portly man, who had just entered the bar, blushed and looked down at his feet. "Yeah, it's me, Juni. The years have, uh, come kind of fast to me." Keisuke's face was as red as a tomato. He walked softly, with hunched shoulders, as if he were a child caught somewhere he didn't belong.

"Not as fast as donuts to your face," Shota roared out, splashing his drink across his chin.

"Shota, bad form," Juni said.

"No, no, it's alright. He's always giving me crap. It's just because he hasn't found a woman willing to stand him longer than a week." Keisuke nearly whispered the last part, almost as if he realized how stupid it was to challenge Shota like this. In public, of all places.

Shota let out a laugh, stood up, and slapped more than hugged the man. Keisuke's face relaxed, and he sat down at the table.

Juni recalled Keisuke the last time they had met. Then he was slim—slightly muscular, even — and had just started dating girls. His personality had always been gentle. Next to Shota's crassness and the meek Keisuke, Juni fit right in the middle. Keisuke ordered his drink, Cassis Orange, and they toasted to the three of them, their health, and their futures.

Juni caught up on the local news. Keisuke had two children, a boy and a girl, both in middle school. He had married a girl named Hitomi, who was at least five levels out of his league. Got a job with the municipal authorities checking waterways and maintaining water quality. Shota hadn't changed a bit. Took over his father's fishing business after getting fired by Juni's dad. Times were tough for him. Juni's father dominated the industry in the area, leaving very little room for smaller enterprises like Shota's to thrive. Juni avoided talking about his personal life beyond the fact that he hated teaching high school science. He contented himself with listening.

"Hey man," Keisuke began, "I'm sorry about your dad."

"Don't be. I'm not." He took a swig of the lukewarm beer and couldn't wait for Mrs. Sato to get his next whiskey out. Even Shota raised an eyebrow at him, but neither of his friends pushed him on the subject.

Shota got up, announcing to the entire room, Mr. Ando included, that he had to pee.

"So, you still living near the school?" Juni asked.

Keisuke smiled sheepishly. "Actually, we moved to the Table Top."

Juni almost let his glass slip from his fingers. "Seriously? Not to be rude, but how can you afford it?"

"Oh, I just got lucky. Hitomi's uncle came into some extra cash and wanted to help us out with buying a house."

Juni couldn't believe that. The amount he would need to own a house up there was beyond "running into some extra cash."

"That's good for you, man," Juni said, putting on his best smile to keep from showing what he really thought.

"But don't talk about that when Shota comes back; it'll bring up bad memories."

Juni raised an eyebrow.

Keisuke continued, "He didn't tell you, I think, but he had a son. He died seven years ago, and it was the same time I got the house on the Table Top, so it's better not to talk about anything that could remind him of that."

"Are you serious? His son died? How?"

Keisuke glanced at the bathroom door and lowered his voice. "Shota took him out fishing; he was only five at the time. He put him in the boat and went back to the car to grab something for just a minute, and when he came back, his boy was gone. He jumped in the water, couldn't find him. Police never recovered a body. Shota was a mess, man, like borderline-suicidal. Everyone said the kid fell over and drowned, but he never accepted that. But anyway, best not to bring up anything that could remind him."

Juni's heart cracked in two. Immediate shame over his comments about his own daughter consumed him. "Shit, I didn't know. Poor Shota. Thanks for telling me."

The bathroom door opened, and Shota lumbered out and back to the table.

"What I miss?"

"Keisuke said we should call your girl in Aomori and see if she's real," Juni said. Keisuke blushed. Shota nearly spat his drink all over the table.

They ordered more drinks. Ate dried squid dipped in mayonnaise. Had meaningless conversation. Even did a few rounds of karaoke. For the first time in months, Juni was happy.

ELEVEN

The sofa was a crime scene. Wrinkled shirts crumpled into piles. Mismatched socks wedged between the cushions.

Juni was packing his backpack in his usual "chaos leads to order" approach. Toss everything on the floor, and then the path forward becomes clear.

He texted Haruka shortly after he got back from the bar, "I'm coming home tomorrow." The reply, "GOOD."

There was nothing left for him here. Yeah, it was a fun night with the guys, but that was a momentary distraction. Haruto had wanted him to leave soon anyway, so at least he wouldn't disappoint one person in his life. Nothing left for him in the will. The journal was a joke. And to top it all off, the typhoon was coming tomorrow night.

No need to get stranded here longer than you need to be.

Out of the corner of his eye, he saw his reflection in the window wall. Night enveloped the outside world in charcoal hues, tinged with deep grays. Since that first night when he thought he saw something in the corner of this room, he had slept with the lights on. True, it blinded him to potential prying eyes from the outside. But what was out there? Owls and deer? Nothing to worry about.

The living room glare was preferable to clearly seeing that blanket of night, leading out to the sea. Today's experience on the dock convinced him never to be that close to the sea again. The smothered groan came back to him. Something that wasn't a voice, but bordered on one.

He cleaned up the crime scene nicely. Backpack full to the brim. Not a single sock left behind.

Juni went to the bathroom, brushed his teeth, and washed his face. Then he packed all his toiletries. He poured a glass of water and sat back down on the sofa. He flipped through his phone, looking at pictures of Mayu. This reminded him of the photo he kept in his wallet. He took it out and unfolded it. Just last month, they had gone to the zoo. Juni's favorite photo was one of Mayu, God forbid without Keke the Wonderful in tow, crouching in front of the lion exhibit, putting on her best fierce snarl.

This was the last treat he had been able to give her before the notices from the bank started coming in and reality choked out his life.

Next to the photograph was the picture Mayu drew for him the morning he left.

Tears clouded his eyes. Juni wiped them away with his sleeve. He put the photograph and drawing on the table, got up, and looked at the window wall. Walked over to the light switch and killed it. The moon cast a pale line of light across the distant water. A few lights shone in the village below. The forested hill between the house and the village was black as soot.

Rain fell on the window. The sound of the splattering drops was almost soothing.

I have life insurance.

He smiled at the idea.

There was a clause in the policy that stated death by suicide would leave his family with nothing. But if he could make it look like an accident? Just take a boat out tomorrow night and let the typhoon do the rest.

The thought of being buried beneath the heavy waves shook him to his senses. No, death was not an option, if for no other reason than that he was terrified of the idea of meeting his end *that* way.

His dreams came back to him.

Floating in nothingness. Feet dangled above something down below.

A shadow in the corner of this very room.

A dark stain on the bathhouse ceiling and the sauna.

Haruto raving about the man in the drain.

Nonsense.

He turned back to the sofa and sat down, tired enough to fall asleep without his nightlight.

Then he heard it.

A scream.

Coming from the direction of Haruto's home.

Not again.

Juni resolved not to go over and bathe the man again. He did his good deed already.

A second scream broke the night. But this was not his neighbor's. This was the scream he mistook for a fox several nights ago. Only now, he wasn't so sure.

Juni sat up straight.

The high-pitched wail was beyond what any human vocal cords could make, but at the tail end of the screech, a deep and guttural growl, almost human-like, reverberated.

"No!" was what he thought he heard from the direction of Haruto's house. Followed by muffled words from the man, too quiet to hear clearly.

Breaking glass.

Haruto let out a primal and fierce cry of pain that didn't seem possible for any person to make.

And then silence.

Juni stood still in the dark room, grateful that he had turned off the lights, giving him some cover. He went to the front door and looked out the peephole. Nothing but darkness and rain.

What if Haruto needs help now?

Juni was about to call the police, knowing for a fact that the closest station was over an hour's drive away. But what would he say? And if he needed help, an hour was too long to wait.

Just see what's happening first.

He opened the door, turned on his phone's flashlight, and went outside. Almost immediately, the rain stopped. Juni stood still for a moment and listened. Nothing but the last remnants of raindrops falling from tree branches.

He walked down the driveway, turned right, and walked up to Haruto's home. No lights in the window. He walked down the driveway, keeping his footsteps light, though he wasn't sure why.

Knocked on the front door. "Haruto, you okay? Been drinking too much again?"

No response.

Something rustled from the side of the house. Juni clenched his fists until he heard a lamb bleat, followed by the cluck of the chickens.

He released his pent-up breath.

Juni opened the door slowly. The inside of the house was even darker than the other night. No source of light, aside from Juni's phone.

The white light washed over the clutter of cardboard boxes by the entrance. Juni moved into the house and walked past them and into the kitchen.

"Hey, Haruto, you around?"

Nothing.

Juni walked deeper into the house, checking each light switch he came across, but none worked. The last time he was here, Haruto only had a lantern on in the kitchen, entirely possible the man didn't pay his electric bill, nothing too strange with that. Juni walked by the living room, but didn't linger, and gave it a quick glance. Nothing but a pile of boxes in the middle of the room.

He checked the bedroom: nothing. The bathroom: nothing. He even opened the back door that led out to the animal pens. He saw two sheep near their fence, staring at him. But nothing else.

He went back inside and headed for the front door, passing the living room. His light reflected off something on the floor he hadn't seen when he walked by the first time. It lit up multiple tiny fragments like diamonds in the dark. Moving closer, he saw it was glass. He went into the room and skirted around the boxes. Shining the light through the window in the living room, he noticed it was gone. Not just smashed, but the entire frame was ripped out of the wall. Sections of the wall itself were torn away when the window was removed.

A whimpering rose from behind him. Juni twisted around, clutching his phone like a dagger, blunt and nearly useless, but better than nothing.

It was Haruto. Sitting on the floor in the dark corner of the living room. Wrapped in a blanket, muttering to himself and crying.

Juni ran to him and bent down. "Hey, you okay? What happened?"

From this closer vantage point, Juni saw the blood running from his forehead.

"Come to count the cost. Come to count the cost. After all these years."

Haruto wouldn't meet his eyes. Juni wasn't even sure the man knew he was there. He grabbed Haruto by the shoulders and shook him. The man's frail neck caused his head to bob like a rag doll's.

"Haruto, snap out of it! Did someone break your window, or did you do that yourself?" Juni only half-believed in that. Give Haruto an ax and an hour, and he wouldn't have been able to damage the wall like that.

Suddenly, Haruto snapped his focus onto Juni. "You. Because of you, *it* has come to count the cost." Spittle fell in sticky webs down the man's unshaven face.

Haruto threw off the blanket. He was naked. His emaciated frame was lit by the ghostly light of the phone. He stood up and ran out of the house. Juni followed him, catching up to him in the driveway. Haruto stopped at the edge of the woods surrounding his property. The moon lit up his feeble body in a ghastly glow. He looked at Juni with eyes that spoke of both accusation and terror, maybe even a little guilt thrown in, and then he ran into the forest.

For half a second, Juni thought about chasing after him.

Nah, fuck him. I've done enough for him already. He wants to go psycho and run into the woods? Fine, *let him do it.*

Juni went home.

TWELVE

Juni walked into his father's house, then shut and locked the door behind him. Shame danced on his heart for leaving Haruto out there, but why was it his responsibility to do something? The old man made the choice to do what he did.

But the window.

He had no answer to that. Haruto was far too weak to have done that himself.

But he's gotta have tools, like a chainsaw or something, right? Then he'd be able to. But did I hear a motor revved up? No, I heard something else.

Enough.

Juni went to the liquor cabinet and poured himself a full glass of whiskey, straight. The liquid fire went down his throat and into his bloodstream. His eyes stung, and he gripped the glass for support. Finally, he let out a gasp. Whether out of satisfaction or pain, didn't matter; the end result was the same.

Dull the mind.

The lights in the room went out.

Juni had left his phone on the sofa and had nothing on him to shine into the darkness that now filled the space.

"Shit."

Maybe the typhoon winds were coming in early? It was raining a few minutes ago, so maybe a power line got knocked down.

He stood still for a moment, trying to remember where the breaker box was. Never needed to use it when he lived here as a child. He remembered Dad going down the stairs into the basement, cursing up a storm, every time a big one swept by and killed the lights. He could try there first.

He stumbled across the room to the sofa, seeing the furniture lit under the moonlight streaming in through the window wall.

The feeling of eyes boring into the back of his head.

The hair on his neck tingled and stood straight. He heard nothing. Fear froze him in place as if he had anesthesia coursing through his veins.

He needed to turn around and see what was there, and of course, it had to be nothing. But some ancestral fear told him to play dead. If you don't look, it's not there.

He looked.

In the corner of the shadow-filled room, at the far left edge of the window wall, was a black shape, deeper and darker than the rest of the room. A black hole sucking in even the natural darkness of night.

It moved.

He saw its mass walk across the window, a faint glow of moonlight outlining its form. A thick belly. A bald head. Something tall.

"Dad?" Juni's voice came out of quivering lips.

The dark shape stopped moving.

A wheezing sound. Air being sucked in by someone with weak lungs. It exhaled weakly. Almost like someone choking on water. Gurgling out their last breath.

Two white orbs appeared from the shadow's head.

A drowning voice, coming from nowhere and everywhere all at once, "It gives, and it takes."

A woman's voice, from somewhere outside the house but still as clear, "The sea is an open grave."

The lights came on.

No shadow. No Dad. No woman.

The fuck? I'm losing my mind.

Juni let out a deep breath, surprised that he had held it in for so long.

For another minute he stood there, straining his ears for any other sounds.

His reflection in the window wall regarded him coolly. Juni saw himself hunched over, hands spread out at his sides as if bracing himself to get hit.

Get it together, man.

He went back to the kitchen to fetch one more glass of liquid fire. Get drunk. Go to sleep. And tomorrow, leave this hellhole.

He stopped in his tracks as if hit with an invisible wall.

There on the counter, next to the whiskey bottle, was something that was not there before.

The journal.

The same one he had tossed into the ocean. Water glistened on its cover. A small puddle formed around it. A thread of seaweed clung to its side.

Juni's mind raced with all the possibilities. *Whoever did this, did it while the lights were off. Was it the same guy who broke Haruto's window? Was it Haruto? Did he watch me throw the journal away and jump in after it later?*

Juni approached cautiously as if it were a bomb that could detonate at any second.

An alert sounded from his phone, causing his heart to shatter against his ribcage. He took it out of his pocket and saw a notification from his bank.

His mind raced with what it could be: a final notice for the mortgage, a closure of his account?

He swiped open the lock screen and opened the banking app. What he saw squeezed out a cry of joy from him. This morning, his account was empty. Now, the numbers have rocketed into the hundreds of thousands of yen.

Juni's heart fluttered, joy blocking out the strangeness of the moment. This was enough money to cover half of what he owed the loan shark.

Euphoria seized his brain. So much so that he forgot about the journal. The shadow and the voices were now long-lost memories as well.

Finally, he got over the surge of happiness and put the phone down on the counter.

He picked up the journal.

The three instructions were circled in red. The color was smudged and smeared dark-brown in places. It didn't look like the stroke of a marker, more like paint, make-up, even blood. The next three pages, which were blank the last time he checked, were now filled with writing.

"Holy shit."

Juni sat down at the counter and started reading from where he had left off.

Most of the pages were filled with incoherent nonsense. Several of them were filled with lists of names.

The first few names:

Machida Mako 1987 X

Sato Harumi 1989 X

Yajima Nana 1991 X

Morita Sara 1993 X

The list went on like this. Mostly women's names. Two men. All spaced two years apart. All were checked with an X by their names. Juni scanned the list; it went on to the next page. A few names in the middle were scribbled, and he couldn't make them out.

The last few names:

Sakagawa Kentaro, 2017, the third and final man's name.

Takeuchi Mona, 2019, woman's name.

Morita Rachel, 2021, a foreign woman? Fifteen women in total.

The list ended with a blank spot—presumably for another name—and the year 2023. No X by it.

At the end of the list, there was a messy set of calculations. It was like looking at someone trying to budget their life on a napkin. The amount started off small, but grew bigger by the end. And though he couldn't make sense of what it meant, seeing names and these perfectly spaced-out dates, every two years for the past three decades, unnerved him.

Juni flipped through the pages and found various phone numbers and addresses. Nothing seemed important, or at least he wasn't capable of sifting through the silt of information for the gold of knowledge.

The one address of note belonged to Tachibana Sakura: Tanosawa, 2-Chome, 45-2. Juni knew Table Top was the entirety of 2-Chome Street. This was the only legible address; everything else was the scrawling of an epileptic. He grabbed a red pen from the counter and circled the address. Then the meaning of the name came to him: Dad's friend, the one he gave all his money to.

Rage and jealousy replaced the happiness in his heart.

The last page: a photograph taped onto the paper and a message written in red letters in a script he couldn't read, scrawled on the page multiple times. The picture was a grainy black-and-white shot of some kind of procession in front of a stone shrine. Not quite in the Shinto style, it more so resembled Stonehenge than anything. The surrounding land was rocky. Dead trees, looking like they were burnt, stood behind the shrine.

Three figures, their dark clothing blurred into the background, stood before the shrine. In front of them was a fourth, their head covered by a hood. They were on their knees before the altar. One of the hooded men held a misty white object that Juni thought could be a knife. A dark shadow on the ground, too smudged to make out any details.

One legible phrase under the photograph in his Dad's handwriting: YOU'RE ON THE RIGHT TRACK. KEEP GOING.

Juni shut the journal and threw it back on the counter.

Then he sat down on the sofa and looked up at the ceiling fan.

"What...the actual...fuck?"

Too many questions. But the one thing he knew is that he had enough money to at least pacify the thug stalking his family.

Ka-chuck, ka-chuck, ka-chuck.

From the depths of his subconscious came the pachinko parlor in all its neon and head-splitting glory. If he played his hand right, he could double what he had now and be done with the sunglasses-guy for good.

Or...

What if there was something to the journal? It was all beyond his ability to explain at the moment, but the evidence that something was happening and it was real was now sitting in his bank account. Not to mention the soaking journal on the counter, with newly added pages.

What if... I take a different kind of gamble in the morning?

Just test the waters.
See what happens.
Ka-chuck, ka-chuck, ka-chuck.

THIRTEEN

The golden rays of sunrise fractured the gray sky here and there. The storm of the previous night had passed, leaving behind that post-squall mix of iridescent colors in the sky. Mist flowed and weaved between the buildings.

The Table Top, true to its name, was a flat area of land, a large shelf, really, set above the village of Tanosawa. In total, twenty homes filled the Top, each one of them massive, attached to huge lawns, high-end cars out front, all the homes facing the sea with an unobstructed view. Ten homes were set above the ledge's edge, with a sheer cliff dropping down to the sea. The other ten were more inland, set against the mountain that acted as its second natural border.

Strange to think that even Keisuke had a place here now.

Juni left his car parked on the side of the road outside the gate and walked up to an intercom posted outside. He entered Sakura's address into the keypad and waited.

"Yes?" came a woman's voice.

"Hi, is this Tachibana Sakura?"

"She just left for the day about a minute ago. May I ask who is trying to reach her?"

Juni left his information, and the intercom went silent.

He thought about giving until the gates swung open and a Mercedes drove out. He looked inside the driver's window and saw a middle-aged man. Since this looked like the only exit to the neighborhood, and this wasn't Sakura, maybe he could catch her on her way out?

Juni walked through the gates before they shut.

He felt woefully out of place. He didn't even understand what he was doing. His debt to Aido-sama was due today. He had half of it now, somehow, but that wasn't enough. It might be to give him a few day's grace, though.

This was his only option. He refused to think about the sunglasses-man showing up at the apartment. But the only way to stop that from happening was to come up with the money.

He walked down 2-Chome, craning his head back to take in the view of the homes. None of them were as large or as unique as his father's house, but they were light years beyond anything down by the harbor. Two worlds existed here: the shacks by the shore and the mansions of the Top. And never did they meet.

Juni wondered where these people got their food and did their other shopping; Tanosawa was certainly not the place. Did that mean they all drove hours away each week to get groceries? If so, why stay here? Why not set up their homes in more populated parts of the peninsula?

Juni never visited this neighborhood growing up. Though his father could be seen in the same class as these rich neighbors, Dad always spoke ill of them. And since none of their children attended the local schools back when Juni was a kid and the elementary school was actually open, Juni never had the cause, or the spine, to enter the community.

On his right, he passed house 45-1 by the mountainside, which meant 45-2 would be on the opposite side, on the ledge. The home was built in a traditional Japanese style. Well, traditional for lords and samurai, not the average farmer and fisherman. A four-sided courtyard wall surrounded the property. Beyond it, Juni could just barely make out the top of the home itself, a structure that rose like a medieval pagoda.

The top of the outer wall came to a point with shingles, like a roof just for the gate rested on it. The entrance was set in the middle of the wall. The closed doors were wide enough for two trucks to drive in side by side. On top of the gate, two bronze figures, acting as guardians to the house, much the same as at a Buddhist temple.

The one on the left was a serpent-like dragon. Its body was bronze, but it had blue eyes—some kind of stone — placed in its face. The one on the right was a catfish, frozen in what had to be a mid-jump out of the water. Its eyes were red. As Juni approached the intercom, he felt watched by the lifeless eyes of the statues.

He rang the bell.

He halfway expected nothing to happen. Yet immediately the sound of gears turning made him jump as the doors opened inwards.

Inside the courtyard, a woman stood as if she were about to leave. She was middle-aged, yet retained the beauty of her youth. Her black hair, with a single faint streak of gray, was tied back tightly, ending in a ponytail. She wore a black skirt suit with freshly polished black heels.

Her teeth flashed into a smile behind her crimson lipstick.

"Sorry, are you here to deliver something?"

"Tachibana Sakura? This is going to sound weird, but—"

"Junichiro?" She took a step back, and her perfect smile faltered for just a second. "You look just like him." Her smile altogether vanished, and her voice became grave. "Why are you here?"

"Umm, this is awkward, so I'm just going to say it. Dad left you all his money in the will, I know that." Juni fought back the emotions as he spoke. "And that's okay; that's not why I'm here." *Liar.* "But he gave me a journal with some weird instructions. Actually, that was all he left me, and your name was also in that, so... I don't know what to ask exactly, but..."

Doing a great job, buddy.

She looked down and seemed to contemplate bad news. She looked up. "Fine."

She briskly turned away and started walking, half striding, towards the house, expecting him to follow, and follow he did. The gate came to life once more and shut behind him.

To Juni's left, under a carport, were two cars that looked more expensive than his entire apartment. He wasn't sure of the make of one of them, but the one nearest him was definitely a Rolls-Royce. The path to the house was curved and filled with gravel. The rest of the courtyard was made up of Zen gardens of raked sand, stone altars, and bonsai trees.

The house itself was a castle, the type which Mayu would have loved to see and fill with stuffed dragons. It looked like a miniature of the kind he had seen on trips to Osaka and Nagoya as a kid. A pagoda-like structure painted black and red. Catfish and dragon statues dotted the curved roofs.

If it weren't for the luxury cars behind him, Juni could have sworn he had been transported back in time by a few centuries. It wouldn't have surprised him to see servants in topknots and sword-wielding attendants run out to greet him.

Sakura opened the front door of her home. She took off her heels and went inside. Juni followed and took off his once-white-now-brown sneakers, fully aware of the dust and mud caked on them, and tried to hide them in the entrance's corner as he came in.

Sakura noticed the attempt and smiled. Juni avoided her gaze, embarrassed even to be here. The front hall was cavernous. A single wide hall was the only thing he could see. It was lined with several doors, behind which the other rooms must be hiding. The ceiling — which was pure glass, letting in a deluge of sunlight — was high up, about where the third-story roof should be. Various paintings, vases, and flowers sat smug along small shelves on the walls. Sakura opened the first door on her right and bade Juni to come in.

She sat down at a large conference table in a room with bright white walls, large leather chairs, and abstract art that looked like fluorescent roadkill on the moon. The room stood in stark contrast to the more traditional aspects of the home. This area was thoroughly modern and chic.

Sakura rang the intercom. "Yukina, a cup of tea and...," she looked at Juni expectantly.

"Uh, black coffee, please."

"And a black coffee." No voice replied. Sakura cut the intercom.

"Thank you," Juni said as he sat down across from her.

She looked at him and studied him for a moment before speaking. "Now, let's skip the pleasantries and get right to it. I'll tell you upfront that if this is about your father's estate, you'll have to speak with my lawyers about it, assuming you can afford to hire your own. So, if not that, then why are you here? Tell me about this journal."

"Like I said, my father left behind some pages filled with strange instructions for me to follow. Your name and address are in it, with a few others, but only yours is legible. Anyway, I followed the steps he wrote for me, and, I don't know, maybe they worked. I know this is vague, but if I said everything out loud, you'd laugh me out of here. So..."

Juni stopped to catch his breath. He realized then and there that he had no questions for her, no concrete piece of information to ask her aside from, "Why is your name in my Dad's probably magic journal?" Nothing that a sane person would dare to ask a stranger.

Sakura stared deep into his eyes the whole time, not once blinking.

A knock at the door. Sakura said, "Come in," and a young woman, maybe in her twenties, dressed in a silver kimono, came in with a tray of drinks. She set the tea and coffee on the table. Juni said, "Thank you," and she left the room. He took a sip from the mug. Even her coffee was high-end, better than anything he'd ever bought before.

"Hatayama-san, your father was very close to this community here at 2-Chome. And to put it bluntly, you are not one of us."

"What does that mean?" Juni asked sharply.

"Quick to temper, I see, Hatayama-san. I knew another man in your family with similar attributes."

Juni's face went hot, because of either anger or shame; he himself wasn't sure.

Sakura went on. "If you would be so kind as to let me finish." Juni nodded. "Good. You are not a part of this community, but it would seem that your father has entrusted you with his legacy, because he left you instructions. I must confess I am shocked to hear that he gave you the journal, if it is indeed what I think it is."

"Can we stop being cryptic here? What is this legacy you're talking about? Because he didn't leave me shit." The offense of his father's will outweighed his reticence at being in a high-class home. He no longer felt uncomfortable being where he thought he shouldn't be.

"The legacy of your father is not found in his wealth, or in his home, or even in his fishing business. Those are just the fruits that have grown. The seed—the source—is something far greater."

Sakura leaned forward. Juni felt an odd mix of suspicion and arousal as she spoke.

"Have you heard its call? At night, when the rains come?" She didn't blink at all as she spoke.

A twisting in the pit of his stomach. "You mean the foxes we have around here?"

Sakura laughed. "No, Mr. Hatayama, not the foxes. But I can see that you have heard its call, if only by the way you squirm at the mere mention of it. You are not ready—or deserving — to know much more. Not until I know I can trust you. But, unfortunately for us all, if your father has chosen you to be his successor, and if you have indeed heard its call, then there isn't much time."

"Time for what?"

"Do what your father said in his journal. You must be the one to give it what it needs. I'm assuming you've tried it, yes? Maybe threw something valuable, but small, into the water?"

Juni nodded.

"Baby steps. From now on, you must give something of greater value every time. And with each offering, venture further out to sea to give it. Closer to Tajima Island each time. An act of devotion. It will let you off light at first, but not for long."

Juni could no longer contain the fire in his belly. "Bull. Shit. What is this fairytale crap? Offerings? Devotion? To what exactly?"

Sakura regarded him coolly. "Follow the instructions, and you will see for yourself."

Juni got up out of his chair and headed for the door.

In a calm and even measure, Sakura said, "You believe, though. Because you already received something for what you gave, didn't you?"

Juni's back to her. He said nothing, but he didn't open the door.

"Juni, if I may call you that, I hope you take my words to heart. Because the consequences of inaction for you, me, and everyone in this village will be severe if you ignore the call. I'll be checking in with you soon. And if you aren't up to the task, well, let's just say we don't want to talk about what will happen then."

Without another word, Juni left the house.

Juni reached the gate, and it opened automatically for him. He got in his car and drove down the road that led away from the Table Top.

I don't actually believe any of this shit, do I? Magic and wishes being granted?

The road ran down the side of the cliff overlooking the sea. The waves were calm. Sun poured itself out over the surface of the still waters. Mist had burned away. It was all so peaceful. Could there be something *more* down there? Some veiled world full of horrible things, right out in the open? Sakura's words were ominous and vaguely threatening.

The car came to the bottom of the hill and entered the village. He passed by Tanaka's, two older women outside the shop doors laughing and looking at a pair of onions they had just bought. In minutes, Juni found himself back at the harbor. He hadn't intended to do it; his brain must have been on autopilot, and he just ended up there.

He sat in the car for five minutes, contemplating his next move.

Before he was willing to accept any of this, he had to be given a sign. He would test it out. Isn't that what he always told his students in class? "Don't just accept things as they are; test what people say and come to your own conclusions."

He got out of the car. He walked by the same dirty truck with fishing gear in the back as before and walked down the pier. That meant Shota was probably nearby, but at least his boat wasn't. His fear of the water hadn't gone away even in the slightest, so he made haste with his steps.

Arriving at the midpoint of the dock, he took off his wristwatch. Haruka gave it to him five years ago on his birthday. Many times he had thought about pawning it to help with the debts, but could never bring himself to do it.

But if this bullshit was legit, he needed to give something of value, right? And he needed to wish for something that couldn't be explained away. For all he knew, Sakura and Dad were actually part of some weird ocean-worshiping cult. She was a woman of means, and it wouldn't be that difficult for her to plant money into his account and make it seem like something supernatural was happening. But to what purpose? Juni couldn't see her doing it as a sick joke. Maybe the ranks of the faithful were thin, and they wanted a new devoted member?

He looked out at the sea: dark storm clouds were rising out of the horizon, like black ink spilling upwards into the sky. The typhoon was supposed to make landfall tonight, and it was supposed to be monstrous. He checked his weather app, and the village was in its direct path. There would be no natural way for it to miss. He was looking straight ahead on its path of assault. The forecast was for the entire peninsula to get hit.

So that's it. If I give the watch, and if the typhoon misses Tanosawa, and only Tanosawa, then I might believe and we might be onto something here.

He held the watch above the water. Two thoughts struck him. One, why just ask for this one thing? The deadline for Aido-sama's money was also today, wasn't it? And two, if he wanted greater results, he would have to go further out in the water than last time.

He forced himself to walk to the end of the pier. Sweat stung his eyes, and his hands shook so much, he almost dropped the watch. The end of the pier that was closer, wasn't it? He refused to think about doing a third offering and what that implied. This had to be good enough for now.

The sea surrounded most of his peripheral vision now. He refused to look down.

"From what is mine to you, so that what is yours will be mine. I want the typhoon to miss Tanosawa tonight, completely. And I want enough money to pay off Aido-sama, by the end of today."

Juni felt eyes on him.

Looking from side to side, he saw no one.

Juni dropped the watch and heard it splash.

Muffled, as if it were coming from under the dock, a man's voice said, "This isn't what I want."

FOURTEEN

Juni pulled into his father's driveway. Haruto was waiting outside the front door, clothed in his khaki pants, his usual striped collared shirt, and bowler cap. He was holding a bouquet and a glass bottle wrapped in a golden cloth, as big as the man's torso, nearly. A bandage wrapped his head.

Juni got out of the car. "Haruto, you feeling better today? Going to go running into the forest again tonight?" Juni knew that was cruel, but his patience was stretching thin with this man.

Haruto limped his way forward to meet him in the driveway. He bowed, smiled, and said, "I have to apologize for the way I've been acting since you came back. It's been improper, and I've burdened you too much since you came."

"Haruto," Juni felt a barrage of scolding forming in his lungs, the same he had doled out on his students, but halted. "It's okay. But you have to stop drinking, or at least cut down a bit. You hurt yourself last night and broke your window."

Haruto was smiling in humble apology the whole time, nodding his head in agreement, until the window was mentioned.

He said, "Oh, I'll make sure to be more careful from now on, don't you worry about that. Say, have you finished what you came here to do?

Not that I'm trying to get rid of you or anything, but the business with the will must be done by now, surely?"

He looked up at Juni like a child, eyes wide and glassy and expectant.

"There's one thing I need to do, or wait for, actually."

"No!"

The explosion of not quite anger, but entreaty, shook Juni.

"You must leave now. Before the typhoon strikes. You can still make it if you drive now. I'll help you pack. I'll take care of everything here. But go, please."

Haruto dropped the flowers and the bottle. Thankfully, it didn't break. He fell to his knees, grappling Juni's shirt.

Juni tried lifting him up. "Get it together. I can't leave, not yet. And this is the second time you've told me to leave. Why?"

"It's not safe for you here."

Juni picked the man up, set him on his feet, and handed him back his gifts. "Explain more."

"I can't. They'll... they'll come for me if I do."

"They? Do you mean Tachibana Sakura?"

"No," Haruto said as his eyes wandered around his surroundings, seemingly devoid of focus. Then, in a whisper, "I mean, the one who comes in the rain. The man who talks to me from my drain. He lives in the bay, but make no mistake, if there's water, like from a storm perhaps, he can move. And he comes to count the cost. He will destroy you."

Haruto backed away from him. "I've said too much. This might be the end for me, Junichiro," he said and locked eyes with Juni, tears streaming down the man's sunken face. "Don't make the same mistakes your father and I did. Run while there is time. As long as you don't make an offering, you can still run."

Haruto, listening to his own advice, ran back to his home.

Juni lay on the sofa, staring at the ceiling fan.

He weighed Haruto's words.

Bullshit, all of it.

But if it was the delirium of a senile man, then why did he throw the watch in the water?

After the odd encounter with Haruto, Juni spent the rest of the day in the house, eating the rest of the fruit in the fridge and most of the fish. If he stayed here any longer, he'd have to go shopping at some point. He messaged Aido-sama that he could wire him half the money. No response had come in yet. He also wondered when Sakura would kick him out. After all, this was her house now. Why she hadn't done so already was beyond him.

He looked at his phone and refreshed the bank app. The money from yesterday was still there, which was good. Problem was, it hadn't gone up. Maybe this was all a farce. In that case, he wouldn't have to worry about Haruto's warnings. But if it were true, he could save his family from financial ruin.

And how dangerous could it be if Haruto and Sakura also messed with it? They're still alive. Sakura is bangin' rich. Haruto not so much, but the man has a ranch and damn goats walking around. Juni's place has cockroaches and centipedes.

Juni rolled his feet, dropped his phone on the coffee table, and walked over to the window wall. The sun was dipping just below the horizon. Blood-red, its light splattered across tin-colored skies. Dark clouds coalesced out at sea. He could tell the wind was picking up. The trees below swayed in fury.

No money. And the typhoon was still coming. It was too good to be true.

Either I fucked up by asking for two things, or I fucked up by not going further out into the water, or I fucked up by believing in any of this to begin with.

In his restlessness, he wandered away from the living room, the only part of the house that he felt comfortable in. Aside from the kitchen and the bathroom, he had until now refused to go into any of the other rooms. Not thinking about where he was, mind fixed on his troubles, he walked down the hall to his father's room. He paused in front of the closed door, grasped the handle, and walked in.

The curtains were shut. Juni hit the lights. A haze seemed to fill the room, slightly brown, dust swirling around the space like the air itself was burnt. Nothing inside, save for a bed in the middle of the room. Blankets tucked in tight under the mattress. Undisturbed.

Above the bed, against the wall, was a deep black stain. It radiated out like a Rorschach inkblot. Glistened as if still wet. It might have been the overall haze in the room, but for a second it looked like some vapor was coming off the mark. Juni's stomach constricted, and bile rose in his throat. He slammed the door shut. He couldn't stay put another second in this house, not with the knowledge he'd be sleeping in a room next to *that*.

He went back to the coffee table and checked his phone one last time. Still no updates. The money was due tonight.

He had one last recourse.

Juni stood in front of a massive three-story home.

Bright floodlights in the garden washed over the place. Hues of pink and baby-blue splashed across the surface of the home, making it look like a toy more than an actual domicile. Shouts erupted from inside. The front door opened, and Keisuke emerged, out of breath, his full face flushed red, sweat pouring down his forehead.

"Whoa, you okay?" Juni asked.

Keisuke reached into his pocket, took out a handkerchief, and wiped his face. "Totally, why ask?"

"Daddy, come back!" came the high-pitched voice of the little boy standing behind Keisuke.

"Sorry, buddy, we'll play later. We have company."

The boy pouted and stuck out his tongue before running away. Keisuke gave an embarrassed smile. "We were just playing hide and seek."

Juni thought it was funny that the man who had killed it in track and field back in high school could get so winded playing a kid's game. "Ah, I see."

Keisuke let him in. As Juni passed through the house, he marveled at its size, its newness, and the money that seemed to drip off the walls. Keisuke opened the back door and showed him to a large wooden deck overlooking the sea. The water was so close that they could hit it with a tennis ball from here.

Juni sat down on a bench in front of a table. Orange string lights lit up the backyard like little campfires protecting their home. Night swallowed the view of the sea. The wind blew gently but seemed to pick up in intensity.

"Worried about the storm tonight? It's gonna hit around midnight, right? You guys are so close to the ocean," Juni said. "I'd be pissing myself."

"Nah, we have storm shutters, see?" Keisuke pointed out the steel sheets folded above the windows. "And the waves have never been that bad before. Even if they were, we can take it."

"That's good." Juni looked around. "Good, you're doing good, man, I'm impressed."

Keisuke blushed a little. Despite his considerable size, sitting across from Juni, wedged into his seat, he looked like a child in a man's body.

"Juni, you seem off. What's up?"

"I'm alright." Juni looked down at his feet. The nearby waves drowned out the silence that followed.

"No, you aren't. You look like you need to ask me something difficult."

Juni sucked in his breath so fast it made a hissing sound. "It's not easy, but..." Juni swallowed, took a deep breath, and got on his knees, face to the ground in front of Keisuke. "I need to borrow money! Five hundred thousand yen if you have it."

Juni wouldn't look up from the ground, couldn't face his friend at eye level. If he saw disappointment or even anger there, he could never live it down.

Keisuke grabbed him by the shoulders and guided him back to his wobbling feet.

"Umm, Juni, I want to, I really do, but..." he cast his eyes out towards the sea. "We're trying to have another baby now. And Ayumi is going to need money for cram schools soon and then university. Then it'll be Kaito right after her."

It felt like Keisuke was apologizing for a great offense. "No, don't worry about it. I get it. I'm sorry I asked."

They sat in silence again, the crash of the waves failing to wash away the awkwardness.

"Did anyone hear about Mr. Sato?" Juni asked.

"No, but everyone in the village is talking about it. It's not too weird for someone to go missing when a storm is kicking up the water, but this makes three people in the past week."

"Three?"

"Yeah, I guess you only knew about Mr. Sato. A few days before you got here, some big shot from Tokyo rented a speedboat and tried taking it around the peninsula by himself. Dumb guy, didn't even know how to pilot a boat. So it turns up near the harbor, no sign of damage or nothin'. But the guy is gone. Police did a search but didn't find him."

"Sucks."

After a few more minutes of stilted conversation, Juni excused himself to leave.

"Wait, stay for some food at least. Hitomi will make something."

Juni wanted to be anywhere else at that moment. Wallow in his misery. Until he realized he hadn't eaten since the afternoon.

"Sure, just for a bit."

"No way, I had no idea," Juni said, almost spilling the glass of beer on the table. He was laughing so hard.

"It's true, Keisuke asked me out in front of my manager," Hitomi said. "Here was this tall, beefy guy at the hostess club. Everyone thought he was so cool. But he couldn't talk to girls. Everyone tried to make him feel comfortable, get him drunk, load on the compliments, all to get him to lighten up and smile."

Keisuke's face flushed red as he tried to hide his face behind his beer.

Hitomi seemed to relish his torture. With the kids in bed, it was just the three adults drinking on the deck outside under the stars.

It was getting windy, but not so bad that they needed to get to shelter just yet.

Hitomi continued, "Nobody could get him to budge—until me, that is. I come over to his table, and he's just sitting there with his coworkers, looking at his drink like he doesn't really want to be there and all. I say to him, 'Hey, move over.' He does. Looks shocked that this tiny girl just ordered him around. Then, I spend the next hour basically berating him for his bad manners. His boss looks shocked. I think I might get fired over the whole thing, but I was mad that this guy was being so difficult. Time is up, so they all get up to pay for their drinks. Keisuke stays behind. Grabs my hand and asks me to be his girlfriend then and there, in front of everybody."

"And you said yes? I can't believe that," Juni said.

"No, I said no. But he comes back every Saturday night for the next month, and the same thing plays out each time. He won't talk. I get mad at him. He asks me out. Until one day he finally breaks down and tries to tell me a joke."

"Please tell me what it was." Juni's face was now red with amusement.

"Can't. I think it was so bad, my subconscious blocked it out of my memory. But, you know, it showed me that under all the muscle and dumb aloofness was a good guy."

Keisuke's face was now in full-on meltdown. Juni was nearly choking on his drink.

Hitomi took a sip of her champagne and asked, "So, how did you meet your wife?"

His smile became more rigid. "In university. We worked at the same cafe on campus and, I don't know, it just sort of happened."

Hitomi's mouth was open as if dumbfounded. "That's it. I tell you this hilarious story, and you guys just sort of, kind of, happened?"

"Yeah. We're fine, but you know, time can dull things."

Keisuke sat up, presumably to give Juni an out.

Hitomi went on, "But you love her, right?"

"Of course." By the look in her eyes, he could tell she wasn't buying it.

"Alright, I think Juni's got a big day tomorrow, so he should head out. The storm will be here soon, too," Keisuke said.

Thank you, brother.

His hosts got up and led him to the front. Hitomi waved cheerfully at him. As Juni went through the door, Keisuke caught his arm. "Hey, take this."

Juni looked at his open palm: he was holding a ten thousand yen bill.

"It's not much, and I'm sorry I can't do more, but here."

Juni took it. "Thank you."

An inflatable soccer ball smacked Keisuke in the back of the head. Kaito and now his older sister Ayumi were in the hall behind him giggling.

Juni smiled. "You have a good thing here; I envy you."

Keisuke looked at his feet. "Yeah, we had to give a lot to get it." His words sounded almost mournful. A sudden cloud covered the jolly man's face.

"Hey, you alright?"

Keisuke snapped out of it. "Yeah, it's nothing."

Keisuke wished Juni well, shut the door, and returned to his parental duties.

Juni left the house full of screaming children and marital bliss. He was acutely aware that he could be experiencing the same thing right now had he chosen to go home.

Juni got back to his father's house late and tipsy. He turned on all the lights. Checked his already packed luggage. Washed his face.

He took what he thought would be one last look out the window wall. The wind lashed the trees in fury, and the waves, dark without the light of the moon, writhed and churned.

So long, Tanosawa, thanks for nothing.

The deadline for Aido-sama's money had passed. He was sure his family was fine. Maybe that guy came by and knocked on the door, but Haruka was at her mother's, right?

His phone sent out a chime.

It was the bank app.

He swiped it open.

His heart beat fiercely. He could feel a pulse in his throat. Tears blurred the image on the screen.

Aido-sama's debt would be paid tonight.

He fell to his knees, gripping his phone so tight, it felt like he could crush it. He called Aido-sama, but the phone just rang. Texted him he had money now; he just needed his bank information to wire it to him in the morning when the banks opened.

If the money is here, what about the storm?

Juni ran to the window. As if in tandem with the bank alert, the trees had become still. The waves calmed down. The heavy storm clouds dissipated and revealed the stars.

"Holy shit, it's real."

FIFTEEN

asegawa Taiki walked the streets of Shinjuku like he owned the place. Well, he didn't, but his boss Aido Takanori did, parts of it, anyway. The Kimura-Gumi crime syndicate wasn't as entrenched as the other factions, didn't have the weight of history and connections backing it. But fuck if it wasn't the fastest-growing one.

And Taiki was there from the start.

He slouched as he walked, not out of insecurity, but out of an oafish relaxation that came with being untouchable. A defiant laziness. A shield that kept anyone from confronting him. It was night out, the city lights drowned out the sky, and he saw the world several shades darker than it actually was, thanks to his Ray-Bans, which never left his face.

He had gotten used to seeing things darker. Natural and artificial light irritated him. The inky blue of his lenses brought the world into a calm state where he knew what to expect. Everything made sense that way. Everything and everyone looked the same to him. Means to ends, chumps and whores.

Taiki wasn't always the thug, the one who broke noses and dealt meth without his boss knowing. At least Taiki hoped he didn't know.

No, Taiki was a sweet boy growing up. His mother told him so, and he believed her with all his heart. He loved his pet hamster, Chupa, watching soaps with mom after school, and hanging out with the girls in his class more than with the boys. Dad, on the other hand, thought he was too much like a girl. Too soft-spoken. Too passive. Bad at sports. Destined for a life of insignificance.

Weak.

So, Taiki carried that burden his whole life. Not wanting to be the weakling that his dad was terrified he'd become. He'd do anything to shake that off.

He beat up Yamada Sora when he was thirteen for the crime of trying to kiss him. Didn't matter that Taiki liked boys and was the one to instigate the kiss; what mattered was that his father walked in on them and he needed an excuse for the close contact. The violence amped him up and made him strong. Fuck, even his father cheered him on that day.

Taiki was in control.

Untouchable.

Dad bounced and left Mom all alone when Taiki was fifteen. She turned to the world's oldest profession to support herself and her son. Taiki both hated and loved his Mom for that. Whatever confused emotions he felt, one thing was sure: he'd get her out of that life.

And he did. He made so much money working for Aido-sama that he could support her now. Problem was, Taiki was getting good at pushing crystal meth, and Mom was a regular customer.

He never reflected on this. On his role in his mother's undoing. Could never see things clearly.

Taiki walked past a supernova-bright pachinko parlor. It reminded him of what he was supposed to do later that night. Visit that prick Hatayama, break down the door if need be, and get the money. If he couldn't, he was supposed to come back to Aido-sama with several of the man's fingers. Maybe even one from his wife or daughter. Motivate him to try harder.

Taiki turned down an alleyway full of hostess clubs, pink salons, soap lands, and other fine establishments that he often frequented. The neon signs above the stores, the posters of photoshopped girls in bikinis, all were a welcome sight to him. Places like *One Love, Cherry Top, Jungle*. All the places where he knew the roster of girls by heart. He wasn't just a customer; he was their muscle.

Men in suits and earpieces stood in front of the high-end shops while fat fucks in dirty tank tops slinked in the shadows to pull suckers to their shops. They all nodded to him as he passed.

Rina was working tonight. His girl. Or at least his for the hour whenever he saw her. He liked to relax a bit before having to do the more unsavory aspects of his job. Tonight was going to get violent for sure. He knew Hatayama couldn't have put together the money so fast. He didn't mind hurting men, but when it came to women and children, he felt kinda bad about it.

Kinda.

He might have to see Rina afterward as well, to wash his mind of the guilt. Taiki turned down another alley and came to *Blue Angel Bodies* where Rina worked, at the dead-end of a quiet alley. Nobody was on the street in this part of the neighborhood, though a few people walked by the entrance to the alley now and then. Not the most popular joint, it needed little security. That, and nobody would mess with the girls here knowing Taiki was a preferred customer.

Smiling, with his cigarette balanced on his tongue, Taiki made for the front door.

The smell of rotten eggs filled the alley. He coughed and covered his mouth. A slight brown smoke, barely visible, seemed to fill the area. He ignored it and went to the entrance again.

Right before he could touch the door handle, a muffled voice of a man said, "This is not what I want."

Taiki turned around. He slipped a butterfly knife out of his pocket. "Who the fuck?"

Nobody there.

"The stars are so beautiful tonight," came the voice of a young girl. Taiki turned on his heels and saw no one.

"Are you going to kill me?" Another feminine voice, huskier than the one before, as if the woman was a heavy smoker.

"Come out, fucker, not the time to be messing with me," Taiki said.

In the alleyway's corner, in the dark space just below a pink neon sign of a banana with whipped cream on it, something moved.

The electric buzz of the sign was the only sound in the alley.

The bright colors reflected off his glasses.

Taiki walked toward the shadow. "Think you can mess with me? Know who I work for?"

Two white eyes opened in the dark.

Taiki froze.

"No! Watch out. They're in the water," came a young man's voice. "Don't look at the lights. The eyes!"

Taiki noticed more shadows above the sex shops. Standing on the roofs, looking down at him with fluorescent eyes. The shapes were of adult men and women, one of whom looked pregnant. There were even a few child-sized ones.

Taiki lunged at the shadow in the corner. Nobody there.

Something touched his shoulder. Without hesitating, he spun around and swiped his knife in front of him. Nothing.

The neon lights faded, and thick darkness filled the alley. The smoke and the stench grew more intense.

For the first time in years, since good old dad beat the habit out of him, Taiki cried. His hands shook, and he dropped the knife. "What do you want? I have money, just take it." He pulled out a rolled stack of bills from his tracksuit pocket and threw it on the ground.

"This is not what I want," came the muffled voice from somewhere beneath him.

Taiki looked down at the storm drain and screamed. He turned to flee but was pulled down by his ankles, his face hitting the asphalt, shattering his sunglasses, and breaking his nose. The screams continued as two elongated arms dragged him towards the drain. His fingernails chipped and broke as he tried to hold on to the asphalt, all to no avail.

He yelled out, "Mama!" His legs went into the drain just fine, but the size of his waist saved him from being pulled in fully. He flailed and tried to pull himself out. Whatever had a hold of him yanked him harder. So hard that he felt a crunch near his tailbone. Another snap. Ribs collapsing. Incredible pain. Before he lost all consciousness, he felt his insides rush to his throat.

The door to *Blue Angel Bodies* opened, and a woman in her forties with red-rimmed glasses and a single red streak in her otherwise black hair stepped out into the alleyway. Tonight had been rough for Rina, and she needed a smoke. She knew Taiki would come by later and needed to build up her resolve to deal with the guy.

She lit up her cigarette, covering the match with her left hand. Rina puffed smoke into the air and sighed. Amid the gray smoke, something odd took shape. Waving the cloud away, she gasped and pivoted around to shut the door and call the police. She wasn't paid enough to deal with what she had just seen.

A smear of blood led down into the sewer. A severed arm lying in the gutter. Bits of bone and muscle and organs clogging the storm drain. Shards of Ray-Bans strewn across the ground, reflecting the white lights of the dark denizens above, the only witnesses to what had happened.

After the door shut, a singsong voice of a young girl filled the alleyway and the cloud-covered evening.

"The stars are so beautiful tonight."

SIXTEEN

Floating above the dark waters. The waves beneath his dangling feet rose like jagged teeth, seeking to consume him. The island of Tajima, deserted and barren, stood motionless in the tempest.

A pale form swimming in the sea. Rising to the surface and diving again. Serpentine yet human-like in its movements.

Falling.

Hitting the water.

Drowning.

Empty black space surrounding his body.

Suffocating.

Something moving in front of him in the depths. Flashes of murky white flesh shrouded in muddy water. Moving towards him.

Powerful yet bony fingers grabbing onto his waist. From a hand that was too big. The cloudy figure right in front of him.

Flashing a row of serrated teeth.

Juni woke to the sun bathing the living room in clear and golden waves. The warmth of the rays on his face woke him up to clear skies.

Since he last checked, no high winds last night. Not even a single drop of rain.

His body felt rested, but his mind was far from any sense of peace.

His dreams. The thing in the water. Each time he had the dream, something was getting closer. Obscure darkness at first, but now something was making itself solid and visible. Getting closer to him. He tried not to think about what Haruto said: "The one who comes in the rain."

Juni flung his legs off the sofa, stood up, cracked his back, and stretched out his arms.

Looking out at the bay, at the golden light of the sunrise, it still wasn't easy to dissociate from his dreams. They were getting worse. Becoming more visceral. Creating in him a feeling of siege. Of the impending danger from which there was no escape.

But the view before him was one of tranquility. Whatever his father had been doing, giving offerings to the sea, it clearly worked.

Juni had enough money to pay off his most dangerous and shadiest of debts. He still had the mortgage payments to worry about, but soon, after calling Aido-sama again—and hopefully getting through this time—he wouldn't have to worry about getting his knees capped.

And that's what we call progress.

And then there was the weather. He checked his phone and saw that the area around Tanosawa had a forecast of a sunny day. The rest of the peninsula was currently being pummeled by the typhoon.

The sky above Tanosawa didn't show the slightest hint of a cloud.

That's three times now. Three requests, and three responses, all exactly what I wanted.

True, what he really wanted was for his debt to be completely done away with, but he remembered a line from Dad's journal: *From what is mine to you.*

Maybe the reward given was in some way proportionate to the offering? So far he had only given a coin and a watch. The latter had sentimental and some cash value to it, but not that much.

He took the journal from his backpack. No new pages had appeared.

If I want all my debt gone—and some more, why not?—then I'm going to have to give something bigger. And what did Sakura say? Something like, "The more that I wanted it to work for me, the further out at sea I'd have to go."

A thought that made him queasy.

First things first. Aido-sama.

He dialed his number and paced the room.

A woman answered, "Who is this?" Her voice was rough. To the point. Blue-collar in its accent, but full of confidence allotted only to the rich and powerful.

"Sorry, I think I have the wrong number."

"You're trying to reach Takanori, right?"

"Yes."

"I'm his wife. Now who is this?"

Juni explained his situation to Mrs. Aido.

"Well, the police have been here all morning sorting shit out. My husband is dead. I took his phone before the cops could confiscate it. Gave them one of his other phones. Didn't want them to know too much about what he did, but I guess they will sooner or later. So, I guess you think you're lucky, Hatayama-san. Can't owe a dead guy anything, can you? That's what you're thinking. No, wire me the money you owe now, and maybe I can let this go."

Juni got her bank information and hung up.

He stood there in shock. For a second he felt bad for the joy bubbling up in his gut, but that second soon passed. He was free. Sure, sad to hear the guy died, but he wasn't the nicest one out there. Juni wouldn't be surprised to hear that he had been killed as an act of revenge for murdering somebody else.

Juni opened his bank app and made the transfer to the account number Aido-sama's widow gave him.

Juni looked out at the sea. Normally, a thing that stirred up the deepest emotions of fear in him. But today, he smiled in gratitude. The upset in his stomach subsided. He extended his car rental by a few days on the app. Chose the "pay upon delivery" option.

He then took out his phone and dialed Haruka to tell her the good news.

"You want me to take you out there to do *what*?" Shota asked as he tightened a bolt on his motorcycle, the sweat from his forehead cutting black and gray streaks down his cheeks.

They were just outside of Shota's place, a shack more than a house. The sidings may have been wooden once but were now hobbled together with fragments of metal welded on. The roof was two or three corrugated tin slats bolted onto the walls.

The front door was open, revealing a one-room living space, a tiny sink next to a gas-powered stove, and a mound of beer cans, fishing equipment, and magazines. The place looked like a literal trash can, but Juni kept that to himself.

"I know it's weird, but it's like a final send-off for my dad. I want you to take me to Tajima Island, and I need to throw something overboard. I'll say a word or two in remembrance, and we can come back right away."

"You know I can smell bullshit a mile away, right? Your dad didn't ask you to remember him, and even if he had, you wouldn't do it. You're not the superstitious type."

Well, he would have been right if we were talking last week.

"Okay, yeah, you're right. But what I need to do is strange, and I thought it would sound better couched like that."

"Who uses a word like 'couched'? Big city boy through and through now, huh?" Shota laughed, pushed out the bike's kickstand, and left it leaning against the shack.

"Fuck you," Juni said with a smile. "So, you gonna help me, or?"

"Sure, I'll take you there. For your stupid-ass ritual or whatever you're doing. But I can't promise I won't laugh at you while you do it."

"Thanks. I mean it. When are you free?"

"Wanna go now? I can take us down on my bike."

"Sounds good."

Shota revved up the bike, and Juni got on the back part of the seat, holding onto Shota's waist. He offered no helmet. Shota drove the motorcycle out of his driveway and turned right onto the road.

Shota didn't live far from the harbor. They'd be there in just a few minutes. The tiny homes of the village, all of them the same sad design: boxes with small holes for windows, piled right up against one another, some of them in worse condition than Shota's. A few of them had sections crumbling into the river that ran alongside the perimeter of the village.

Again, Juni noted the dearth of humanity walking the streets. The odd elderly man or woman walked here and there, listless and waiting for death. Juni couldn't wait to leave this place. But there was one last thing he wanted to do, one last thing he wanted to test.

Haruka didn't take the news of Aido-sama's death the same way he did. Similar to how she acted when first hearing of his father's death, Haruka was more mortified than happy.

Why couldn't she see this for the blessing that it was? In the end, he pacified her by saying their problems were ending. "How?" she asked. He left it vague.

Maybe one day he'd tell her.

The buildings blurred. The bay came into view. The waters were still; with the sunlight shining off them. There were only two boats tied to the dock, Shota's and one other smaller boat that maybe was once a speedboat, but now resembled a canoe due to the march of time.

Shota drove the bike up the steps from the parking lot and onto the pier itself. The *rata-ta-tat* of the wood beneath the rubber tires was strangely melodic and soothing.

It reminded him of a time when was a kid. Dad was driving up to Mount *Osore,* and Juni was in the backseat. The road was narrow and wrapped around the side of a mountain. Carsick, stomach feeling like it wanted to escape out the closed window, Juni lay face down on the seat. The motion of the car hitting the bumps in the road, rocking his body, didn't make him feel worse. It was entrancing and invited him to sleep.

He remembered seeing Buddha statues on the side of the road as Dad drove to the temple where people went to pray for their dead. Juni hated these visits. The temple sat next to a sulfuric lake, resting in a caldera above the still-active magma deep underground. Ugly demon statues guarded the bridge that cars had to drive over to enter the temple grounds.

Dad went to see the *itako* often: blind women who could commune with the dead. Dad made him come along, for what purpose Juni had no clue. He just sat on the ground and played with rocks as Dad talked to the women.

The itako entered their trances and spoke in hushed tones. Dad would lean forward and nod along with the show. Juni's skin crawled and tried to flee his body every time he had to witness the grotesque conversation. The smell of rotten eggs gagged him. The faces of the demon statues, with their tongues sticking out, terrified him.

The only pleasant memory of those days was the soft thump of the road on the car's belly as they drove those roads.

Juni felt that comfort now as Shota brought the bike to a halt. The last moments of safety before being confronted with something beyond his understanding.

But he felt compelled to do this.

They got off the motorcycle, and Shota leaned it against a post. He untied the rope from his boat to the pier, took the keys out of his coverall pockets, stepped onto his boat, and turned it on. Juni helped push the boat away from the dock, jumped on, and sat down on the bench behind the captain's seat. Shota's flashy boat, imperial flag waving madly in the wind, veered away from land and headed out to sea.

Juni kept his eyes closed the entire trip. He tapped his knees nervously and tried to focus on the goal: the reason he was out here.

He knew exactly what to offer. It was in his wallet, resting warmly against his left thigh as the boat bounced up and down. Giving this object, close to the island, had to work. If it did, Juni would be free of all his debts; he'd be a new man. Not only liberated from the demands of gangsters and banks, he also imagined being freed from the indentured servitude of catering to whiny teenagers and their vulture parents all day, of having to bow to his decrepit boss, of having to live in that coffin of an apartment, of staying married to a woman he no longer loved.

Shame slapped him in the face at that last thought. But it was true. Whatever this thing was that he was making offerings to, surely it knew what was in his mind, anyway. No use in hiding his desires from it.

The chance of a new life was right before him. All he had to do was drop this in the water.

And why Tajima? What was so special about this island that Sakura had to mention it?

It had appeared once in his dreams already. He was also sure that that was the place where the weird ritual in the journal's photograph took place.

What does it—

"We're here," Shota called out over the dying engine. "Never been this close before. Ugly rock."

Juni opened his eyes, the sun's glare stinging his vision.

"Do what you need to do. I'm gonna fish while I wait." He grabbed an anchor, tied it off to a cleat, and tossed it overboard. "Don't know how deep it is and whether it'll set, so don't be too long." He set up his fishing pole in the rod rack, sat down on a lawn chair, lit up his cigarette, pulled his baseball cap over his eyes, and seemed to fall into a coma all while keeping his hands on the rod.

Juni moved to the port side and gazed out at Tajima.

A dead rock. Like a meteorite that fell from the sky, from some barren waste of infinite space, it stood out of the water as if it didn't belong there. Juni never knew what made him feel this; was it the color, a dreary gray mixed with jet-black that was at the same time bright? Was it at the height of the island? The rocks jutted straight out of the water and so high, he couldn't see what was on the other side of them, like a stone drawbridge raised by some mad king on an isolated outpost.

The skies were blue, lighter near the sun, a dark cobalt straight above. Juni took out his wallet and opened it. It wasn't the money, his maxed-out credit cards, or the picture of Haruka that he was going to offer. No, it had to be valuable, more than anything he had given yet. He took out the folded picture Mai-Mai had drawn for him the day he came to Tanosawa. For the last time, he beheld the red dolphin-dragon and the warrior princess riding above the marshmallow clouds. Tears welled up in his eyes. He loved his daughter, and that was one reason he had to do this. He'd be able to give her anything, right? Keep her safe. Send her to art school someday.

All good things require sacrifice, don't they?

He glanced back at Shota. The man looked asleep, maybe even dead, but the way he held the pole told Juni he was wide awake and could hear everything he would say. But no half-measures. If he was tossing in the picture, he had to be sure it would work.

"From what is mine to you, so that what is yours will be mine. I want all of my mortgage paid off. In full. I want my credit card debt erased. I want enough to live on so that I can quit my job."

He held the picture above the water. He looked down at the steel-blue waves. Darker indigo depths beneath the surface, fading to an almost black expanse, obscured anything that might be under the boat.

He let go of the picture. It floated down and side to side, like a leaf falling from a tree. It landed in the charcoal water. The paper went from semi-rigid to limp as the water soaked it. The colors ran and streaked across the page. The red of the dragon bled out like toxic blood, washing out the picture. It stayed on the surface, and Juni feared what it would mean if it didn't sink.

"The stars are so beautiful tonight."

The voice of a young girl jarred him. He took a step back from the edge of the boat. He had heard some strange phrases since coming here, but this one was new to him. Up on Tajima's ridge, dozens of shadows stood, eyes blazingly white even in the light of day, looking at the boat. Or was it the water they were gazing at?

"What the fuck was that?" Shota asked, standing up from his lazy stupor.

"No, please don't. I want to live," came the words of a sobbing woman, gasping for air.

"Juni, what's going on?" Shota cursed when he saw the figures on the ridge.

Then the familiar muffled protest, "This is not what I want."

"Juni!" Shota yelled as he grabbed his arm.

Juni looked back at him, eyes wide and lips shaking.

Then came a string of words, what might be called a sentence, that nearly broke Juni's mind. A unique voice delivered each phrase. Some were ones he had already heard before; others were new. Most were women's voices. It was as if something had dissected human speech, picked what it wanted to use, and tossed out the rest.

"I want... beautiful...please don't...give me...here...are you going to kill me? Kill. Kill me? Kill."

Then came the screeching. A high-pitched wail shook the underside of the boat. The two men fell to their knees and covered their ears with their hands. Shota fell onto his side and gnashed his teeth.

"No...not again...give me...kill."

Something hit the boat, and it rocked so hard that even though they were already low on the deck, they almost fell into the sea.

"Kill. Kill. Kill."

These words were hoarse, from the throat of a woman who had drunk her vocal cords into oblivion. But there was something overlaying her voice, behind her voice, using her voice. A growl, deep and resonating and throaty, menacing and cold. Wet and belonging to some great mouth.

The voices stopped. The boat stood still. Juni helped Shota to his feet. The figures on the ridgeline had gone. The picture was no longer floating in the water.

Deep in the darkness of the navy waves, he glimpsed something. Pale flesh of a large body. Something longer than the boat. It was just for a moment before it sank out of sight.

But Juni knew what it was. It looked exactly like what he had seen in his dream.

Which meant it had a set of teeth he'd like to never see.

SEVENTEEN

"What the flying fuck was that?" Shota shouted, near a full-on breakdown, clutching at Juni's shirt. "You said nothing like that was going to happen!"

"I don't know, I didn't know that would happen, but—"

"But what, buttercup? Out with it."

"But I knew something supernatural was going on, yes. I'm sorry for not saying anything, but I didn't think you'd believe me. I wasn't totally on board, either, but, fuck it, yeah, something strange is happening, but Shota," Juni took the man's hands off his collar, "but it's saving me. Dad wrote about it in his journal. Whenever he gave something to it, he got rewarded. Like money, fame, or whatever he wanted. Yeah, this is all sorts of fucked-up crazy, but it's saving my life, Shota."

Shota backed away from him. "You shouldn't have anything to do with this. I shouldn't have anything to do with this. And give what exactly and *to what?*"

"Anything important to me. Like pictures, money. What is down there? I don't know. It's weird and scary, but it's not hurting anybody. I'm about to lose my house. The bank is going to reclaim it. I've already gotten the loan taken care of with some bad guys. All of it gone! And if this works again, the bank. I know what life has been like for you, living in that shack, fired from my dad's company. If you want to help me here, join me; it can help you too."

Raving lunatic. Madman. "Straight-jacket to dinner every night" kind of speech. Juni was aware of how he sounded, but the truth of what had been happening to him was pouring out, and, fuck, it felt good to be honest for once.

"No. I don't want to come one inch closer to this shit. Now shut up and let me take us back home."

Shota hoisted up the anchor, started the boat, and sped out of there like their lives depended on it.

Back at Dad's house.

The sun was now extinguished. In the sky, red hues like blood washed out of a garment, spreading out from the sea to the village. The cicadas were screaming their last songs of the day, mating calls shrill in desperation, calming down before the coming night.

Juni stood on the patio, hands on the railing. Eyes fixed on the waves. They reflected the crimson sky, like a sea of dull blood.

Shota didn't understand. Couldn't understand what Juni did. He was on to something here. Was it beyond him? Beyond all the rules of science he had professed to believe in? Yes. But it was working.

Any moment now, I'll get a notification saying that everything will be okay. Maybe it will be tomorrow at the latest, but it's coming.

After dropping him off back at Juni's car, Shota said he didn't want anything more to do with this. Juni tried to reason with him, but the man wasn't having it. Juni hit up the Sea Breeze for a few silent drinks next to Mr. Ando and went home.

A goat bleated, and one came into view off to the left, from the open backyard between his house and the ranch. Haruto was following the animal, patting its back, whistling a song to it. He looked very different now. All Juni had seen of the man this week was a disheveled and paranoid drunk. In the red sunset, tending to his animals, the man looked at peace with his simple existence. Juni wondered what Haruto's connection to all this was. At first, he thought the man was on the brink of mental deterioration, but now he could see that Haruto knew what the thing in the water was. His last words to Juni were ominous, as if he wasn't long for this world.

The man in the drain?

"Hey, Haruto!"

He looked up and smiled at Juni. In a way, he looked much younger then, despite the obvious signs of age. It was the youthful way he walked with the goat. Like a child would with a puppy. Or a stuffed animal.

Juni walked down the stairs from the patio to the side of the house, near where Haruto stood. There was no fence between their properties, and they met in a small field on the edge of the hill.

"I'm still here. See, Haruto, nothing to worry about."

"Oh, that. I'm so sorry. I keep on troubling you with nonsense."

"But it's not, is it?"

Haruto looked up from petting the goat, eyes wide and perplexed.

Juni continued, "I did it, Haruto. I gave an offering. Three of them, actually. And the things I've gotten in return. My life is changed. What is it? What were you and my dad into?"

Haruto's lips trembled, and his hands shook. He must have spooked the goat because it backed away from him. "You? Why?" the man cried. "Oh, my boy." He wandered away from Juni towards the edge of the hill, looking out at the sea. "Then it is done. And your life is over, son. It will come for you in the water. They will come for you in the shadows. And they will not stop until the cost is paid in full."

"What are you talking about?"

"There is a Dark within the dark. The floor of the sea moves and writhes. In amber light comes the end of Man."

Haruto turned around and walked back home. As he passed Juni, he put his hand on Juni's shoulder. "Your father woke it up. And I helped him keep it awake. Now you are part of this. And we will all pay for our sins."

The doorbell chimed. Juni was sitting at the kitchen bar chewing on Haruto's words.

We will pay for our sins.

Juni went to the front door and opened it.

Sakura was standing there. Dressed in a scarlet dress, with the slit of a thigh flashing between swaying silk, a black hat with a black ribbon and feather sticking out of it. She looked like a cross between a 1920s flapper and a geisha, both absurd in their anachronistic style. But Juni found her strangely attractive in that moment.

"Umm, hi. Didn't expect to see you again. What are you doing here?"

He could have blushed at the idiocy of his embarrassment and word salad.

"May I come in first?" She brushed her way past him, took off her shoes, and entered the house, leading him to the kitchen bar. "Nothing's changed since I came here last. Disappointing. Except where are all my paintings?"

She sat on the bar stool, crossed her right leg, and leaned back against the counter.

"I burned them."

She laughed. "Why would you go and do that? Anyway, have you been doing what your father asked of you? Have you given to the waters?"

"Yes, three times now. It's amazing, I've gotten so many—"

"And have you been going further out to sea, towards Tajima, with each offering?"

"Yeah, and—"

"Good. And have you seen anything *unnatural*?" She seemed almost excited, like she was asking a recently returned friend about a country she had always longed to visit but couldn't.

"Fuck, where do I start? Well, there's been shadows with white eyes. Ghosts? Voices. Repeating the same lines. And let's not forget about the thing I saw in the water by the island."

Her eyes widened, for a moment stretching her skin so thin that the façade of makeup and her perfect smile revealed her age. "You saw it? And you went as far as the island?"

She stood up, nearly tripping over her own feet until she caught herself by grabbing the counter.

"Yeah, I did. What was it? I really want to know."

She turned and placed both her hands on the counter as if to catch her breath. "Junichiro, no one, save for your father and those that it takes has ever seen it. And no one has ever approached Tajima without their boats running aground."

Juni let out a nervous laugh. "Sakura, I've been there before with my Dad when I was a kid. And a friend took me there today. It was totally fine."

"You don't understand: no one except for you and your father, and those who were with them, has ever made it that close. Many in this village believe and serve, but none has been granted such access. I didn't think it would let you get that close."

"Why do you look so scared?"

"It can't be what I'm thinking."

She got up to leave.

"Wait, you can't just come in here and drop some cryptic shit like that on me and leave."

Juni blocked the door. Her eyes flashed fire at him, but he didn't move.

'Fine," she said as she sat back down. "You really want to know? It means it has accepted you as the one to bring offerings to the Wave. I don't know why you, so don't ask me. It was your father first, and now it's you. Tanosawa hadn't had someone in this position for hundreds of years before Ryotaro filled it. It's a privilege that some would kill to have, Junichiro, if you catch my meaning."

Too many questions to ask.

"You mean my life is in danger? From who?"

"But you don't need to worry about that, not if it has indeed chosen you. It will protect its investment and not let anything happen to you. But you better listen to this clearly. If you do not give it what it wants, it will take it by other means."

"What does it want?"

"I think you know."

The gnarled phrase at Tajima this afternoon. One word repeated over and over.

Kill.

"Okay, what is the Wave?"

Sakura looked out of the window wall. "Something I wish to see someday. It doesn't matter." She got up and went to the door. Holding the handle, she sighed. "I'm sorry this happened to you. But if you will not give what is required, and soon, it will take freely as it chooses. Time is short. Decide."

She got up and left him alone.

Night had come to Tanosawa. The cicadas were as silent as the dead. Darkness ruled the skies.

Juni was lying on the sofa, reading the texts from Haruka he had been ignoring the past few hours.

WHEN ARE YOU COMING HOME?

THIS IS SERIOUS.

It was the last one that convinced him to call home.

I'VE BEEN HEARING VOICES IN THE HOUSE.

Followed by five calls that he missed with the phone on silent since he went out on the boat with Shota.

He dialed Haruka's number.

"Juni!" She sounded happy to hear him. The shock of it momentarily stunned him. "Are you there?"

"Yeah. Is everything okay?"

"Juni, we need you to come home."

"Are you at your mom's?"

"We were, but came back."

"What? After I told you to leave? Did that man show up again?"

"No, nothing like that. But I don't feel safe in our apartment or Mom's. It started at her place. Mayu's been having bad dreams every night. She was telling me she had heard something screaming outside her window and that there were voices, too. I thought it was just her imagination, but yesterday I heard something. At first, I thought it had to be a catfight or maybe the neighbor's TV was too loud. So, I opened the window to see what was going on, and I heard someone whisper in my ear, Juni! From ten floors up, where Mom lives. Nobody was there. I thought I was losing my mind, but it happened again this morning, so we came back to our home. And just an hour ago, while I was washing dishes, Mayu had headphones in and was watching anime on her iPad, and I heard a girl say something to me. In our house! Right next to me. I know this sounds crazy, but I swear I'm not losing it."

She spoke quickly and ran out of breath.

Juni didn't think she was crazy at all. This rant terrified him because he believed it. "What did the voice say?"

"It was a girl, maybe in her teens or twenties, and she said something about the stars being beautiful."

Juni felt his body plummeting through the crust of the earth down to the core. "Did... did she say anything else?"

"I don't know; I'm losing my mind here."

"No, you're not, I believe you, honey. Try to think, did she say anything else?"

"Why the hell do you believe me?" She laughed, but the fault lines of fear were in her voice. "I heard a girl in the kitchen, and a man's voice, like he was underwater, like he had a blanket or pillow over his mouth."

"Did he say, 'This is not what I want?'"

"No, it was more like, 'Soon, you will see.' It was hard to hear because it was raining hard outside. Juni, I know I'm going crazy, but why are you so calm?"

"Honey, I'm coming home. Tomorrow, first thing. I know this will sound strange, but don't go near the water, I mean like any pond or lake or something, and don't go outside when it rains. Or go near any drains!"

Juni felt his blood rush to his head.

"What is happening?"

"I don't know, but I'm going to fix it. Love you."

She didn't reply for a moment. Maybe she wasn't accustomed to the word, but she finally repeated it back to him.

They hung up.

This was too far. Juni was fine testing the waters himself. Skeptical at first, but ecstatic when he saw the results. But now, whatever was happening here was seeping its way into his family's life. Like the black mold in his roof, infecting his home. Like the stain in his father's room and in the sauna. The dark spot on the ceiling of the bathhouse.

All his insides felt like they evaporated at the thought, *Was that really mold in my house these past few months?*

He didn't like this. And he really didn't like the new phrase, one he hadn't heard yet, "Soon, you will see."

See what?

This had to stop. Would it stop? If he just gave nothing more to the waters, would it all go away?

But Juni knew what it wanted.

Blood.

And for whatever awful reason, he was chosen to give it.

He got up and went to his father's room. The door was shut, just as he had left it. He couldn't feel his hands as he reached for the knob.

This is so stupid. It's just rotten wood or some water damage, so why even bother with it?

He turned away to make for the living room. Some magnetic pull refused to release him. He had to know. Opening the door, he walked inside.

The miasma had gotten worse since the last time he was here. The brown, charred air was thicker. The overwhelming scent of sulfur filled his nostrils. Coughing, he backed out of the room, pulling his shirt up to his mouth. For a moment, he thought a fire had broken out. He tried to remember where the extinguisher was in the house. As he thought this, the haze rose to the ceiling of the bedroom and stayed there. Everything under the cloud was clear of the toxic air. There was no fire in the room.

But this air, it has to be poisonous.

He made to close the door and then stopped. The stain near the bed had grown. It was just the other day, uncomfortably close in size and even shape to a person. Now it took up most of the wall. Tar-like sap oozed out of what looked like a gangrenous wound. It fell in clumps on the bed. From the substance came the brown smoke. The sheets were dissolving under the stuff. It didn't produce smoke. The brown clouds. It was as if the very air transformed into something new, something this world had never seen, and poured out from what was being eaten by the touch of the mold.

The wall pulsed as if thousands of insects were clawing their way out of the wood. The sound of their scratching mandibles chewing through the plaster wormed its way into his head, echoing throughout his skull.

Juni's phone buzzed in his hands. It broke the spell. He opened it and looked at the notification. It was from his banking app.

Looking back at the room, the stain had reverted to what it was yesterday. As did the haze. Nothing melting, nothing pushing its way out of the walls.

Still, Juni was done here. He slammed the door shut and walked back to the living room.

He looked back at his phone. Never had he been so nervous to open a message before. The bright green bubble popped onto the screen.

Juni covered his mouth with his hands and dropped the phone. With the amount that he saw, the mortgage would not be a problem anymore.

EIGHTEEN

Laughing and crying, Juni lay on the floor. Confusing emotions swelled up in his chest. He had to go home; he knew that. What was happening here was pushing him towards madness. It might even be dangerous.

But all of his money problems were gone. Poof. Like they didn't exist anymore. What he had struggled to solve for months through gambling and loans and even hard work was, in a moment, nullified. The pendulum swinging above his head for the past few years, blade dulled and gritty, caked with dry blood, was now a non-issue.

Was the thing in the water evil? Yes, it was terrifying. And he hated that it had somehow reached his family in Tokyo. But how could something that gave so much be so bad?

But no, this was enough. It had to be. He fought off the thoughts of staying. Of giving more offerings. Of building up his empire and kicking up his feet for the rest of his life.

There was nothing left to give, aside from the photo of Mai. A small part of him couldn't give that up. He also doubted the rental car would make much of an impact. He would have stayed and figured something out and braved the potential risks if it weren't for the fact that his family was now being affected.

Then there were the implications of what Sakura had said.

Blood.

That was a line too far to cross.

Unless, could I give one of Haruto's chickens?

He laughed at the thought. It might work. But things were getting too intense. Best to stop it before it got worse.

Just then, rain started pelting the window wall. The metallic clang of the water sounded almost like hail.

The lights went out.

Juni got up off the floor and turned on his phone's flashlight.

"Shit."

Maybe the lights would turn back on quickly, like last time. He sat there for a full minute; the rain ramping up its assault against the glass.

Then came the screaming.

The high-pitched wail broke through the torrential rain. Now Juni knew, at least somewhat, from where that sound emerged. Which meant that *it* was here. Not far away, buried under the smothering waves. No, it was on land. Right outside the house.

Juni went to the window wall and cupped his hands against it. A blanket of deep night. The rain made it worse. He thought he saw something moving, but it could well have been the trees getting knocked about by the storm.

A howling wind slammed against the house. It shook a little. Was this the typhoon? It came out of nowhere.

If I wished for this to go away and it's here now, what does that mean for my money?

He checked his phone. No signal and no Wi-Fi. Must be the storm. He'd have to wait it out first.

Haruto's voice broke his train of thought. The same pained scream as before. As if something was torturing him beyond his limit. Earlier, Juni had assumed that he was just drunk, attacked by demons no more real than his nightmares. Now he thought differently, because he knew that something swam in the waters of Tanosawa, even making landfall in the rain.

Glass shattering.

More screams.

Then a boom that could have been thunder but sounded much more localized. It came from right next door.

Then the screaming stopped. The lights came back on. Rain started fizzling out to a light patter. The wind settled down. Soon, the light of the moon graced the windows with its silvery touch.

All was still.

Juni could ignore Haruto. He was fine last time, wasn't he? Sure, his window was broken and he ran off into the woods naked, but otherwise he was fine, all things considered. Juni waited for a sign, for some sound to tell him that Haruto was up and about and fine.

Then it came; the bleating of the goats and the sheep, from far too close to be on Haruto's property. Juni looked out the peephole. At first, nothing but the dark silhouettes of the trees with moonlight lighting up the front yard. Then they came. Two of the goats ran across Juni's driveway as if escaping a predator. The only way they'd be able to make it over here is if the fence was left open or destroyed. He very much doubted they could jump it.

Juni opened the door and went outside.

"Haruto!" he called out as he walked and made his way over to his house. As he turned the corner onto the old man's drive, he saw nothing but a black expanse. No lights on. Same as before, except for the dark forms strewn about the lawn. As Juni walked up to the door, he saw they were pieces of the fence, tossed about the entire front yard. He knocked and called out again. No response. Feeling all too familiar. Which was a good thing, right? That'd mean the old man was okay, the same as before.

Juni opened the door, turned on his phone's light, and walked in.

The first thing he noticed was the smell of iron, thick in the air. Mixed with the stink of rotten eggs. He shone his light across the dirty kitchen area. The second anomaly quickly became apparent. Black, tar-like mold covered the walls, the floor, and even the kitchen ceiling. It looked exactly the same as what he thought was an illusion back in his father's room. Juni walked past it all, careful not to walk directly under the substance. He studied a spot of black on the ceiling. The wood surrounding it was slowly absorbing the liquid—if that's what he could call it. The parts already covered were dissolving. Holes appeared at the epicenter. Soon, the plaster was eaten away, and Juni could see the wooden support beam of the ceiling. They too, were falling apart. The substance spewed out thick brown air.

"Holy fuck."

He had to move fast; if it continued at this rate, the entire home could collapse in minutes.

"Haruto! We need to get out of here!"

Juni turned down the hall into the living room. The hole in the wall was boarded up with cardboard and duct tape. Guilt pierced his heart. Not once had he thought about helping Haruto fix the damage, even after he got all that money. But whatever home repairs the man had done, no amount of tape or super glue could fix what Juni saw next.

The entire wall behind the TV was gone, as if something had ripped it away. From this vantage point, Juni could see the animal pens outside. The goat and sheep fence was smashed, and some animals wandered about like refugees of a calamity. The chicken coop alone remained intact.

Inside the living room, rainwater covered the furniture. As did the black mold. Haruto's leather chair was overturned, covered in the slime, and shredded to pieces. Black streaks across almost every surface of the room. The burnt air was slowly filling the space. Juni coughed and felt lightheaded.

Blood pooled in front of the chair. Every now and then, black drops from the mold fell from the ceiling into the blood, rippling out concentric waves.

Haruto was nowhere to be found. Not hiding in any corner.

Drip.

He hadn't even noticed the black stain right above him. Some of the dark sap fell next to his face, grazing his left ear.

Searing pain.

Electric signals firing in his brain.

Juni shouted in agony and instinctively moved his left hand to his ear. Then he remembered how the stuff ate through the ceiling and forced himself to lower his hand. He clenched his teeth and punched the wall.

Then the pain subsided mostly. Enough for him to stand. He hazarded a touch of the ear. Nothing burned his fingers. He felt the fire in the ear fade away.

Juni left the house. He called out Haruto's name into the forest. A creaking sound came from the man's house as the roof caved in. He wasn't inside, and he was nowhere nearby.

Juni went back home, checked his ear in the bathroom mirror, and ran some cold water over it.. It must have been just a drop of the mold and not enough to do major damage, because his ear wasn't dissolving before his eyes. There was a hole in the upper part of the cartilage. Nobody would have noticed without being told about it. No blood poured out. The wound looked cauterized.

But, fuck, it still hurt.

He splashed some more cool water from the sink on his ear and pressed a towel against it until the pain was pretty much gone.

Enough.

Gotta make sure everything is locked.

Juni ran like a madman through the house, making sure every door, every window, was locked. He checked his phone for a signal to call the police. It would take them forever to get here, but he had to try. The storm must still have been going on: not a single bar, and the house's Wi-Fi was still down.

Juni looked up at the window wall. He had felt unnerved by it the entire time, but more in an "I think something's watching me" kind of way. Now the window was more than just that; it was the easiest point of access into the house. The window stood on a hill and was too high for anybody to walk right up to it. But still, it was glass. Juni knew there was a storm shutter outside. He had seen his dad use it before, but that would require him to go *out there*.

Why the hell did Dad put the controls outside?

Juni stood in the kitchen, grabbed a butcher's knife, but remained unsure of what to do and where to go.

Something moved outside the window wall. A black shape with the briefest flash of tiny white lights, like fireflies. A thud against the glass. Juni did not dare go near.

He felt his arms shake and his throat go dry.

Another thud. Not hard enough to break the glass. Not yet.

Juni stood in front of the fridge, knife in hand, for what felt like over an hour before he could move. During this time, nothing made a sound. No rain. Even the sheep next door fell silent.

When he finally stepped forward, electric shocks of numbness shooting up his legs, limping from the inactivity, he made it as far as the sofa and sat down. Still no signal on the phone.

He sat there, eyes transfixed on the window wall until the first signs of dawn cut through the darkness. The brighter it got outside, the clearer Juni could see a smudge on the glass. It was spread all over, from top to bottom, side to side.

When the sunrise lit up the room, Juni sighed in relief, because he could now clearly see what was left on the glass.

In clear Japanese, written backward so that he could read it, in chunky black and red wet clumps and streaks, a message:

"This is not what I want. Kill. Kill. Kill."

And behind the bloody words, out in the bay, a large shadow, beneath the morning light, taller than any building in the village, dove into the water.

NINETEEN

Juni's phone chimed. Without even looking at the notification, he swiped it away and called the police.

"This is the Mutsu City Police Department, please state your emergency," said the woman on the line.

"This is Hatayama Junichiro. I'm staying at 37-6 in Tanosawa. On the north side of the peninsula, near Oma. Someone has just attacked my neighbor and vandalized my home."

"Okay, sir, we can send a patrol car out to you now, but it will take at least three hours, maybe more, since the typhoon has caused several landslides on your side of the peninsula. I apologize, but that's the best we can do. Can you describe your neighbor's condition and who attacked them?"

Juni almost told the truth for a split second, but then thought better of it. "I heard him yelling and went to check on him. Someone broke a window, and there was blood all over his house. I didn't see him or who did it. He's elderly, and the storm was getting bad. And there's this stuff all over the place."

"Can you be more specific, sir?"

"This... you know... blood on my window, and this black stuff, too. It burns when you touch it, so be careful."

A long moment of silence on the line.

"Okay, sir, we will take that into consideration. Stay inside with your doors locked until an officer can make it to your residence."

Juni hung up.

Three hours? No problem. It's light out. It's not raining anymore. I'm safe.

Breathless, Juni fell back down on the sofa. He checked his phone. Another notification from his bank. He opened it.

More money had come in.

Double what was there last night. Enough to pay the mortgage, enough not even to have to work for a year or two.

With bile rising in his throat, he laughed, borderline maniacally.

"Good news, right?"

He dropped his phone on the floor and paced the room.

"Okay, okay. Cops will be here soon; show them what I need to. Then get in my car and get the fuck out of here and back to Tokyo. Can't leave now; they have to clear the landslide first. So, just be patient."

But no way was he going to be alone as he waited. Juni poured a shot of whiskey, downed it, grabbed his keys, and got in his car. He'd be back to wait for the police later.

"Shota, open up, please."

Juni banged his hand against the metal siding that served as a door. A rusty screech came from the other side as Shota's considerable frame filled the doorway.

"Juni, I can't handle you right now." He went to shut the door, but Juni stopped it with his foot.

"Something happened last night. I think Haruto is dead. He's missing, at least. Something came to my window and wrote a message in—I think it was blood — the same words we heard yesterday at Tajima."

Shota let him inside. "It came to your house?" Shota's tanned face had become ashen gray. "It can do that? With what happened yesterday, I was ready to give up fishing, and never fucking touch water again. But you're saying it can come out of the water?"

He sat down on his disheveled bed, leaned over to the tiny fridge by the pillow, and got himself a beer.

"I know, and I'm sorry. Things are getting out of hand, and I don't know what to do."

"What if you just stop? Stop messing with it?"

"Sure, absolutely," Juni said as his eyes flitted up and to the left.

Yeah, things are not going in a positive direction, but if you had seen the numbers I saw this morning, you wouldn't give up so easily.

"Can I just stay here for a few hours? I called the cops, and I need to meet them, but then I'm going back to Tokyo right after."

"Sure. But I gotta go soon. Picked up a part-time job helping to clear the roads of landslide damage."

"How bad are they?"

"The south side isn't too bad, should be cleared in a few hours. All up north is really bad, like it'll take days to clear, but nobody's hurt, from what I heard on the radio."

"So I guess this is goodbye?"

"For now. Don't get all soft and cry on me now."

Shota punched his arm and smiled.

"Same to you."

Before Shota left, he turned and said, "This thing... it's not going to come after me too, is it?"

He thought about Aido-sama. Dying at just the right time. All the way in Tokyo.

Shota will be fine, though. Everyone who was harmed was involved directly somehow. Haruto helped Dad with the offerings; Aido-sama was involved with my debt. Shota isn't.

Maybe it would all end when he went home, anyway.

"No, not at all. I'm the one who started it, so you don't have to worry."

"Good to hear." Shota didn't look convinced. "And you'll be fine once you get away from here?"

"Yes. I'm sure of it," he said as his eyes darted up to the tin ceiling. He was struggling to maintain eye contact.

Shota stepped outside and added, "Oh yeah, they found Mr. Sato."

"No way, he's okay?"

"Dead."

"How?"

"Dunno. But I heard the cops found his body ten miles south, floating in the water. Had something jammed into one eye. Gruesome stuff."

"What was it?"

"What was what?"

"The thing in the eye."

Shota furrowed his brow. "I think it was a coin. A guy I know who helps clean up dead bodies that wash ashore told me. It was, like, shoved into the eye, took them a hell of a time to get it out. Anyway, gotta get."

Shota left.

Juni didn't even have to speculate here. He knew it was a five hundred-yen coin.

He knew it was his fault. His first offering, done around the same day Sato went missing, was found on his body. Or rather, *in* his body. A rejected sacrifice.

He will freely take what he wants.

He shivered thinking about the watch and Mayu's drawing.

Time passed as Juni lay on Shota's bed. The summer heat and humidity made the place feel like an oven. Eventually, the reek of sweat, stale tobacco smoke, and seafood became too much, and he needed some air. He got up, went outside, and walked around the house.

Shota's place was just on the outskirts of the village. Only a minute's walk away from the nearest home, but also uncomfortably close to the sea. Juni could see the surf from where he was. Regretted the decision to come here, so close to the water. He rang up Keisuke earlier, but he didn't answer. He also naturally trusted Shota to handle shit better than Keisuke. But the sky was clear and rain-free. And he couldn't stay in his father's house anymore, so close to the carnage next door, so far away from other people, so close to the stain above the bed. He touched his ear. No pain, but still a reminder of what the mold could do.

Juni walked to the back of Shota's home, to a small tuft of land that could have served as a backyard. The stony beach was right there, less than a stone's throw away. No trees, or buildings, or even bushes blocking the view.

If this were anywhere else in Japan, Juni figured Shota could get rich by selling his land. Small as it was, it had a killer view and access to the beach. Sure, it wasn't soft and sandy, but nothing a rich guy with a dump truck couldn't fix.

The heat was intense. The cicadas grew louder. Drowned out his thoughts. But it was even hotter inside the house.

Looking at the sky, he noticed some heavy clouds rolling in. Dark gray and coming in quickly.

The wet heat drenched his white-collared shirt. He was sure the neck of the shirt had a yellowish-grimy stain by now.

He thought about the money in his account. Second-guessing his decision to leave the village.

I mean, did anything actually happen to me? Aside from a scratch on my ear? Just some scary shit, yeah, but I'm fine. Whatever was at my window could have easily come in, but it didn't. Maybe I'm overreacting.

Never mind the words "kill, kill, kill" written in blood. His mind was piecing together the meaning of the fractured sentence.

"This is not what I want." Every time he gave an offering. Then, when he had done it three times, given an unacceptable offering three times, the command: "Kill."

The unease set in his bones. He knew what it really wanted. Not watches or pictures or money. It wanted blood. It needed sacrifice.

The page from his father's journal. The crossed-out names, set every two years apart. Was that what Dad was giving?

People.

But if that was true, then why was Juni being rewarded? Why get any money at all if what he gave wasn't enough?

A sound came crashing into his ears. It blotted out the noise of the waves and even that of the cicadas. A scream. High-pitched and foxlike. His blood froze. Almost a welcome change, given the heat. Juni looked out towards the water and saw something standing on the beach. The sunlight illuminated the entire area, but the figure itself was black.

Like a shadow.

Juni walked over to the edge of the road. He could see it—the outline of a man. And on his head, a round hat.

"Go home," the shadow called out from the beach.

Juni felt a mixture of both relief and terror. "Haruto! Where have you been?" Juni remembered that first night, washing the man's skeletal frame, him running off into the woods, him grabbing onto Juni's shirt and spitting up his crazy words all over him. Maybe Haruto really had dementia. Maybe this all had a reasonable explanation.

Juni jumped over the guardrail on the road and walked down the grassy hill that led to the beach. When his feet touched the stones, he stopped. He looked like Haruto and was no longer obscured by shadow — something he had attributed to the angle of a cloud or something. But he seemed somehow drained of color. The flushness of his cheeks. The gray in his hair. Even the blue of his windbreaker and the black of his bowler cap. All of it was more muted than Juni remembered. Like a photo negative.

"Haruto, what are you doing out here?"

The figure turned around and walked into the water. He moved past the cement pylons used to break up enormous waves and moved further out into the sea.

"Haruto, what the fuck are you doing?"

Juni ran after the man, but stopped short of entering the bay itself. Haruto was now beyond the pylons and was waist-deep in the water. The waves were calm and slightly grazed his chest now and then. But even that would have been enough to knock down the elderly man. Yet on he walked.

Juni took off his socks and shoes. He waded out into the water until it came up to his knees. Yelled out after the figure once again. He lost sight of him. Juni went further out, almost past the pylons. Water waist-high now. He saw Haruto again with the waves up to his neck.

A swell bellowed up and splashed Juni in the face. Then, there was no one there. Haruto had vanished.

It was almost silent, save for the lapping of the water on the concrete structures. A sudden heavy feeling hit his left shoulder. Something gripped it. Something that felt like bony claws. Juni spun around, nearly falling over.

It was Haruto.

Relief filled Juni's heart for exactly the time to notice the details of his face.

"Are you..." Juni began and ended, his lips quivering.

The old man looked normal. But he wasn't wet. He had gone into the water completely, but here he was, clothes and hair dry. Even as the waves rose to his chest and fell, they didn't make his clothing wet.

Haruto's eyes bore into Juni's skull. Red eyes. Bloodshot and wild. Pleading. Desperate. Angry.

Then they turned black.

Like ink spilled into them. He opened his mouth, and a small crab climbed out and scuttled across his face. Its skittering made scratching sounds across the man's face. Juni let out a cry and tried to break free of Haruto's hold on his shoulder. He couldn't; he was pinned in place by a strength the old man could not possibly have possessed. Haruto's face went pale blue. Like a corpse. The cheeks became hollow. The flesh decomposed. All of a sudden, his clothes seemed soaked. All manner of garbage appeared on his torso from nowhere: from ropes to plastic bags to seaweed. Juni screamed and struggled against the thing that had a hold of him.

Haruto opened his mouth wider, to where it surely would have broken his jaw to do so. Seawater, kelp, and crabs all came pouring out. He spoke with a voice that sounded like it was underwater.

"Go home, Junichiro. You have been marked by the Wave. Leave now before it takes you and all that you love."

"W-what are you talking about?" Juni was on the verge of tears.

"The Amber Wave has marked you as it did your father. You should never have gone there. Now, before—" A scream filled the air. Haruto's dead and fully black eyes seemed somehow afraid. He let go of Juni. Juni fell into the water and splashed violently to get back on his feet. When he did, Haruto was gone.

Juni's heart raced as he tried to reconcile what had just happened. It wasn't a dream. He was there, standing in the water, not lying in his bed. If it were an illusion, then he was insane.

A surge of cold water wrapped around his legs. The hair on his neck stood up. It wasn't from what he had just seen. No, this was something different. He looked down at the water, for the first time realizing that he was in the ocean. The drive to save Haruto had momentarily boosted his heroism in the face of his thalassophobia.

A shadow covered the water in front of Juni. From something tall. Something standing out of the water. Something right behind him.

On the back of his neck, he felt a slight breeze, or was it breath? The smell of rotting fish choked him. The heat of the breeze made him sick.

He felt that at any moment he would be pulled under. Juni bolted toward the shore as best he could, his legs moving as if through wet cement. He fell once and bounced right back up. Juni made it to the beach and kept running until he was back on the hillside.

He scampered up the hill and back out onto the road.

He did not look back.

Juni ran to his rental car. Fuck the police. They can deal with Haruto themselves. *Whatever paperwork has to come, I'll deal with it later.*

His clothes soaked the upholstery, and he smeared clumpy sand all over the seat.

Juni drove up the hill that led out of the village. An old man began crossing in front of him, but Juni slammed the gas harder and nearly hit the man as he passed.

Soon, he came to a section of the road with grass shoulders on either side. Above him, the Table Top in all its ritzy glory.

So long. Thanks for all the tea.

He pressed the gas harder and flew up the hill that would take him out of here.

A figure in the middle of the road.

Shredded track suit. Bone sticking out where the left arm should have been. Broken sunglasses on his face. The shards were embedded in his cheeks and forehead. His innards spilled out of his torso, onto the road. Juni sped up and kept on driving. He braced himself for the impact, but it never came. He just went *through* the man, like air.

As he hit the man, he thought he heard him cry out, "Mama!"

"Fuck, fuck, fuck. Must go faster."

He crested the hill and slammed on the brakes. Across the one and only road in and out of the village on the south side, the wreckage of trees and mud and boulders. Looking up at the hillside, a path of destruction sliding all the way down.

Juni got out of the car and started climbing the pile of debris. He slipped and clawed his way back up. Something sharp in the mess scratched his face. But no matter how hard he climbed, he kept on sliding back down. After the fifth attempt, he sat on his ass before the landslide, covered in mud and wet debris.

This had to have just happened. Shota said the roads would be fine just a few hours ago.

It doesn't want me to leave.

Just then, it started raining.

Juni ran into his father's home and locked the door. He left behind muddy footprints wherever he went, but didn't care.

"What do I do? What the fuck do I do?"

He looked at his phone again— no signal.

"Fuck!" He threw the phone across the room. It landed somewhere in the open bathroom.

The rain grew thicker. It was midday, but the clouds quickly turned a deep stony gray. It felt like sunset was only moments away.

He did not want to be here, but it was safer than Shota's place, so close to the sea. It might be the safest building in town, for all that was worth.

Suddenly, the house shook. The fridge fell over. Juni swayed and had to hold on to the kitchen bar for support.

Then came the sirens.

Woeful and foreboding.

The wind picked up fiercely. Even so, Juni could clearly hear the tsunami-warning sirens. A sound tattooed into his mind through countless school drills. He remembered telling his students to take each drill seriously and make for the designated safe spots. They never did, laughing and checking their phones as they sluggishly meandered to where they needed to be.

As a kid, Juni had taken part in dozens of these drills in Tanosawa. He hoped with every atom in his body that this was not real. If it were, the whole village would make its way to Tanosawa Elementary School for refuge. It was the highest point of safety, aside from Dad's place and the Table Top, and the most accessible for the people.

But the sirens kept on blaring. No voice came on saying it was all a test.

That eerie wail clawed into his stomach. Juni went to the window wall and looked outside. Still light out, though the rain and gray clouds dimmed what he could see.

"Oh, my God."

The tall shadow he had seen before in the water. Standing up straight. The seashore receded behind it, exposing the rocky floor of the shallows.

Towering over the harbor. The few boats on the pier didn't even reach the shadow's midpoint. It had white eyes, blazing bright in the murky weather. It was looking at him.

Then, it was gone. It vanished in an instant.

In its place, a wave rose.

A wall of black water.

The tsunami came crashing into the village.

TWENTY

The waters covered the few homes that Juni could normally see from the window. Roofs completely submerged under the wave. A sea layer that invaded far inland where it was not welcome. He saw several of the smaller homes swept away by the force of the ocean, falling apart like tissue paper in water.

The sirens blared like mournful ghosts beholding the end.

Glass shattered. Wood splintered. Homes upturned. Trees mowed down. Juni couldn't see people but imagined their bodies ripped from the streets and carried along the violent torrent of the wave.

Juni wept. He pounded his fist against the window.

"You motherfucking..." His speech failed as snot ran down his nose, tears blinding his vision. He fell to his knees, head lowered.

He hoped everyone had made it to the school in time. He knew deep down that wasn't possible. The timing from the sirens to the wave was less than a minute. Those nearest the evacuation point could have made it to the hill road and been saved in time. Anyone a few more blocks out from that point had to be lost.

The house rumbled so hard that the cupboards in the kitchen flew open and spewed out the dishes over the floor. He heard the shattering of glass and porcelain throughout the house. A crack tore its way into the wall next to the window, like some giant insect was trying to burrow its way into the home. He felt the home shift, the foundation on one side lower. A lantern fell off its pedestal and rolled down to the window wall.

The quake wasn't powerful enough to knock Juni over. But he noticed that the view from the window showed more of the hill now. With terror, he realized that; the house being on a hill as it was, it could slide down that hill at any moment if the soil was disturbed enough or the rains were powerful enough.

He got up and froze. A shadow with white eyes was standing below, looking up into the house.

Something came flying through the glass, ripping right by Juni's face, and landed on the sofa. It rolled across the now slanted floor and stopped at Juni's feet.

Dazed. Unable to comprehend all that was happening, Juni went to the broken window. The jagged glass around the small hole suggested something the size of a soccer ball or smaller came through. He turned to the object that had broken through his thin veil of security.

He found Haruto. The little that was left of him.

TWENTY ONE

Haruka woke, sat upright, and put on her glasses. Her heart was racing, and adrenaline filled her system. She didn't know why she woke so suddenly, or why she was so afraid. The space next to her on the futon was still warm from where Mayu had been sleeping. It was empty now. Only a vague indentation on the sheets told the story of the little girl who was there.

"Baby? You in the toilet?"

No answer.

Red light from the alarm clock resting on the nightstand illuminated just enough of the room for her to see the foot of the mattress. Beyond that, it was darkness.

Mayu used to sleepwalk when she was four. Haruka had grown used to her own nightly panic attacks induced by her daughter's absence. She and Juni would take turns, decided by lethargic rock-paper-scissors, for who would find her. Mayu hadn't done this in two years. Haruka feared the return of those sleepless nights. Things were easier now that she could stay at home all day with her. She had to admit, though, that life had become boring and predictable in those years. At least there was stability.

But now life was full of Juni's fake smiles. Letters on the table ringed with old coffee stains. The man in sunglasses at her front door. The voices in her ears.

If this were stability, what meaning did life have?

Haruka got out of bed and stood up. The room was dark, but she could see light through the crack at the bottom of the closed door. She opened it. Walked down the hall. Turned on the light in the kitchen.

"There you are. Why didn't you answer me?"

Mayu was standing at the window in the living room, holding the curtain open. She didn't respond to her mother.

"Mai-Mai?"

"I saw Grandpa again."

"Baby, not this again. Come back to bed." She moved over to her daughter. She felt chills throughout her body. "It's just another bad dream. It's okay."

Haruka was embarrassed to admit that she felt fear. For days now, strange whispers had been plaguing her. Even Juni seemed concerned on the phone. She desperately wished he wouldn't believe her. Of course, that would have been just another crack in their relationship, but that was almost better than the alternative. That she wasn't insane. That there weren't actual voices haunting her.

Mayu heard nothing, thankfully. Aside from the dreams, of which Haruka knew no details, she seemed okay. A little restless for her dad to come back home, but not losing her mind like her mother.

Haruka put her hands on Mayu's shoulders and grabbed the curtains out of her hands to shut them.

"He brought friends this time," Mayu said.

"What do you—" Haruka froze. Before she could close the curtain, she glimpsed something in the alley. It could have been a cat whose eyes caught the lights of a passing car. Two reflective orbs. They were gone now. Haruka drew closer to the glass and looked down into the alley. There was nothing.

"Mommy, I don't like him anymore. His friends woke me up by yelling too loud."

"Yelling?'

"Yeah. Like a lady screaming. They need to be quieter."

"I'm sure it was just a dream, honey. Come on, let's go."

She took Mayu's hand and led her back to the bedroom. She took one last look at the window as she did so. What Mayu said unnerved her, but it was nothing to be afraid of. She never knew her grandfather, never met him. Just knew him from photos. It must be the confused feelings of a little girl who never knew her grandpa, finding out that he was dead, and not having her dad around.

Not to mention, Mommy was going a bit nuts this week.

If she were being honest, Haruka missed her husband. A first in a long while. She would feel a lot safer with him around. Mayu has been having these episodes ever since Juni left. Haruka couldn't wait until he got home and things went back to normal. Loveless though the marriage was, at least things could go back to better than this. Better than insanity.

This week cast doubt on Haruka's plans to leave him. But she would still do it if he didn't pull his act together—and fast. When it came to her daughter's nightmares or very real gangsters showing up at her door, she knew which one she'd rather deal with.

"Okay, missy, back to bed."

Mayu went under the covers, clutching Keke the Wonderful close to her chest. In seconds, she was out. The picture of innocence resting in the safety of a parent's love.

Haruka laid back down and pulled the blankets over her. She knew things wouldn't be normal again. Juni said that everything was okay with the will, but she could tell from the tone of his voice that he was lying.

She could always tell.

Haruka rolled over, her back to Mayu. She could hear her slightly snoring. Haruka's eyes grew heavy. She opened them. A thought just occurred to her. The cat's eyes in the alleyway. There were no ledges, railings, or anything else on that wall that a cat could climb up on. Their apartment was on the third floor. They had a fire escape attached to their side, but there were no windows or landings across the alley in the next building, where she saw the eyes.

She sat up and looked out the bedroom door she'd left open to the dark hallway.

Immediate regret.

Just need to be sure. She got up and went into the hall. Closed the bedroom door and turned on the hall lights. She stilled her breath and listened. Nothing but the tick of the kitchen clock, the gentle hum of the refrigerator, the voice of the next-door neighbor softly talking to his wife—a nightly occurrence for years now.

She looked at the closed curtains at the window. She was about to go to them and look outside. A sudden fear struck her.

What if I see something?

She couldn't do it. Back to bed. On her way, she passed the bathroom. The noise of her neighbor's conversation was unavoidable. A sound she had gotten used to in the four years living here. But something was off here. That wasn't his voice. She was here all day, every day, so she knew exactly what the guy sounded like. This voice was were gravelly compared to the softness of the neighbor's.

Where is it coming from?

She turned to the bathroom. She went in. Above the bathtub, she noticed a thick black stain that hadn't been there just this evening before she brushed her teeth. The smell of sulfur. The air was wavy, as if someone were burning meat on the grill.

The voice, too quiet to hear any words, was coming from the bathtub drain.

Forget this.

Haruka shut the door, wedged a dining room chair against the handle, and went back to bed.

She kept the lights on all night.

TWENTY TWO

It was a severed head. The ragged neck looked like someone had ripped it off, not cut it. The eyes were missing. It was wet and draped in kelp. Rot had set in, and the stench of it filled the room. The mouth sagged open as if it had grown tired of screaming. The flesh hung loosely on the bone.

Juni braced himself for the emergence of a crab from the mouth, but none came.

He slapped himself. He rubbed his eyes, put his hands on his knees, and bent forward, nearly retching on the floor.

This isn't real. This is just another hallucination. He stood up straight and looked at the head once more. It was not going anywhere and was very much real. Accusation and terror lived in those rotting eye sockets.

"Haruto, dear God, what happened to you?"

Tears stung his eyes, and Juni broke down into a sob. The head was leaning against his foot. He backed away from it, and it rolled down to the window wall. He sat down on the floor and cradled his knees. Thought about Haruto, the man who had always lived next door to his family. Back when Juni was a child, Haruto and his wife Asuka were constant pillars for him. When his Dad was out at sea, or in the big city drinking away his fortunes, it was Haruto who would come over and check on him.

Even Juni's mother couldn't do that. She was a wraith, a nonentity in his life. Whenever Dad was gone, Mom would also disappear. Where to? Fuck if he knew.

But not Haruto. He was always there. Juni never would have said it out loud, but the man was the closest thing to an actual father figure he had ever known. The weight of sorrow threatened to bury Juni deeper into the tilted hardwood floor.

No, this is not the time.

Juni stood with shaking knees and forced himself to look at the head. Shattered glass from the window surrounded it. Someone had clearly thrown it. That someone was both a murderer and a monster. An executioner of sweet old men. This gave additional weight to Juni's visions earlier in the day. Mental instability did not bring it on, but that they were—he almost laughed at the thought—actual ghosts.

The man in the road. Aido-sama's thug. Was he dead too?

Then he remembered the coin found in Mr. Sato's eye. He had to know. Juni went over to the head. Haruto's face was turned upwards, mouth open in a silent and eternal scream. Something caught the light inside that mouth.

Juni knew. He knew what he would find. But still, he had to see it for himself. He grabbed a blanket from the sofa and wrapped his hands in it like gloves. He put his covered hands on Haruto's cheeks and angled the head so that the light of the room would shine into the mouth.

"Fuck!"

He stood up. Now dangling out of the mouth, he could clearly see, was the watch Haruka had given him. The one he had cast into the sea.

He took hold of the bit hanging out of the mouth and pulled it out. It was only half of the watch.

This proved it.

First Mr. Sato, and now Haruto. Two deaths for two offerings. Why only half a watch? Didn't he wish for two things when he gave it? Which meant that there was someone else out there for whom he was responsible.

"I did this," he whispered. The roar of the waves now consuming Tanosawa resounded in agreement.

He assumed that the police might have found an interesting artifact on Aido-sama's body—maybe even the thug's as well.

Was it worth it? All these deaths for the money?

He honestly couldn't answer himself then.

He stood there in the middle of the room, not knowing what to do next. Eventually, he pulled himself over to the window and looked out the hole the head had come through. Dim gray light still illuminated the landscape. The dark water of the bay was closer than it should have been: it now reached inland, covering everything at sea-level.

It really happened. Tanosawa was gone.

The rain blew into the house through the gap in the glass. The thick clouds were quickly turning coal-black.

That's it, I need to close the shutter.

The house wasn't stable, but it had stopped moving. He knew it wasn't safe to stay, but it was even deadlier outside. Whatever broke into Haruto's home was out there.

Juni went over to the sliding glass door and opened it. He was immediately hit in the face with rain. The wind threatened to rip the shirt off his body. He went out onto the patio and searched for the shutter controls. Half of the deck was cracked, but it was still level.

Lightning lit up the darkening clouds, followed shortly after by booming thunder. A gust of wind pushed Juni along and nearly tipped him over the railing. He pushed his way through the gale and found the control box on the side of the house, next to the window wall. There was a switch for the backyard floodlights. He switched them on. He opened it up and pressed the "lower" button.

A mechanical grinding kicked in, and the metal shutters rolled down over all the windows. Juni ran back into the house and shut the sliding door.

Inside, he saw the metal sheets envelope the windows. The rain from the hole in the glass ceased. He was sealed inside.

The scream came again from outside the shuttered window wall. It was much louder than should have been possible to hear through the walls and the storm.Whatever made the sound struck the shutter almost as soon as it was closed. It shook and rattled it with a sound that set his teeth on edge. It reminded him of a drunk he had seen in Tokyo banging on a closed store's shutters, demanding to be let in at 3 a.m. But this came not from human hands. Whatever struck the barrier did so with the force of a truck hitting a tree. Dents appeared in the metal. It bent in the middle. Part of the ceiling above the shutter cracked. A screw came loose from the shutter's gearbox and fell to the ground. The bottom of the steel curtain rose. Something was lifting it up. It rose a few inches off the ground and then dropped back into place.

Juni stood frozen in place. Shaking himself out of his stupor, he frantically looked around for something to block the potential opening with. He pushed the sofa against the shutter on the window wall, wet shoes slipping and struggling to find their grip on the floor. The shutter rattled again from a mighty blow. Something sharp scraped against it like nails on a chalkboard. A tear appeared in the sheet high up. More glass shattered. Rain spilled into the room. Juni felt dizzy and sick.

"The police are coming! Get the fuck off my property!"

His voice barely rose above the whirlwind of the typhoon that was growing even stronger. It got lost in the storm and became useless. A deep roar emanated from the other side of the shutter. Juni felt the vibration in his bones.

The shutter shook violently, more than it had so far. Juni fell to his knees and cried out, "Go away! Please!"

The noise and clatter rose to a fever pitch, blocking out all sane thought.

Then silence.

The shaking ceased. The wind died down. The rain stopped.

He could hear something sliding across the ground outside. Like someone dragging a body. A large body. Through wet, squishy grass.

Juni went over to the window wall. Something shredded the shutter in multiple places. He looked out and saw a deep cobalt covering the sky: either it was night, or the clouds were just that dark. But the wind died down. The typhoon was dwindling. The terrible pounding on the wall had stopped.

Half of the shutter had been ripped off the hinges. Huge gashes were taken out of the middle. Juni looked out through the shredded metal. The dragging sound continued, but he couldn't see its source. The only things visible were the trees painted dark in the low light, the wet sheen of the broken patio, and the black void of the waters that had covered the village and refused to recede.

A sizzling sound. Juni backed away from the shutter.

The black sludge, the acidic mold-like substance, was dripping off the shutter at the gash marks. It ate its way through the metal, dissolving it and producing the disgusting brown haze that wasn't quite smoke—it was almost as if the very air surrounding it was transforming into something else, something that didn't exist in the world.

The mold started spreading from the roof of the house. In moments, it ate through the wood like an alien termite and dripped acid to the floor. From there, it spread even more. The floor started breaking away. More burnt air. Juni coughed and had to cover his mouth to save himself from the noxious fumes. He thought that at this rate, the mold would eat the entire home in just a few minutes if it didn't slide down the hill first.

Even before that, the brown air would make staying here unbearable. If the mold destroyed what it touched, he didn't want to think about what the haze would do to his lungs.

No more shelter. He couldn't stay here.

The mold melted onto the roof even further; the stain growing to the size of a person. It wasn't an amorphous blob. It took shape. He thought he could even make out the bony fingers of a hand, the teeth of a lower jaw, the narrow neck.

The sliding sound came near the window wall once more. Juni skirted around the stain on the roof and the melting puddle on the ground beneath it, and peered outside the tear in the shutter. Juni could see the branches of a nearby tree move as if something had brushed past it. Every now and then, he saw something bob up and down between the tall trees and the sky. Moving away. It was round, like a giant head. The black mass paused. It seemed to turn towards the house.

Two pale yet bright eyes shimmered in the dark. Looking directly at him.

From behind him, near where the stain was, "The Wave gives, and it takes."

The breathing of a drowning man. The wet smacking of a throat trying to clear out water.

The voice was so clear to him now despite its alteration. This was Dad.

TWENTY THREE

"Why the fuck are you doing this?"

No response, save for the labored breaths.

Juni couldn't bring himself to turn around.

Dad repeated, "The Wave gives, and it takes."

"I don't want this."

Laughter intermingled with wet coughing.

The sounds ended. Juni turned around. No one there. But the black stain had grown. No longer human-like in its appearance, it was now much longer, bigger, but there was still something animal in its form, like a shark or a whale, but also like a man. It may have been the teeth that he could clearly see forming at one end. The end of a tail at the other. The brown miasma was thickening.

Juni wanted nothing more than to be near other people right now. Not isolated in his father's house, with the nearest neighbor dead, the shutters now useless and the windows shattered, and whatever the fuck this was consuming the home.

He couldn't stay here. This creature could enter the house if it came back. Maybe the shutters slowed it down this time. But if the rain started again, it could easily come inside.

Was it just playing with me?

And even if it didn't come back, the black mold would soon consume the house. He shuddered at the thought of what would happen if human flesh were to touch more of it than what had grazed his ear.

Regardless, the next course of action was to get somewhere safer. He had two options: the village's tsunami evacuation center in the elementary school or the Table Top. Keisuke would let him in for sure, but Sakura had a thick-walled courtyard and had to know something about what was going on. Plus, they'd be surrounded by people.

The problem was that the Table Top was on a separate hill, with the only path to it cutting through the center of the village, which was now underwater.

The school was closer and on the same hill. Juni could take a path down the hill from the house, cross the reservoir of Amagase Dam via a maintenance path—just like when he was a kid—and walk the ridge to the school, never having to go down near the sea.

Juni was done with this shit. He'd take the money he had in his account and use it for sure. But he wasn't going to give another offering. If possible, he had to undo what he had done.

Guilt weighed him down. He realized now what he had unintentionally done: with each offering, someone had been taken. He did not give blood, so blood was taken in another way.

"I did this. All of this is happening because of me."

No time to lose. Juni took off his wet clothes and put on his dirty sweatpants and red T-shirt from his bag. At least he had the mind to bring a hoodie—not as good as a rain jacket but better than nothing.

He got ready, left his bag behind, and exited the house. Before he closed the front door, he took one last look inside, back at the stains devouring the structure. He could have sworn the large one on the roof moved. What looked like a bulbous head seemed to turn and watch him leave.

He shut the door and ran.

The sound of waves was the first sensation to hit him. Waves far too close inland. Crashing water and swirling roars. He gave one last look at Haruto's house before he took the path down the hill. It was a pile of rubble now. Sepia smoke rising from the ruins. As if hit by a missile, Haruto's home was no more. Despite the recent rain, it was still smoldering. Black and charred wood, covered in mold.

Haruto's animals were walking around the property. He saw a single goat and two sheep. The chickens were nowhere to be seen.

Juni ran down the path, fully aware that the colossal figure had been nearby mere minutes ago.

It was still technically daytime despite the surrounding darkness, but there was no heat in the air and even the cicadas were silent. The pine branches overhead absorbed the little light of day that remained. Juni turned on his phone's light and guided his feet over the overgrown roots and grass. The village once used the trail for leisure, but Dad bought up the land here too and soon put a stop to all of that. Haruto was hired to keep the trail clean and maintained, along with many other responsibilities. By the looks of it, he had been slacking off for years.

Juni flew down the path, something he had done a hundred times before. He ran as fast as he could: no telling when the rain would return. But would he be safe even without the rain? He knew nothing about this thing chasing him. But it was too late to debate this. Keep on running.

A baby's cries. Juni stopped in his tracks.

"Hello?"

The infant wailed in desperation, a cry that pierced his heart.

The crying intensified. Before Juni went towards the sound to save the child, he paused. He had heard this before. This exact cadence of wailing. When he saw the shadow of the pregnant woman in the house.

No, he would not fall for this. He ignored the child and kept running. Minutes later, he was happy with his decision to leave. The crying did not dampen the further that he ran—it kept pace with him. Almost as if the ghost of a newborn was chasing him through the dark woods, flying just overhead.

He came to the end of the trail, which stopped at a ledge overlooking the reservoir. A set of decaying concrete steps led down to a lake of black water. The surface rippled as the rain started pouring again.

On the left side of the water, a concrete wall acted as a dam for the rivers that came down from the mountains. To the right, the spillway for gradually releasing water to prevent flooding. Above the reservoir, a half-finished concrete bridge connected a mountain road. Rebar stuck out of the semi-complete structure like an incomplete formation of a skeleton.

The lake reflected nothing but deep darkness. Almost impossible to differentiate between the water and the sky. In the middle of the man-made lake was a wooden raft used for emergencies and maintenance, attached to a pulley system of ropes connected to the other side.

A cacophony of screams came from behind and above him. They sounded like they were coming from his father's place, or somewhere near it. More screams now to his left. Up on the dam's concrete wall were four more figures. Human-looking. One looked vaguely female. All of them with ferocious white eyes. Somewhere off behind that line of ghoulish spectators, the baby cried even louder now.

"The ocean is an open grave."

The voice came from behind him. Juni couldn't turn around. He felt a wet and cold hand on his shoulder. A small hand. The crying became so loud, Juni couldn't hear his thoughts. The shadowy figures raised their hands to the sky.

"Open grave."

"The stars are beautiful."

"They're in the water. Beautiful... in the water."

"Grave."

Each phrase in a different voice. Men and women both.

Juni flung the hand off his shoulder and turned around. Nothing there. The shadows on the bridge remained as they were, hands outstretched. Thankfully, the baby had ceased its screams.

Juni looked for the maintenance path, which should have been along the dam side, just above the lake. There was nothing but water now. The rain had filled the reservoir too much and submerged the path.

A roar erupted from the forest path behind him. He saw the trees up the hill sway violently as something big pushed through them.

Juni went to the water's edge. There was only one path forward, much as he dreaded it. Despite the protest of his muscles refusing to go in, he forced himself to jump into the lake and swim. The water was lukewarm. Its tepid embrace made him queasy. He could hardly see anything above the water. Below was a world of horrors waiting to seize him. He kicked frantically, accidentally gulping in water, coughing it out, and making a fool of himself as he swam.

He could feel the eyes of the ghosts—he had now fully accepted that's what they were—on him as he propelled himself through the water. Witnessing his feeble attempts to flee something he could not understand and could not hope to fight.

He made it to the raft and pulled himself onto it.

Juni stood and considered his next step. He could swim the second half of the way, or he could pull the raft along by the ropes that acted as a pulley to the other side. On the other side, he could see the maintenance ladder that led down to the ridge path.

He looked once more into the abyss below. Pulley it is.

Whoever left this in the middle of the fucking lake deserves to be shot.

Although he supposed it could have been left near the ladder, forcing him to make the whole swim to the other side. The little mercies of life.

He grabbed the rope and pulled. The raft jerked forward slowly, but it moved in the right direction. He looked up at the dam wall. The spirits were still there, calling to the skies with splayed fingers, but their eyes were on him. He heard a murmur, almost like a chant, from the bridge.

The words were muted, too far away to hear clearly, but too close for comfort. A rhythmic chanting of just a few words, over and over again.

Then came the sound he had dreaded the most.

A splash in the water from behind him. Juni turned his head so fast, he pulled a muscle in his neck. But there was no time to register pain. He saw a pale tail, too much like a whale's to make any sense in this environment, recede into the water. He saw ripples extending from something large that had just dived in. Then he saw the spines. Boney things, white as chalk, that came to a sharp end, at least six of them, standing out of the water, coming closer, moving side to side as if attached to a large snake sidewinding its way in the water.

They went under the surface. Juni pulled the rope faster until he felt his palms rip and the blood pour out. The sound of something rising out of the water and splashing back down. He pulled faster, his voice sputtering out of a weak throat, entreaties to some higher power to make him go faster.

The ladder was only ten feet away now.

So close. Pull faster.

A force from under the raft rocked him forward and sent his face right into the wooden platform. He groaned, the pain crackling across his nose and jaw. He got to his feet. The rope was gone. The metallic wheel that held it to the raft was no longer attached. The raft was launched forward by the impact, right next to the ladder, save for a space of water three feet wide that separated the ladder from the raft. The rungs went down into the water. He had to either swim to it or jump.

Movement to his right. The bony spines emerged, along with something else. The top half of a bulbous head rose out of the water. Its skin was sickly pink, stretched tight over its skull, almost human-like in its fleshiness, but the hard edges of bone underneath were anything but. No eyes were present, none that he could see, but he could feel it looking at him all the same.

Juni leaped off the raft, arms open wide to catch the ladder. His body smacked against the metal. He felt a sharp pain in one rib. But he made it, clinging to the ladder like a long-lost lover. He climbed, slipping once but catching himself, and made it to the top.

He pulled himself onto the platform above the reservoir, level with the ridge path that would take him down, and looked back down into the water. The thing was still there, looking up at him. As were the spirits on the bridge, still chanting.

Two long arms—with what could be hands webbed between gnarled claws instead of fingers — came out of the water and gripped the ladder below. The creature started to rise and pull itself out of the water.

Juni didn't care to see what it looked like. He ran down the path to the school.

TWENTY FOUR

"Mayu, where are you?!" Haruka screamed into the rainy night.

She was leaning out the bedroom window that she didn't open. Mayu was nowhere to be found. Not at the window where she said she saw grandpa's friends. Even Keke the Wonderful was left behind, lying on the windowsill, drenched by the rain. Haruka looked out into the alleyway that ran parallel to their apartment. She climbed out the window and onto the fire escape, still wearing her white nightgown, white bunny slippers the only thing protecting her feet.

She had just gone to sleep after thinking she had seen something out there. Now, not even a few hours later, she was mad with terror at the disappearance of her daughter.

She climbed down to the ground floor. She was in the alleyway now, hyperventilating, screaming out her daughter's name. A small shadow at the end of the alley. About the size of her daughter.

"Mayu, what are you doing?"

The girl's silhouette darted to the right and out of sight. Haruka ran after her. She slipped on the wet cement and fell, hitting her head on the ground. She pulled herself up to her feet, the world fading in and out of focus. The rain smeared the lenses of her glasses and blurred the world even further. She stood and ran once more, barefoot this time. She came to the corner where Mayu had turned and hit a deadend. Nothing but a concrete wall of some other apartment building. Her chest felt like it was going to explode.

"Mayu!"

The sound of feet running through a puddle came from somewhere high up. Haruka looked up and saw her daughter on top of the building, looking down at her.

"Oh, honey, what are you doing? Move away from the ledge, okay? I'm coming up there."

Before she could turn, she froze in place. Behind her daughter, a man's figure, eyes burning like fluorescent bulbs.

She shook Mayu's shoulders until the girl opened her eyes. Tears mixed with the rain as both cascaded down Haruka's face. Mayu opened her eyes and looked around her in a daze. She didn't respond to her mother's questions. She just stood there with a confused expression. Haruka held her close and buried her face in her daughter's nightgown.

She scanned the rooftop for any sign of the man who had been next to Mayu, but there was nothing. An empty expanse with several satellite dishes and a water tank for the residents below. No place for someone to hide. Haruka had flown up the staircase with feral speed. There was no elevator in this building. Nowhere for the man to have fled unless he jumped to his death. She took Mayu's hand and led her back down to street level. In a few minutes they were back in their apartment, having entered through the open bedroom window—Haruka didn't have her keys on her when she ran outside.

She undressed Mayu, dried her off, and put some warm clothes on her. Then, Haruka dried herself off and changed. She turned on the teakettle. Haruka stood there in the kitchen, leaning against the counter, waiting for the water to boil. Mayu was sitting on the floor, watching TV with a soaked Keke. Some cartoon about superpowered breakfast foods. It was nearly midnight, but neither of them would sleep anytime soon.

Haruka wondered if she should call the police or not. On the one hand, she had seen the man, meaning he may have abducted Mayu out of the bedroom. But there was no one else on that roof. She told herself she had imagined it. Fear was coursing through her body like an electrical current. And people don't have glowing eyes. She tittered. The sound felt inappropriate considering what had just happened. The water finished boiling.

She poured matcha powder into two cups, added the hot water, and took them over to Mayu.

"Here you go."

Mayu took the cup, blew on it, and sipped at it, not taking her eyes off the cartoon.

Haruka lowered herself to her knees, cup in hand, thoughts lost to the stormy night.

"Honey?" Mayu looked up at her. "Can you tell me why you were outside?"

Mayu furrowed her brow and went back to her cartoon. The French toast hero was now fighting off some tooth-cavity-looking bad guys in spandex.

Haruka put her tea down and gently tapped Mayu's arm. "Mai-Mai, this is serious. Look at me. Thank you. Tell me what happened."

"I don't think I'm supposed to tell you."

Haruka's blood ran cold. Was there actually a man in her house? Did he tell Mayu to keep it secret?

"Who said that?"

"Umm... It was Grandpa."

"Honey, Grandpa passed away. I know it's hard to understand that, but—"

"I know. But it was still Grandpa. He said he wanted to take me to see his friends. The ones who are making all that noise outside every night."

Terror seized Haruka's heart. She was definitely going to call the police after hearing this.

Haruka moved closer to Mayu on the floor and put her arm around her. She gently guided her daughter's chin to face her. "This is important, baby, tell me everything."

Mayu bit her lip, and eyes fixed on the TV screen. Haruka pressed her again.

"Well, every night when you leave me in the bath, he talks to me from the water under the tub."

"So you can't do anything?" She felt like screaming at the officer but refrained, Mayu having fallen asleep. "There was a man with my daughter; he might have taken her out of here from our window! He was in our house!"

"Hatayama-san," said Officer Rei, a woman in her early thirties with a stone-serious expression. "You yourself said that the windows were locked from the inside, and we found no evidence of a forced entry. We will look into it, but based on what you told us, there is no actual evidence for us to follow up on. We'll check surveillance tapes from around the alley and see if anything comes up. If there really was a man, he'd show up there for sure, correct?"

Haruka couldn't believe they weren't taking this seriously. Over the past few days of hearing voices, of seeing strange eyes and now strange men at the window, she felt like she was losing her sanity. The way the officer eyed her suspiciously just now, as if she believed Haruka was on the verge of a breakdown, made her sober up. No matter what, she wouldn't give people ammunition to say she was a terrible mother. Especially if she and Juni went to court for custody.

"Okay, understood. Thank you for coming by, and please let me know if you find anything."

Officer Rei nodded and let herself out.

Mayu was asleep next to her. The clock on the bedside stand read 3 a.m. in red letters that looked like glowing eyes in the dark. The only reason the lights were off was that Mayu complained they kept her up. Haruka was wide awake, staring at the ceiling.

It had to be Mai-Mai's dream, not an actual intruder in her room. Her father-in-law was dead. It was clearly a product of her imagination. Even so, it disturbed Haruka that her daughter would react so intensely to the death of a man she had never even met before. She weighed whether to get her some help. Have the doctor look her over.

No, it's my responsibility. She'll be fine. I just have to do better with her.

Her thoughts drifted toward her husband. They met in her first year of university in Tokyo. He was a few years older than she was. Confident. Charming. Ambitious. She was madly in love. She had big dreams herself. Was going to be a doctor. Not a nurse, like every older man around her assumed she'd be. She was going to go into pediatrics and make the world a bit of a better place. Now, she's thirty-two and stays home all day. Sure, she loved her family; there is no doubt about that in her mind. But sometimes, she dreamed of that other life. One where she hadn't quit school to be a housewife. One where she made a difference in the world.

She turned in bed. Mayu's hair was splayed over the pillow like a modern art display.

No, she was making a difference. With this little one in front of her. She'd die to protect her.

But she didn't want to do this alone. She couldn't do this alone. Where was Juni? He wasn't answering her calls. She checked the news, and the drizzle now pouring over Tokyo was a full-blown typhoon up in Aomori. It made sense why she couldn't get through, but even so, it disturbed her that she had heard nothing from him in days. How long would he be gone? With the storm as bad as the TV made it out to be, it could be a week.

Rain fell against the window, now locked and triple-checked before she went to bed. Keke the Wonderful was hanging on a clip by the window to dry. Haruka's eyes grew heavy. She forced them awake. Too afraid that she'd wake up and find her daughter missing again.

She closed her eyes. Sleep began flooding her restless mind.

A creak of the floor at the foot of her futon.

The air grew heavy, as if somebody had entered the room.

She opened her eyes and screamed.

Standing there was a man with white-hot eyes.

TWENTY FIVE

Tanosawa Elementary School stood on a grassy hill overlooking the village. When Juni graced the halls of this temple of wisdom, he was a terror. He, Shota, and Keisuke used to save up their rice at lunchtime in their pockets only to launch the rice grains at their teacher during gym class. Keisuke always went along begrudgingly. Even then Juni knew people feared his father, because he never got in trouble. Not once. Not even when he moved to the nearest high school several miles away and got caught selling cigarettes to junior high school kids. Just a onetime thing, but still.

The school used to overflow with children, or at least that's what Dad used to say. Juni remembered his homeroom, all thirteen kids. He was sure that by now that number could even be zero.

Sprinting until his calves felt like they were splitting, Juni rocketed out of the tree line and came onto the soccer field behind the school. He had no idea what time it could be; his phone must have gone missing when he swam in the reservoir. The sky was like charcoal. It felt like it should only be five or six in the afternoon, but given everything that was happening, it very well could be midnight. For reasons he didn't want to think about, he no longer had his watch, either.

He shambled across the overgrown field; the grass whipping his face as he shuffled forward, careful not to trip in the dark. Yeah, this school had to be derelict by now. But there were lights in the auditorium at the back of the school, by the soccer field. Through the smudged windows, he could make out figures walking inside. The rain continued, but far off over the sea, the moon peeked through the clouds, providing some light. As he now ran towards the building, the view of Tanosawa came up to greet him. Normally, it would have been a small collection of roofs and narrow streets, a tiny park and a few shops. What lay before him was a void.

Water the color of coagulated blood filled the village. Some of the two-story homes poked their upper halves above the dirty water. Everything else was lost. He paused for a moment to take it in. He saw several people still on their roofs, the ones that lived the furthest away from the school, and were lucky enough to own slightly taller homes. Their cries for help were soon drowned out as the heavens opened and the light rain became a deluge pouring out of the black sky.

Before he turned away, he saw something that nearly made him cry out. Despite the torrential rain, the moonlight still shone out over the sea. The rays highlighted bony spines in the water, circling the few homes that stood out of it.

No, how could it have gotten there so fast? It was just behind me.

Then, as if sensing him, it ended its circular pattern and headed straight towards the school. Juni ran to the gym's front entrance and pounded on the doors. Someone opened them almost immediately, meaning they weren't locked, and he wasn't thinking straight.

The startled face of a diminutive elderly woman in glasses and a wool cap greeted him. Juni pushed past her and shut the doors behind him. The cavernous gymnasium could fit about three hundred people, but no more than two or three dozen strolled the room, making it seem lonely and desperate inside. Most of them were in their sixties and upwards. Juni spotted a young family with a few children near them.

He noted the ways in and out: four windows on the left and four on the right walls, none on the back, all too small for an adult to squeeze through. Rear exit doors big enough, he reasoned, that the creature could come in through, same as the front ones.

"Everyone!" he yelled, causing the woman at the door to clutch her chest. "You're not going to believe me, but we need to barricade the doors."

Juni didn't even wait for a reply or a shout of ridicule. He ran over to the wall by the bleachers, where he remembered the school kept its gymnastic equipment: pommel horses, vaulting boxes, heavy mats, anything and everything that could give them a chance of keeping that thing outside.

"What are you talking about?" said a man in his early thirties, with heavy black-rimmed glasses and a hairstyle that swirled around his forehead, surely against his will, or at least one could hope.

"There's a—" Juni paused as he threw open the door by the bleachers and began pulling out chairs and tossing them to the ground. "A monster, okay? A fucking —" a chair nearly hit the man in the glasses as he dodged it, "giant thing in the water. It'll be here soon, and it'll kill us all."

The man put his hand on Juni's shoulder. "My friend, a horrible disaster just hit us, and you're scaring my kids."

Juni stopped his mad frenzy of pulling out a pommel horse and locked eyes with the man. "I'm sorry, and I know that this is a horrible time. But if we don't do something, everyone in this room is going to die."

The man was about to say something when a familiar voice rang out from the other side of the gym. "Juni? What's going on?"

It was Shota coming out of a side room with two other men dressed in construction coveralls. They were carrying jugs of water. Shota put his down and walked over.

"Shota!" Juni ran over and embraced him. Shota's face lit up in extreme embarrassment because of the affection being inflicted on him in front of his work buddies.

"I thought maybe you were down in the village when the wave came," Juni said.

"Me and these guys," he threw his hand back almost dismissively at the other two, "just finished helping with the landslide I told you about. We were up in the hills driving down when it came. Did you see it? That fucking wave came in and demolished everything."

"Great that you're here, but *it* is also here. The thing we both saw in the water. It killed Haruto and broke into my house. I saw his head, it threw his head through the window! It chased me here. I saw it. I fucking saw it. And I saw *them*, ghosts, spirits, I don't know, but..." Now Juni's voice was shrill as he clutched Shota's arms, spittle flying out as he spoke.

Stark raving mad.

If Shota hadn't seen it, hadn't heard it for himself, he would have looked at Juni the way everyone else was just then: with fear and disgust, possibly even anger at the man who was making an awful situation even worse. But he had seen the thing in the water that spoke with mutilated human voices. It was here.

Come to count the cost.

Shota's face drained of all color. He said, "He's right. Katsumi, Shun. Help us block the windows and the doors."

Shun? Juni hadn't even noticed. One man with Shota, the man now smiling at him like Juni was a freak, was the same guy who tried to fight him, naked, dick to dick, in the bathhouse.

The man who was presumably Katsumi said, "Shota, what the fuck?"

Shota, a man of gargantuan size compared to anyone else in that room, bellowed, "Do it. Now!" Katsumi dropped the questioning and rushed alongside Juni. Even the man with glasses, whose wife shouted, "Kojiro!" after him, came and helped.

"Oi, Shota, why the fuck are you listening to this pussy?" asked Shun. He walked over to Juni just as the latter was grabbing a mat. Shun put his foot on the mat and stomped down, tearing it out of Juni's hands.

Juni snapped. He grabbed Shun by the collar and growled, "I don't give a shit about what you think of me or why you hate me for whatever reason, but if we do not do this, you are going to die."

Murmuring from the crowd. Juni caught the words "insane" and "needs help." Some mentioned his father's name.

Shun must have seen Juni's plea as an intimidation move. He slapped Juni's hands away. "Get your fucking hands off me, queer." He cocked his hand back as if to slam it into Juni's face.

A bigger hand came crashing down on Shun's, gripping his wrists and spinning the man around.

"Shun, you touch him, you'll have to jerk off with your wrists instead of your hands," Shota growled. He pushed Shun away.

"Whatever," Shun muttered as he walked away.

The woman with the cap came over. Now Juni could clearly see that it was Mrs. Sato, fear having blinded him earlier. "Juni, are you telling the truth? Look at me when you answer, and I'll know."

Juni felt like a teacher was scanning his soul for an admission of cheating. "Yes, I am."

"I believe him," she said to the crowd. Then, to Juni, "Is this what happened to my husband?"

Juni nodded, fighting back the urge to confess his sins to her.

She nodded back firmly and walked away, resignation and solemnity etched on her face. She went to help some younger men carry a tumbling mat to the front door. Aside from Shun, who now sat in a corner glaring at them and drinking from a flask, everyone else helped pile items against the doors. The scene was an anchor of human decency in the hellish storm that had broken out over his life. He could have cried seeing how people came together in a crisis.

He knew that most wouldn't believe him. At least the more powerful voices in the room did.

Most of the people helped pile the gym supplies against the front doors and the windows. At least three windows were left bare, the supplies having run out. Katsumi produced a chain from the back room and locked the rear exit doors' handles with it. In mere minutes, the ragtag group of survivors did their best. Juni told himself that it wouldn't be enough.

He thought about the acidic mold that the creature left behind and how quickly it ate through everything. He thought of the shape taking form on the roof of Dad's living room.

He also wondered if the thing would leave the school alone if he were to run. The dread logic that came with the idea that it wanted Juni specifically wasn't something that escaped him.

But what was he going to do? Stay out in the rain and let it take him? And there was no guarantee the thing wouldn't hurt these people regardless of what he did. The time for heroic morality was gone; this was survival.

Having mollified his conscience, Juni sat on the ground next to Shota.

"So, your project blew up in your fucking face, didn't it?" Shota accused. "Was that wave connected to all of this? Do you know how many people are probably dead because of you?"

"I didn't know."

"'Didn't know,' he says. Fuck. You messed with something that was clear, I don't know, evil, man. That thing in the water wasn't natural. You getting money for throwing crap in the ocean wasn't natural. You should have known better."

"I was desperate, okay? You would have done the same in my shoes."

"Buddy, I *am* in your shoes. You've seen my house. I have nothing. But you, you piece of shit, you have a wife and a daughter, something to lose, and what do you do? Make a deal with the fucking devil."

"You're right. I was wrong to do it, and I'm not going to make excuses anymore. But that doesn't matter now, does it? What matters is making sure that thing doesn't get in here and that nobody else dies."

Shota grimaced. On the verge of dressing Juni down again, with a tinge of empathy somewhere in there. "Alright. Can do. But what is it? What do you know about it?"

"I saw... *something* back at the reservoir. Don't ask. I can't handle thinking about it too much. It was huge. Like, so big it wouldn't be able to fit through those doors over there. But it leaves this black stuff around. Don't know if it spits it out or secretes it or what, but it eats through things like acid.

It can appear anywhere where water is present. Not just in the sea, I even saw it back in the onsen in town a few days ago. Didn't believe it fully at the time, but looking back, yeah, it was there, just watching me from a stain in the ceiling. I think it might use them to, I don't know, travel through? At least look through? So, basically, a supernatural god-monster. Easy to deal with, right?"

Juni realized how insane everything sounded in that moment.

Shota exhaled so long it seemed like his soul had left his body. "Shit. So, we're fucked?"

"Yep."

An hour passed as they waited. Rumblings bounced around the crowd, calling Juni a liar, an attention seeker, just like his father. Some of the elderly complained that they felt trapped inside and that it was too stuffy. The few children were too tired to cry.

The air was rife with animosity towards Juni. But where could they go? The people's homes were submerged. The rain was hitting hard. They had to wait here anyway, with or without a psycho in their midst. They at least tolerated him.

Juni and Shota sat with resolve in their eyes, facing the front door. The only two that knew for a fact what was out there, one more than the other. Shota held a large wrench in his hands, the best weapon anyone could find.

But why was it taking so long? Juni saw it before entering the gym, not too far away. Was it planning an assault? Feasting on the survivors up on their roofs? Waiting for everyone to come outside for an easy catch?

The power went out.

Gasps immediately filled the tense atmosphere. A child's cry rose and became muffled, presumably burying their face into mom's side. Emergency lanterns went on, along with a few candles. There was even a floodlight, the kind used for nighttime road work, flashing from the back of the room. It cast everyone as shadow puppets against the harsh light. Devoid of all features. Swallowed in blackness.

Rain struck the roof and the windows harder. The building's frame shook and groaned in the wind.

Juni and Shota jumped to their feet. Shota held the wrench out like a sword.

Lightning flashed, adding its cold light to the interior of the room.

It was still raining out, but the intensity lessened. It was almost silent outside.

Then came the screaming. At least it sounded like it. Faint and far-off, it could have been the wind. Juni imagined they were the cries of those left stranded on their roofs. Men and women cried out in abject terror. Their words couldn't be made out, but the tenor of their horrified screeching could. These were people ignited into pure animal fear. Un-restrained screaming. The kind that left people uncomfortable, slightly awkward, and not knowing what to do.

They were dying.

Silence engulfed their cries. Nothing made a sound in that part of the village. Inside the gym, even the child stopped crying. Juni's chest started heaving. He hadn't even realized he was holding his breath.

A deep and guttural growl emanated from outside. At least Juni didn't have to endure the people's accusations anymore. It was undeniable that something was terribly wrong.

"So beautiful... in the sea."

The girl's voice, slipping into the man's, sang out clearly from some dark corner of the gym. White eyes appeared behind the floodlight, near the rear exit. Juni heard Mrs. Sato exclaim something in a shaky voice. The people shouted, some sobbed, and a few yelled out in anger; one even tripped over nothing and fell to the floor.

A new voice came from the shining eyes, one Juni hadn't heard before. It didn't sound human.

Almost as if it were an amalgamation of men, women, and children, blended together in some horrid concoction of speech, "I want... blood. In the sea."

"By your hand."

"So beautiful."

"If no. I take."

"Everyone."

The white eyes folded into shadow. The floodlights burst and crackled, sending out a silver flare before disappearing. The lanterns burst. Only the candlelight remained untouched.

"Juni," Shota whispered, "it's talking about you, you know that, right?"

"I think I know exactly what it wants. But I can't."

"What?"

"It wants blood. It wants me to kill."

"Holy shit. Like a person?"

"I don't know, but if I don't do anything, it's going to kill everyone."

"Well, what the fuck can you do, then? Can we kill it?"

Juni waved his hands frantically in the dark, not caring that Shota couldn't see. "Kill it? How?!"

"It's him!" Kojiro yelled. He had been standing so close, but Juni hadn't even noticed. "He brought it here. It's Junichiro."

Shun's voice rose from nearby. "It's Hatayama's fault."

The crowd exploded. Fear and fury mixed with the desperate need to survive. The crowd was a pressurized bomb waiting for the right trigger to set it off. Someone grabbed Juni by his sleeve and tried to drag him to the front door. He easily pushed them off.

"Everyone, calm the fuck down." Shota tried to reason.

A heavily built man grabbed Juni by the right wrist and twisted his arm behind his back. Juni gasped in pain and tried to wrench himself free, but the man's hands were iron clasps. Juni glimpsed his attacker; it was Shun.

Juni tried to turn around, but Shun had his arm pinned behind him. Every effort to hit Shun wrenched his shoulder in pain.

Shota rushed over and punched Shun in the face. Juni fell down with Shun but pulled himself free from the hold and got to his feet.

The crowd pressed in on them, shouting. Some stood off to the side and watched.

An older man stepped forward and said, "Explain yourself. Is this happening because of you?"

Before Juni could answer, he heard a crashing sound from the front doors. Shun and Kojiro were knocking down the barricade. Kojiro's wife yelled at them to stop.

A few more people joined them and began tugging and pulling the objects off to the side of the doors.

"We need to get out of here!" Kojiro shouted.

Mrs. Sato yelled for them to stop.

This was insanity. Fear and anger and mistrust on almost every face.

The entrance was cleared. Somebody unlocked the double doors and flung them open.

A dark figure from outside filled the doorway. A deep, shadowy mass. It was bending down, its hulking mass rising above the doorway. In the center of the exit, it flashed a smile.

Eyes burning white.

The mouth was a world of jagged teeth.

An invitation to come and explore.

TWENTY SIX

The long, needle-like teeth clenched shut in a steely smile. The pale eyes, dead and glassy, yet bright, peered into the room, searching. A light mist of rain blew in from above the creature. Juni could see now that it had no neck. Its head connected directly to its torso, with a slight impression of shoulders. Sickly pink skin color looked almost white in the little light. Its skull was too human-looking for comfort. No nose, or ears. Just a smile of teeth and burning eyes.

Shun didn't have the time to realize what was about to happen. An arm reached out from the outside world; an appendage at least the length of a car stretched into the room. Its hand, if that was the correct word for the mangled, twisted collection of claws and webbed finger-like protrusions, wrapped around Shun's throat. It ripped the man out of the room in an instant.

The creature raised Shun up to its face, its grinning and hungry face. The man punched the monster with a free hand, right in the eye. It did nothing. The thing bent down and poked its head into the room, lifting Shun in its hands to the side as if he meant nothing. Someone screamed. The sound of their footsteps raced away, followed by a loud crash into the now-defunct floodlights.

The monster found what it was looking for. It locked eyes with Juni. His heart went into overdrive, banging its way out of his ribcage for an escape.

Shun still flailed in its hand, losing his voice; his screams were so primal. He kicked at the creature and twisted his body to get free. The thing brought Shun to its face again, cocked its head to the side as if trying to figure out its new toy. It opened its mouth slowly. Sticky saliva stretched and ripped as the mouth widened. Widened to the point that it could swallow a man whole. The jaws unhinged, like an anaconda. It slowly, methodically, put Shun into its mouth.

"Please, please stop!" he cried and pleaded.

The thing seemed to enjoy the torture, the slow march to the inevitable.

Something came flying at the creature's face from behind Juni, striking it in the eye. A metal wrench. Once again, the creature did not react.

"Let him go, you fucker!" Shota yelled out, now by Juni's side. The thing paused for a moment and regarded Shota. It narrowed its eyes. Shun's body was more than halfway into the mouth, feet first, he was still screaming, hands clawing at the side of the mouth that was sucking him in.

It bit down.

The thing that struck Juni first was the sounds. Wet tearing of flesh. A brief snap from the man's spinal column. The elongated cry of terror and pain, transforming into a gurgle, a sputter, a drowning sort of sound from the man's throat. Shun's last words before he went silent were, "Help me!"

Then, the upper half of his body flopped down to the floor. Surely dead, but the nervous system was still active. He opened his mouth like a fish flung from the ocean onto a boat's deck. His hands reached forward, failing to find a hold. Then he stopped moving altogether. It reminded Juni of watching the movie *Aliens* with a friend back in high school. The bit when the android Bishop gets ripped in half. Except in real life, one had to contend with the smell of death. The toxic iron stench in the air. The bowels that surely let go in the last moments.

Juni had never seen a dead body before today. Now he had seen two. Or one and a quarter, depending on how you look at it.

The crowd screamed in terror and fled to the back of the gymnasium. Cots were overturned, useless lanterns knocked over, someone kicked a candle across the floor, the flame attaching itself to a long curtain.

The creature stood mostly still, aside from lifting its head straight up, and the bulging in its throat as it swallowed the lower half of Shun. Then it lowered its massive head, revealing that smile of teeth, newly painted red and black with viscera.

But it didn't come inside. It ducked part of its head into the room, but the rest of it remained rooted outside.

Juni remembered what Haruto had said—that it could move in the rain. He hoped that meant it needed rain, or water, to move. The thing moved forward, but always kept most of its body outside.

The fire, a mere flicker of light on the curtain a second ago, was lighting up the inside of the gym in a pulsating orange glow. It spread to the end of the curtain near the ceiling. Several people tried throwing water from plastic bottles onto it, to no avail. A man in his fifties ran over with an extinguisher and started blasting the blaze, most of it snuffed out in the white and foamy cloud.

But it couldn't reach the ceiling.

The creature followed the chaos of the fire's spread. The living light reflected in its pale, pupil-less eyes. It seemed more focused on that than on the people it had presumably come to kill.

Before the fire could spread to the wood of the rafters, the same man with the extinguisher grabbed the ruined lower portion of the now-cool curtain and tugged at it. Juni finally broke free from his paralysis and ran over to help. Shota was already there with a few others. All of them pulled at the curtain until it ripped and came floating down in flaming glory, embers and ashes falling like rain.

Everyone cleared away from the wreckage. The man with the fire extinguisher doused the ruins. The fire went out, even the flames higher up the curtain.

Not forgetting the real danger, Juni spun back around to the open front door. The creature was gone. But in its stead, at the doorway, Juni saw a pool of black. Steam rose off it. It spread from the floor to the doorposts slowly, but corrupting and disintegrating what it touched.

The window nearest the burned curtain shattered. The people screamed. A death smile flashed from where the glass once stood. Then it vomited a torrent of the black mold into the room. It smoked and ate through the floor. The wall under the window began melting away. A splash of the liquid hit one older woman too close to the window. She howled in pain as the skin by her left ankle and her abdomen sizzled like an egg on a frying pan.

Another window towards the back of the gym broke apart. More of the tar-like mold came streaming inside.

"Holy shit, Juni, it's eating through the walls. Is it going to get in?" Shota asked.

"It needs to be in water. Like from the rain. It can't come inside, so it's going to bring this whole fucking building down on us. I've seen that stuff before. It dissolved Haruto's house in a few hours. But this is more aggressive." Another window blew apart. More of the sickly acid poured in. "I doubt we'll last twenty minutes."

A pounding on the side of the gym from outside. The sound banged its way up to the roof.

Someone cried out, "What is it doing? What does it want?"

Then, from somewhere *up there*, "Help me!"

It was Shun's voice. But the man lay dead a few feet away. A spot in the center of the ceiling smoked. Someone pulled out a flashlight and lit up the area. A dark stain, much the same as Juni had seen already, was growing. Something crawled its way out of the blackness. A dark shadow of a man's upper torso, moving like a spider along the ceiling, cried, "Help me!" It skidded away from the epicenter of the mold, yelling out as it went.

The woman who was hit with the mold stopped screaming. The crowd surrounding her cried out in horror. Juni glimpsed a skeletal leg, and an exposed ribcage but couldn't bear to see any more.

Then came a digging sound. Soon, the head of the creature pushed through the now wet and dissolving wood of the ceiling. It retracted its head and began ripping out the wood. Rain came pouring into the center of the gym. The walls near the broken windows were now collapsing. The entire gym would be gone in minutes. Nowhere left to run.

The creature hung from the ceiling and looked down. It unhinged its jaws and poured out a stream of the acidic vomit. The people ran from the deadly splash and kept their distance. The stains grew rapidly across the floor. Too many to count, they streaked across most of the gym floor by now. The brown smoke filled the auditorium. The creature moved away from the hole and disappeared.

In the far back right corner of the gym, a group of three people ran for cover. Katsumi was among them, along with an elderly man and woman. He had his arms held out in front of them as if to protect them.

Then came a scene that stretched Juni's mind beyond its limits.

The puddle of mold in front of that group stretched outward, like someone covered in a blanket and struggling to break out of it. It came alive as if something was breaking through it. Two arms ripped through the puddle on the floor, and the creature emerged. Sticky strands of the mold clung to it as it pulled itself out of the hole. Katsumi let out a yell and charged the monster. The thing lunged forward and caught the man by his right arm in its teeth. In seconds, the creature dove back into the black puddle, taking Katsumi with it.

No trace of either of them.

Kojiro ran to the front door, holding a little girl to his chest, a woman following close behind.

The puddle at the front rippled, and the creature's head rose out of it slowly, eyes piercing-white, sharp teeth set in its horrible grin. The man and his family backed off. The creature dipped its head under the mold and vanished.

Parts of the roof fell and came thundering to the ground.

They were surrounded. Whatever this mold was, the creature could move through it like a portal. The thought of seeing it in his father's bedroom and in the sauna, so close to him while he slept and relaxed, nearly broke Juni's sanity.

The gym was falling apart quickly. The smoke was making everyone cough. They couldn't stay here, but the black pools were at each potential exit point.

Shota shoved Juni forward. "Go; I think I know how to help."

Before he could protest, Shota ran to the back of the gym, yelling at everyone to move to the front. He went to the back exit, near a steaming black lake of death, and roared, "Come out, you fucker, I'm here!"

Juni saw the creature's steel smile rise from the depths. It jumped out of the blackness and into the gym. Shota picked up a nearby lit candle and threw it at the creature's face. It screeched, not as it had done so many times before, but in terror. The monster flew back from the candle, and as it fell to the ground, it stumbled backwards out of the pool to get away from the flame.

If he was going to move, it had to be now. Juni ran to the front entrance. Kojiro caught on to what Shota was doing and beat Juni to the door while holding his kid. He jumped over the puddle, his wife right behind him.

Juni followed them and ran outside. He could hear the screams and pattering footsteps of others behind him. And the last cries of Shun, "Help me!" as they descended into a gurgling, choking noise.

He hoped Shota was okay but couldn't spare a thought for him in that moment.

Kojiro was just ahead, running along the side of the school to his right, with a steep incline of trees on his left. In front of them was Tanosawa, completely underwater. Where the fuck could they go from here?

A shadow fell in front of Kojiro. It was so fast. A hulking shape, shrouded in the downpour of heavy rain. But the eyes were bright, and the teeth glistened. Kojiro turned and threw his daughter behind him, to his wife, who caught her.

The creature grabbed the man by the waist and lifted him up to its face. It looked at Juni, its dead eyes telling him its intentions without having to use the voice of another, the voice of another victim, regurgitating the last words they ever said.

This was blackmail of the cruelest kind. Not even Aido-sama would stoop so low. But Juni knew what it wanted. Which meant this was all for him. To force his hand.

"It wants me, Shota. I know what I have to do."

"What do you mean?"

Juni ran.

In an act some would call cowardice, but Juni knew to be the most heroic thing he had ever done in his life, he ran away. He ran past the monster about to devour the loving husband as if to say, "Not interested."

Perhaps Shota's selflessness inspired him. Or maybe he saw it as the only way to end this nightmare. Regardless, he surprised himself. He never knew he could act against his own self-interest. It almost felt good.

Juni fled to the parking lot of the school that sat on the ledge overlooking the town. He heard people screaming behind him. He heard the high-pitched cry of the monster closing in.

He wanted to believe that it dropped the man to chase after him. But he wouldn't look back to confirm it. Adrenaline flooded his system as he sprinted to the end of the parking lot. He ran down the hill from the lot towards the village.

Juni ran with the black lake of what was once a village to his left. Across the bay of raging waves stood the golden glow of the Table Top. In the midst of everything that had been going on, *that* neighborhood remained untouched. He imagined Keisuke's perfect family watching with horror from their windows. He thought of Sakura sipping wine and smiling as she saw all of this unfold. It was obvious they would not be coming to the aid of the village. This was not their problem unless, of course, Juni failed to perform his duty.

How fucking great for them.

Juni's one thought was, "Make it to Haruto's place." He felt stupid for leaving now. He'd have to make his way back to get what he needed. Juni wasn't even sure it would work, but there was no fighting this thing. He had to try.

He ran into the treeline and hit a trail. It was much darker in the forest, so he needed to slow down to a rapid walk. Going back the way of the reservoir was out of the question. He made it across once, when he had a head start ahead of the monster and was mainly running downhill. There was no way he'd make it now without the use of the raft. He could hear the thing screeching, maybe a few hundred feet behind him at most. There was one way back up the hill: take the winding road. If he could run through the woods that ringed around the village, he might hit the street that led back to Haruto's.

He had no idea if this would take him there for sure, but if he kept running straight, maybe—just maybe — it would.

Branches slapped his face. The rain created thick muddy paths that his feet slipped on and got stuck in. But he kept on moving. The trees behind him rustled. Wood snapped. It was getting closer.

After what felt like an eternity, Juni's feet hit solid concrete. He made it to the road. Trees lay across the pavement, cloaked in leaves and branches. Juni climbed over the fallen logs and flew up the street.

The crashing sounds behind him had stopped. He wasn't sure if it was minutes or seconds ago, but at least for now, there was nothing.

Soon, Juni arrived home for what he hoped would be the last time.

The floodlights still had power and bathed the backyard in pale light.

A pile of wood greeted him. Black and soggy clumps were all that remained of the two homes on this hill, so thoroughly did the creature's black saliva dissolve everything. He shuddered at the thought of the school and those trapped inside. He couldn't spare even a fraction of a thought for the poor woman who had gotten burned by it.

Then there was the fun new fact he had learned, that the creature could travel through the black substance at will. He kept his eyes on his father's demolished home and the mold that bubbled up from its debris.

But this ghost of a place was not what he came for. Juni ran past Dad's ruin of a house and into Haruto's backyard. The chicken coop hadn't been touched by the destruction, but the goat pen was demolished. That was fine with him; he didn't want to deal with a larger animal. The chickens would do just fine. The thing wanted blood, but it never specified from what, did it? Just had to find a blood donor.

How the fuck do you call a chicken?

He wasn't going to start clucking. That was the sort of embarrassment he might just rather die than avoid.

Juni searched the grounds for signs of life. The goats and sheep were nowhere to be found, same with the chickens. The rain came in sideways, harder now, blasting Juni in the face. He ran across the backyard and ducked into the chicken coop. He saw nothing but piles of straw inside.

Then came the crashing of the trees. It was here. Juni went further into the crammed box, nearly overwhelmed by the pungent smell of ammonia and vinegar, and hid himself the best that he could. A tree fell to the ground. The cracking of its trunk and the prolonged sound of its fall shook the ground.

The heavy dragging sound of something moving across the ground. Not footsteps—Juni couldn't remember getting a look at the thing's feet. He assumed it didn't have any. A tail was more fitting to its form.

It screeched and wailed. A sound somewhere between fury and misery.

Would it find me here? Did it even need to rely on senses like sight or smell to do that?

Hoping that it did, Juni held his breath and tried willing his heartbeat to slow down, to no avail. The dragging sound came near the tiny hut that was his last refuge. There would be no running after this. Where could he go?

A soft clucking came from somewhere near his feet. A cooing, even. Juni frantically dug into the straw that made up the floor of the coop. Underneath the pile of it, he found a hen. She may have just now awoken with Juni's intrusion, or she was seeking shelter against the storm while her kin remained lost in the woods. Juni grabbed her by the feet and held her close to his chest. She beat her wings and called out in panic.

The dragging sound outside ceased. Heavy breathing from massive lungs hung over the roof. Juni could smell the decay and rot of flesh in its breath.

The roof came flying off. The walls splintered apart in an instant. Juni was exposed. Hulking over him was the creature. Juni kept his eyes on the ground, where he saw the acidic drool pooling and sizzling on the mud.

The monster overshadowed him so greatly that the rain no longer touched him. Juni dared to steal a glance upward and immediately regretted his decision. He saw the gills that ran horizontally across its chest. He saw a coiled tail behind its bulk. The two arms, each as long as a school bus and bent in two places unnaturally, held the upper half of the thing erect like twisted scaffolding. The round head with no neck, the grove of teeth flashing its wintry smile, the dead eyes set wide apart, were right above him. If he so dared, he could have touched it.

Juni was an ant cowering before something not only far larger than him, but something that did not obey the laws of nature.

From somewhere off in the distance, the voice of the older woman, "Kill."

He didn't need to look to know that her spirit stood nearby, being used as a voice box by this monstrosity hovering over him.

But the creature didn't move. It was waiting. Waiting for Juni to make a decision. It never wanted to kill him; this he knew in his gut. How many opportunities had passed where it could have devoured him while he slept?

It wanted to use him.

The hen fought against Juni's grip with ferocity. She pecked at his hand and drew blood. He didn't care.

With shaking hands, he lifted the animal up and said, "From what is mine to you, so that what is yours will be mine. Please leave Tanosawa. Stop the killing. Never come back."

Juni snapped the hen's neck, wrenched her between two hands like he was revving up a motorcycle. The bird's panicked fluttering stopped after a few twitches, and it hung limp in his hands. He felt the hen's life run through his palms. Juni raised the body above his head.

The creature cocked its head to one side and observed the hen. Then, with gentle and slow movements, it took the chicken by one wing with its teeth. It didn't devour the sacrifice as Juni supposed it would. It simply held onto it like a dog with a toy and backed off.

From behind him, the drowning voice of his father: "The Wave gives, and it takes. Well done, my son. But next time, it needs to mean something to you."

The aquatic nightmare of a thing fell to the ground like a snake and slithered away into the trees. It was so fast that Juni knew it could have caught him at any time during his flight from the school, but chose not to. It was corralling him here, pushing him to make this decision.

And it was made.

Juni passed out.

When he came to, the rain had ended.

The howling wind had died down. Off in the distance, the sun rose. A single ray of golden light pierced through the darkness.

Juni rose off his knees and looked around: the creature was gone. He walked over to what used to be his father's deck. Now it resembled the epicenter of a bomb blast. Juni scaled over a pile of wreckage to get a better view of the village below. The sun's light was turning pink and illuminated the dark waters covering the village. Juni could see the water receding, draining back into the sea. Soon, the carcasses of homes appeared, twisted and mangled by the power of the sea.

Out by the now-devastated harbor, Juni saw a large dark shape dive into the waves. He kept watch over the sea, hoping to see nothing. Ten minutes passed as he held vigil.

To his horror, the white spines of the creature's razor-like dorsal fins did not disappear. They circled and careened near the harbor. It was not leaving.

It was waiting.

In plain sight.

It was still there.

It would never leave.

TWENTY SEVEN

Tanosawa was no more.

Mud and debris buried the paved roads. The river circumventing the town ran overflowing like a ruptured vein, its banks and the homes alongside it nonexistent. Most buildings were gone. In their stead, the exploded remains of what used to be homes. Foundation stones laid bare. Walls collapsed into soaking piles of trash. In the branches of a few remaining trees, some clothing, a bicycle, a dead crow.

Bodies lay in the muck and mire. Dozens of them. Juni couldn't move himself to get a closer look, and he didn't need to. None of them moved. There would be no saving anyone.

He passed by one closely, a young woman in her twenties lying face up on top of a shattered car. Her eyes were wide open, and her hands frozen in a clutching motion. For a moment he thought she should be holding a tray of tea and coffee instead of the cold nothingness she grasped towards.

Of all the buildings, only a dozen remained standing.

Barely.

The windows were blown out, the front doors smashed in, the cars in the driveways sat down the street, piled up against each other. Nobody walked the devastated streets. Up on the hill, in the parking lot of the elementary school, a group of people stood observing the horror that had replaced their lives. They wouldn't come down, not yet.

The white spines poked out of the sea, moving to and fro, back and forth, across the breadth of the village. The sun was out, and the temperature was growing unbearable, but everyone could still see *it*. There was no actual safety up on the hill, but the people couldn't bring themselves to move back so close to the waters, not while the creature stood sentry along their shores.

Juni wondered if anyone would even still want to live here anymore. The population had been minuscule to begin with, but now Juni could only count a handful of survivors on that hill. Maybe the same number he had originally seen in the gym, he hoped.

He stood on the road leading up to the Table Top, his heart breaking over the ruin and the death down below.

Rage pushed him away and forced him to the gates of the affluent community, seemingly untouched by the disaster.

"Open up, you fucks!" Juni banged on the gate, ringing the buzzer for Sakura's house over and over. He kicked the gate and drove his fists into the wood. The intercom switched on.

"Junichiro, what is it?" The voice belonged to Sakura.

"What is it? Look outside! Your god, your genie, your fucking monster has killed almost everyone and ruined the village."

Silence on the other end.

"This is your fault," Juni continued. "You never warned me, not fully, about what would happen if I messed with this 'wave' bullshit. You and my dad did this. You started this and pulled me in."

"Juni," Sakura said, her voice laden with weariness and possibly empathy. "Come inside; let's talk about this."

The gates opened.

Juni sat at the meeting table, but there was no tea, no coffee this time. He wasn't sure if he needed it, though: his heart had been racing for hours on end. His hands wouldn't stop shaking, and he felt his left eye twitching. Exhaustion made it hard to focus on what she was saying. Sakura seemed to pick up on his observation. "Yukina—the one who handles things like this — lived down in the village. I doubt she'll be joining us for a while, if at all."

Sakura did not look like herself. Deep purple bags under her eyes. A nervous twitch in her left hand. She couldn't hold his eye contact. A totally different woman from when Juni had first met her.

He sat leaning forward, his clothing soaked, ripped, covered in filth. Sakura didn't seem to mind the mess she'd have to clean up all by herself now. Her mind was in a different universe.

"You fucks, you killed this village."

Sakura ran her hands through her tangled hair. "Juni—"

"Call me Junichiro."

"Fine, Junichiro. I'm sorry for those people; I truly am. But, if you had followed my advice from day one, none of this would have happened."

A screech from outside made her jump, clutching her chest. It was the sound of a garage door opening.

"You're afraid, aren't you? Because I didn't do what? Sacrifice a person? So what, is the Table Top next?"

Her skin drained of all color, but she didn't answer. She didn't have to.

"Whatever, maybe it's my fault too. None of that matters. What matters is, how the fuck do we get rid of that thing? I gave it a chicken, I gave it blood, and it left. But now it's swimming in plain view out there. It's going to come back, and I don't think KFC is going to satisfy it next time."

"Juni," she said as he raised an eyebrow in objection, but she didn't care or didn't see. "You keep on about the *umibozu*, but that is the least of our worries."

"Umi-what?"

"The name of the creature out there, the Sea Priest. You think that what—it's some monster terrorizing us? No, it's not doing this for itself. There's something much bigger happening, and you have no idea what it entails. Death is a welcome alternative to what will happen if you don't – yes, I'll just say it plainly, if you don't fucking grow a pair and offer a human life to the Wave, to the Wave, Juni, not the creature, else something far more terrible will happen."

"You stupid piece of shit. You knew so much and told me nothing."

"The Wave, it needs you to come of your own accord, to seek it out. I couldn't say more."

"Explain. This Wave, what is it? We're past rituals and pretense; the roads still look blocked, and there's no way out of here. If it comes again, there's no one else to kill, aside from the dozen people down there. Then, when it's done, where do you think it'll go next?"

Her hands ran through her knotted hair, refusing to obey their motor functions, spasming violently.

"No one has seen the Wave aside from your father. The Amber Wave frozen in time. He used to tell us how it called out to him, how it showed him things *under* the water. It showed him, the Slithering God."

"The what?"

"The One who sleeps on the ocean floor. The One who will wake and bury the world in its glory. That's what the Sea Priest does. It's not killing people for food. I don't think it needs things like that; it's bringing offerings to its Master, to wake it up. Your father told us it's been asleep for a millennium, if not longer. That's why the world suffers all the wars and the violence that it does, because it isn't awake yet. That's why humanity is so lost, Juni. Your father promised us a new world, that we would take part in creating something beautiful."

Juni was just getting a handle on the existence of monsters and ghosts, but now gods?

"Tell me more."

"I don't know more," she nearly screamed at him, her eyes filled with tears, her pupils dilated, full of fear.

"This was all okay with you when you didn't have to do the dirty work, huh? It was my dad, wasn't it? Only he could give sacrifices?"

"Yes."

"And all of you here, what, you get to live here in luxury because you covered for him?"

"Some of us, yes. Others because they provided your father with a sacrifice to give in exchange."

Juni's heart dropped. "How could you do that?"

Sakura laughed. Her tired eyes flashed momentarily with spite. "You judge us so quickly. When one of your own friends is among us."

"What are you—" Keisuke's face came to his mind just then. "No, he wouldn't."

"Ask him, then. He's got quite the story to tell. He's got no backbone either; he'll spill it all if you press him."

Disturbed beyond measure, Juni wanted to vomit. But he needed more answers first.

"So what, my dad was chosen to do all this, and I'm next because I'm his son?"

"No."

Juni rose and slammed his hands on the table. "Explain."

"It's because," she took a deep breath, "it's because you are the son of the Wave."

For a brief moment, the image of the pregnant woman, one of the many spirits stalking him, appeared in his mind. He could hear the screaming baby, a sound that not only drove him insane but broke his heart.

Sakura, despite her manic breakdown, picked up on his concern. "You've seen her, haven't you? The one that comes with the child, the one who is always with child. She comes to me sometimes. They all come to me. It used to be once, maybe twice a year. To all of us here at the Table Top. You think the Wave has blessed us." She started laughing uncontrollably. "We're cursed, Junichiro. Cursed!"

She rose from her chair, gripping her hair in her hands. She ripped out a tuft of hair and showed it to him. Its wispy strands swayed as if alive. Gray and black streaks. "And what does it matter? All my life, I've done what has been asked of me. We all have. What your father asked of us, we did it all. Covered them all up so no one would come looking for those people. But now, now that he's gone and left the task to you, not me! Now it is coming to count the cost. Maybe yes, that's it; maybe we can still make the offering ourselves and fix this."

Sakura fumbled in her jacket pocket for her phone.

Juni beheld the woman with morbid curiosity. If it weren't for the events of the past few days, he would have been afraid and felt awkward to witness this spiral into insanity. Today, he was amused. "Good. If you helped my father murder people, or at least helped him get away with it, then you deserve what's coming. I see that you're promptly fucked, which means you can't help me. Before I leave,. who is she? The pregnant woman."

Sakura paced the room like a trapped animal, looking for an escape, scrolling for a number on her phone.

Juni rose from his chair and grabbed her by the shoulders to keep her from fidgeting and pulling out more hair. "Sakura, do one good thing with your life. Tell me."

"She's," her eyes flitted across the room as if expecting someone to enter, someone who meant her harm. "She's Machida Mako, your mother."

TWENTY EIGHT

Haruka woke up under a canopy of unnatural darkness. It felt alive. It oozed into her skin. The wind blew across her nightgown and caused her to shiver. Her back was wet. She groaned and stretched her limbs.

Not my bed. Not my room.

This realization woke her up fully. She sat up and saw that she was lying in the grass. She was outside. Above her, the darkened branches of gnarled trees. Bright stars and clear moonlight filtered from above, but on all sides surrounding her, thick woods, impenetrable by sight. She was in a small clearing. The more her eyes grew accustomed to the dark, the more she could make out some details. A few stones near her. What looked like a wooden sign was close to the treeline. What she did not see was her daughter.

Mayu's name came to her lips and froze there.

I have to be dreaming.

She bit her bottom lip and rubbed her eyes. No glasses. The world was a haze without them. She had never had a dream so real in her life. The feel of the wet grass around her toes told her that no, this was no dream; this was real; this was a living and waking nightmare.

The last thing she remembered chilled her to the bone. The man with white eyes was standing at the foot of her bed.

She rose to her feet and called out, "Mayu! Honey, where are you?"

No response. Only the wind as it brushed aside the haggard branches that blocked out the moonlight. There was another sound. Further off, distant and quiet. A soothing and rhythmic rush of sound.

Waves.

She cried out Mayu's name several more times and was met with the same cool and unsympathetic quiet of nature. Haruka tried to remember what had happened before this moment. All that came to her mind was white eyes in the dark of her bedroom. Despite the heat of the summer night, she shook.

The surrounding woods were an impenetrable wall to the unknown. Where she stood was lit up in a small circle of faded moonlight. What danger could lurk outside this area of relative safety? She had never been the sort of person people would call brave. She would yelp at the sight of a beetle in her apartment and would force Juni to take care of it. Couldn't bear to watch any movie that had a ghost in it, even if it was a kid's movie.

But Mayu wasn't *here*. She was somewhere *out there*.

Haruka took a step out of the light and entered the forest. There was something that could be called a path under her feet, hard to see without her glasses. Somewhat worn down by human feet but overgrown with weeds. As she entered the path, she immediately ran into a spider web that wrapped itself around her face. She screamed. She tore at the web until she mostly cleared it off her face. Though no matter how much she waved her hands, she could still feel the sticky threads clinging to her fingers until she bent down and wiped them off on the grass. The thought that the spider could be in her hair, hiding, laying eggs that would come out in the shower, nearly paralyzed her.

Stop it. This won't help Mai-Mai. You can fall apart later.

Haruka steeled herself and moved forward. The song of crickets filled the woods. A solitary cicada, unwilling to give up its daily mating call, rose here and there. The humidity wasn't as intense as in her neighborhood at night.

I must be somewhere higher in elevation.

This thought caused a near-meltdown of panic. Where in Tokyo could she have gone to feel this relative coolness? She heard no city bustle. No cars. No trains. Just the natural and untamed world.

She made her way into the darkness. The moonlight lit up the path in fragments just good enough to help guide her. On this forest path, she felt incredibly vulnerable. Anything could hide in the thickets. It could be behind her. In front of her. Even above her. The sound of water crashing against rocks became louder. She could smell a faint aroma of the ocean.

In a few minutes, the path opened up wider and wider until she could see a spot of land not surrounded by trees. A field, or a clearing of some sort. Beyond this strip of land, a dark wall of nothingness, spotted in places by small lights. Stars. The sky. It looked so close to Earth that if she were to keep on walking, she might fall off into space.

Haruka left the forest and came into the field. She was soon standing on a grassy ledge above the ocean. Below her, she could see the sheer cliff, the water underneath, and the sharp rocks. Teeth awaiting prey. The waves were splashing angrily against the stones. The water was dark. Black like oil.

The drop extended to her right. Beyond it, a bay. What looked like rocks studded the water until a spot of moonlight splashed over the area and revealed them to be the roofs of homes. To her left, there was a set of stones climbing up a hill to a copse of trees. From the grove, a bridge reached out over the sea and ended at a tall pile of rocks that jutted out of the water.

There was nowhere to go but forward. Not if she wanted to find her daughter.

Haruka climbed the steps slowly, with her hands outstretched in front of her, and walked through the cluster of trees. Soon, she stood before the bridge. It swung and swayed in the wind. Beneath the boards of the bridge, a long way to fall before being dashed against the stones and waves.

Across the bridge, atop the tower of rocks, an orange light glowed. Beneath that light, a silhouette of a child holding something in their hands.

"Mayu!" Haruka cried out.

Next to the figure who might have been her daughter, another shadow appeared. That of an adult. Two glowing white orbs beamed out from the void of their face. The shadow put an arm around the girl and they both walked further away into the orange light, what might have been a fire or a bright lantern.

Haruka moved forward. She placed a foot on the first wooden board. The bridge jerked, unstable. Between each board was a space of about a step. Nothing but air—and the promise of certain death—in between each plank. She put the other foot onto the bridge. Now she was fully suspended above the ocean. She gripped the ropes that served as guardrails. The material irritated her hands. The entire structure shook with each step and with every gust of wind.

She crept her way across the bridge. With each step she took shook the world and brought her own mortality into clear and absolute focus. She would have gone back if she could have. Or even just stayed in place and let her fate take her. If it weren't for the fact that Mayu was on the other side and in the company of some strange man, she would have given up.

One step at a time. Each movement shook the bridge. It took her what felt like ten minutes but she made it across. She nearly kissed the stone ground when she got off the bridge.

The angry sea surrounded the rocky platform. Nothing existed outside of this outgrowth. It was a satellite in the dark.

In front of her was the orange light. It was an enormous bonfire. The fire obscured the other side of the space, but she could see two shadowy figures standing there. Haruka had never engaged in violence. She held no hope that she'd be able to do anything to this person and free her daughter. But she would try for all that was worth.

She drew near the fire, and the heat dried up her tears. Embers shot out and landed by her feet. As she rounded the fire, the figure of the man faded away. Standing there, looking out over the dark sea, was Mayu, alone, clutching Keke the Wonderful to her neck.

"Baby, are you okay?" Haruka ran to her daughter and embraced her. The girl's eyes were glazed over and she appeared drugged. Haruka shook her, but Mayu did not respond.

The waves roared beneath the vertical drop in front of them. An angry growl of water lashing out against stone. Haruka felt it in her bones. Holding onto Mayu's shoulders, she looked out over the vast empty sea. There was no way back to the mainland. They were stranded on this rock.

A thousand questions assaulted her mind now that she found her daughter. How did they even get here? Who lit this fire? If they just stayed put until morning, could they count on someone finding them here?

The ocean growled once more. A reverberation that sounded like metal grinding against metal. No, this sound did not originate from the waves below. The way it twisted her insides and warped her mind made her doubt it had even originated on this planet. Pebbles at their feet vibrated and rolled away.

The rumbling came from the direction of the waves. It grew louder. She couldn't hear the gentle roar of the fire behind her. Couldn't hear the waves. Not even the wind. All that existed was this guttural call from the depths of the sea. A call that reached from some primordial time and froze her in place. It felt like all she had known in her life was this call. Like a magnetic pull of some awful black hole, she felt herself and Mayu leaning over the drop to the sea. She tried to fight it. To keep her feet firmly rooted to the stone. She forced herself to her knees to keep from falling over, hands pushing Mayu away from the ledge.

Out over the black waves, something stirred. The division between water and sky was slight, making what she beheld vague and terrible.

Like a massive wave emerging from the sea, the water swelled up to the sky. A destructive wave large enough to bury any city of man. From its depths came the call.

Deep. Vicious. Uncaring.

Her blood became ice, clotting her arteries. Threatening to strike her dead on the spot. She gripped Mayu until she must have cut her with her nails. It felt like her spirit was rising and out of her body.

From the titanic wave came golden and pink light akin to the sunrise. Haruka felt cold before its light. She might have been screaming, she couldn't tell. The entire world around her, all senses and all thoughts were enveloped in an amber hue.

She shut her eyes and screamed until her lungs hurt.

Mayu remained still, staring at the wave.

Then silence.

The ticking of a clock.

Opening her eyes, she was greeted by the darkness of her bedroom, the warm light of the ladybug nightlight Mayu had brought in, the familiar smell of the fabric spray she used to keep the house fresh.

What she did not find next to her was her daughter. Jumping out of bed, and rushing to each room, there was no trace of her. All the windows and the front door were locked from the inside.

She was gone.

TWENTY NINE

As Juni left Sakura's house, he wondered where his rental car was. He laughed out loud at the thought. Something simple and relatable, not gods and monsters. He couldn't remember seeing it last night when he had his showdown with the creature. Perhaps it was drifting out in the tide, destined for an eternity at the bottom of the ocean.

He smiled. He had no insurance on the thing, and couldn't afford it. But this thought comforted him. Back to the time when money was his chief worry and fear in life. He was done with all of that. A life of poverty it would be. Just give up and let the tide of financial disaster swallow him whole. It was possible that his account still had the money that the umibozu, as Sakura had called it, had gifted him. Though, he wouldn't be surprised if it were gone. He was dealing with something beyond his comprehension, something murderous and cruel. He couldn't see it holding up a bargain in good faith.

But thinking about money was a helpful distraction. He knew he was shielding his mind from what Sakura had told him minutes earlier. He needed the moorings of the familiar, the grounded, to keep his sanity from floating away.

It was the name Sakura said that stalked the crevices of his mind behind his conscious thoughts. It wasn't just that he was the "son of the

Wave," whatever that meant; it wasn't the revelation that the ghost was his mother.

It was the name of that shadow. Machida Mako. The first name written in his father's journal. He supposed was the first sacrifice to the monster in the water. Or to whatever god it served. It made a perverse sense to him. His mother, the woman who pretended to be her, at least, never showed affection to him growing up.

Who was Mako?

Juni knew she was dead, by the hand of his father. But what was so special about her?

Why is she following me? And what the fuck is with the baby screams when she appears?

"And what the hell is the Son of the Wave?!" Juni yelled out over the sea. He climbed up onto the guard railing. "What do you want from me? Why does it have to be me?!"

The mocking crash of the surf and the sight of the white spines, still circling the bay, greeted him.

What was out there? What was this Slithering God and what did it want from him?

He got off the rails and walked down the street to Keisuke's place. No one was outside. Every window was shuttered. Fury burned in Juni's bones. If his old friend was a part of this, he might just burn his house down.

The neon technicolor blaze of Keisuke's dream home reflected the sunlight into Juni's eyes. He walked up the driveway. He stopped at the front door.

There wasn't one.

Glancing to his left, he saw what remained of the door, lying in several splintered pieces on the grass.

Where the door used to be now stood a gaping hole. The sides of the doorframe were cracked and broken in uneven patterns. Black slime stained the floor just inside the entrance, but didn't seem to dissolve anything.

Juni tentatively peeked his head into the house. Fear had now replaced his anger.

"Keisuke, Hitomi, are you guys here?"

Silence.

Though it was daytime, it was dark inside. All the storm shutters still covered the windows. Juni tried the light switch by the front door, but nothing turned on. He stepped inside. He couldn't stand the thought that Keisuke knew about the creature in the water, and presumably its connection to his father. But fear and concern for his friend and his children outweighed his need for justice.

Juni walked inside.

Keeping his footsteps light and slow, he maneuvered his way into the living room. He could hear nothing, and he knew the creature was in the bay, and it was sunny outside, but still, better to be safe. It wasn't really the danger of death that scared him—he no longer believed the monster wanted to harm him — it was the fear of what he could discover in this dark cave of a home. And the kids? Juni prayed to whatever god would listen that they'd been at a friend's house when the Sea Priest came to visit.

A dripping sound came to him as he neared the kitchen. It could be the faucet left on. But it came from multiple points in the room.

A copper smell filled his nose.

Juni turned a corner, entered the kitchen, and froze. He couldn't see the color due to the darkness, but he knew that something wet covered the walls and the floor, something that dripped onto the floor. The dining room chairs were overturned. The table was split in two. Juni entered and nearly slipped. He looked at his feet and now knew what was smeared all over the room.

Blood.

But there were no bodies. Juni went further into the room and rounded the bar that led to the patio. He let out a shout and grabbed his chest. He nearly smacked his face into something dangling from the ceiling. A dark shape, like a ball hanging from a string. He looked closer and saw it more clearly in the dark: it was a chicken. It hung from a rope attached to a ceiling fan. It was a hen, its head slumping to one side as if its neck was broken.

A rejected offering.

There was nothing else to see in this room. He left it, checked the other rooms downstairs; the bathroom, what he assumed to be the parents' room, an office, nothing. There was only one other sign to follow. The dark streak on the wall led up the stairs.

The steps groaned as he ascended them. There was light pouring in from the top of the stairs. As Juni entered the landing, he could see the picture frames on the wall to his left. One of Keisuke looking uncomfortable in a suit, and Hitomi in her wedding dress, smiling. The next was of the family of four at the beach, the kids burying their dad in the sand while Hitomi posed with a peace sign behind them.

Walking further down the hall, Juni saw where the light was coming from. The room on his right.

He wished he had never walked into that room. The wall across from him was gone. As if ripped away by giant hands. Hanging from the roof, leaning over the gap where the wall should have been, was Hitomi. Her dead eyes stared back into his. Blood still ran down her face. She was missing both arms. On the floor beneath her, he saw the lower half of a person. Given the size of the legs, he knew it was Keisuke. He would never know for sure; the upper half was nowhere in sight. He couldn't bring himself to see what spilled out of the wound.

To his utmost horror, he realized he was in the kids' room. Stuffed pigs and elephants on the floor, a spaceship poster on one of the remaining walls.

Were the parents here to defend their children at the end?

Out of the corners of his eyes, he saw a bed on either side of him. A shared bedroom. He couldn't bear to look at them. He forced himself to glance at the one on his right. He assumed it was Kaito's bed since the blankets had giant baseball pictures on them. Now they were shredded, and a dark red mass lay in the center of them. He looked over to his left. Ayumi's bed across the room, pink blankets and giant stuffed animals, painfully reminded him of his own daughter's, was a scene of wet red splashed over the walls.

Juni ran out of the room and threw up on the floor. He sobbed and lay in a ball of suffering in the hall.

It took him an hour to regain his composure. He couldn't even walk downstairs and away from the massacre. All strength had left him. It was easier to look at the floor and focus on the stripes of color in the wood's pattern than to think about what lay mere feet behind him.

He eventually walked back downstairs. Before he left that house of death, he needed an answer for what Sakura had told him. How was Keisuke involved? A morbid curiosity took hold of him. It would be easier to solve this problem than it would be to move on to the next one, the one that still swam in the bay. He looked into the only room he felt would have an answer, Keisuke's study on the first floor.

A light blue MacBook lay on his desk. Juni flipped up the screen, but of course it was locked. He tried a few random passwords and gave up. He sat down in the leather chair and opened the desk's file cabinets. The top two drawers on either side of the chair were filled with documents relating to water and sewage treatment. Dates and forms and budgets Juni neither understood nor cared for. He dropped the papers on the ground after looking at them.

What was he expecting to find? A confession? A secret journal like Dad's?

He walked past a bookshelf. Volumes of titles on Roman architecture and fly-fishing. A Buddhist altar to Keisuke's parents. He saw two photographs of an elderly man and woman. Next to their picture, he saw the name "Kentaro," written on a wooden tile with no picture affixed to it.

Juni threw open the remaining cabinets and tossed out all the papers. He found tax forms and birth certificates and the occasional drawing by Keisuke's kids. Nothing that could explain to him why he was involved.

And why do I care so much?

Juni couldn't answer that, not clearly at least. He felt somehow that whatever Keisuke had done, Keisuke—the nicest and most congenial man he knew — if he could do something terrible to get involved with the Wave, then what did that mean for Juni? He wanted to believe he could escape the same fate. If he found evidence, then maybe he could understand and avoid the call.

The call.

Juni felt it growing inside like cancer. Eating away at his organs much the same way as the creature's acid. Money no longer meant anything to him. He couldn't see himself sacrificing somebody to move into a bigger house.

Because look where that got him! If Keisuke gave an offering, or covered one up, his end was brutal. Juni could never trust the promises of the Wave. Even more, he needed to believe that he was different, different from his old friend. That was his only hope.

Juni yelled and tried flipping over the desk, but it was too heavy. He cursed and grabbed the laptop, flinging it across the room.

"I'm not like you; I can be better."

He slumped down onto the floor.

He had to be better, because he could never let Mayu suffer Kaito and Ayumi's fate. He had to protect her, no matter what. But to do that, he needed to understand.

Juni got up and left the house. He went down the driveway. He was about to leave, but felt an urge to turn around. All that was there was the house in all of its candy-coated glory.

The house. That's what Keisuke got, didn't he? That was his reward. He thought back to his only conversation with Keisuke about moving into the Table Top. What did he say?

Don't bring it up around Shota.

Kentaro. The odd name jammed next to the picture of Keisuke's parents at the altar.

The name in Dad's journal. Seven years ago. When Shota's son disappeared.

Sakagawa Kentaro.

Sakagawa Shota.

Juni's blood went sub-zero, and the hairs on his arms stood as if electrified.

That's what he did, didn't he?

Shota's son disappeared from the boat in a matter of minutes. Body never found. And almost immediately after, Keisuke gets his house.

"You motherfucker."

Juni looked up at the house one last time. He felt great pity for the children. But for Keisuke, maybe even his wife, he only had one last thing to say.

"I hope I see your shadows soon. You deserve to be its slaves."

He walked down the street to the gate separating the Table Top from the rest of the village. As he passed Sakura's house near the front gate, he felt eyes on him. He turned and saw her looking out from her third-story window, looking at him.

"Yeah, fuck you too."

THIRTY

J uni decided to leave.

Fuck this village, fuck the Wave, fuck everyone.

No car, no problem. The road is still blocked? I'll just climb over the debris and walk. Even if it takes me days to get to some fucking civilization, I'm not staying here another minute.

Juni descended the hill from the Table Top and turned onto the village's central road that led back towards Mutsu City. Water still covered the road, up to his ankles. It was only sixty kilometers back to the nearest city, further along the seaside. No problem.

The interior of the peninsula was far too mountainous to make the journey. He'd probably fall, break his legs, and die of dehydration. But was the road any better? He knew that if *it* wanted to, it could come out of the sea at any moment and grab him. But he was done playing by the rules of something he didn't understand. And what little he understood was too horrifying to consider seriously.

"Juni, where you going?"

He looked up and saw Shota, knee-deep in thick mud, pulling some metal bars out of the muck. Juni had been so absorbed in his thoughts, he didn't notice that he had just passed Shota's house, or more specifically, the devastation that used to be his home. Beyond Shota, Juni could see a few people in the distance, rummaging through the wreckage of their lives.

Guess they finally got the courage to come down.

Shota's face filled him with pain and guilt. He resolved never to tell his friend what he knew to be true.

"I'm out of here, Shota. Can't deal with this anymore."

"You're not serious? That thing is still out there; you can see its spiky things poking out of the water if you walk down the street a bit. We have to figure out what to do."

"We? No 'we,' my friend. This town isn't my fucking problem; I wanted none of this."

Shota pulled himself out of the mud. "You didn't want this? You're the one who fucked with that thing to get your money. And now, people are dead. Maybe hundreds. Dead. And you're just going to walk away?"

He thought of Shota's little boy and cringed at the thought of his fate.

"And do what? Help these people? Weren't you paying attention last night? They tried to sacrifice me to that thing. I don't owe them shit."

"Yeah, what Shun did was fucked up, but he got what he deserved for that. What about me? What about Mrs. Sato? Not everyone tried to hurt you. You're just going to leave us? Look at my house, man. I have nothing left, and let me remind you, it **is** because of you."

"Whatever."

Shota's face went violent, rage-filled red. He leaped forward, cocked his right arm back, and punched Juni in the jaw. He went flying backward, landing in a pile of seaweed-strewn cabinets. Something hard jabbed his spine.

"Come on, take it back, or stand up and fight," Shota shouted.

Juni groaned as he stood up. His jaw felt looser than it should have been. Fire crackled in his skull as if it were about to erupt and burst apart.

"Fuck. You."

Juni turned back onto the road and kept walking.

On his way, he looted a destroyed home and found two bottles of water, put them in a plastic bag, and took off. He made it as far as the original landslide he had seen when he was first trapped in town. Not much had changed. Maybe more trees had been added to the mess. But he could do this; he just had to climb. To the left of the debris, a sudden drop off into the sea; to the right, the mountain that spewed out the barrier, similarly clogged with downed trees. Put his feet on the most solid thing he could find, which was probably a tire buried in the mud, and lifted himself up. He made it a few feet before losing his grip and falling down, slamming his tailbone against the ground. He got up and tried again. Juni gained a few more feet before sliding down the pile of trash, completely covered in mud. The entire wall he was trying to scale was slick, ungraspable mud. Three more times he jumped at the mountain of what used to be a forest, and three more times it spat him back out to the earth.

He lay on the ground, gasping for breath, staring up at the sun, now directly above him. The mud provided some relief from the summer heat until it started drying, trapping the humidity closer to his skin. If he kept up like this, with no drinkable water, he wouldn't be able to walk one kilometer, let alone sixty.

The sea lay to his left, with a gradual slope leading down to it. He could just swim across the damaged section of the road.

He laughed.

Yeah, I'm sure that will go over well.

"It's useless."

He thought about just giving up. Going to sleep then and there. If the Wave wanted to take him and rip him apart while he slept, so be it.

He tried to sit up, and a wave of lightheadedness hit him. He sat back down. Gave in to the overwhelming need to sleep.

The Void.

Juni waded in the black waters in front of Tajima. For the first time, there was no fear. The weightlessness was freeing. The current was relaxing.

Dominating.

Just let go.

A red light burst to life behind the island. Like a dull but bloody sunrise. The light outlined two figures on the rocky shore. One bald, overweight, hunched over.

Dad.

His eyes burned like terrible stars of a foreign universe where love did not exist.

A smaller shadow stood next to him, holding his hand. Pigtails. A flowing dress. Something in her free hand, hanging at her side. As the crimson light grew brighter, Juni saw it was a stuffed red dragon.

Mai-Mai. Her eyes were not glowing like her grandfather's.

Because she was alive.

Juni screamed. He thrashed against the water and tried to swim forward. He did not move any closer. His voice came out muffled, as if drowning. The water was like the mud that kept him trapped in Tano-sawa.

Juni's dad held Mayu up with both of his hands. He got down on his knees. He chanted something. A great tentacle, black and falling apart like it was made from rotting flesh, rose from the abyss. It latched onto Mayu. She screamed. Her eyes grew white hot.

"No!" Juni woke, screaming until his throat went dry. He threw out his arms and legs as if trying to escape certain death. He woke fully and saw that he was still by the landslide. But the sun was now just above the horizon over the bay. It was the same dull-red as the light in his dreams. Everything around him was now bathed in the crimson glow.

His throat craved water. He bent over a puddle and drank of the muddy water.

The dream.

It can't be. She's safe in Tokyo.

He went for his phone and found nothing, remembering he had lost it during the chaos of the previous night.

Just then, a ringing. On his right side. Juni rolled over and saw it. Resting on a rock next to his head. His phone. Delivered to him.

Juni grabbed it like he was a starving man clasping onto the last piece of bread on the shelf.

He answered it.

It was Haruka's voice screaming on the other end. Juni's heart died.

"Mayu's gone! It was, it was like a ghost. I know you won't believe me, but Juni, it was your dad! He took her! I was there! Somewhere out in the sea."

Juni stood motionless, unable to process the worst news of his life.

"What do you mean?"

Haruka told him about seeing his dad at the foot of her bed and waking up in some strange place. She told him that his dad was also there, standing with Mayu above a darkened sea. She told him about the terrible wave that rose and washed her in amber light.

"I believe you, honey. I know where she is. I'm getting her back."

"What the hell is going on, Juni?" Her voice was breathless; he could hear the sobs trying to escape at each syllable that she spoke.

"Haruka, I love you. It's too much to explain, but I will when I come home, I promise."

He hung up before letting her speak again. He checked his phone briefly. No signal.

He laughed as tears welled up in his eyes.

"You did that, didn't you? You knew just how to hurt me, and you let me have that one fucking call?"

He nearly threw his phone into the ocean but stayed his hand. He had a better idea. Juni climbed over the guardrail and walked down the grassy slope to the beach. He could see it out there—the white spines, swimming in circles.

Juni walked into the waves with his hands stretched out at his sides.

"Come on! Take me! Take me and give her back! From what is mine to you, so that what is yours will be mine! You want blood, take mine."

He yelled at the creature. Years of pent-up anger and hatred of his father spilled out. He roared with ferocity. Spit flew out of his mouth. He beat his chest with his hand.

"What are you waiting for? You want me, here I am!"

The spines stopped moving. Their angle suggested the creature was facing him head-on, maybe a hundred feet away from him. Juni took a few more steps into the water until it came to his chest. But the spines didn't move.

Then, the creature turned around and swam out to sea.

"No! Come back!"

Juni started swimming after the thing. Soon he lost sight of it as the spines went underwater. A swell rose in front of him and pushed him all the way back to the shore.

He dove in again and swam. Again the swell picked him up and threw him back at the rocky beach.

No more strength. His body was pushed to the limit. Juni collapsed in a puddle of tears on the shore.

He didn't know how much time had passed as he lay there staring into the sun. He was sure he had permanently damaged his eyes. But there was nothing left to do, was there? Just lay here and die.

He thought about Mai-Mai's drawing. The princess riding the dragon.

He came out here for himself, didn't he? To be better than his father, in the process he played along with Dad's desires, regardless.

No more. Fuck the money. Fuck Dad's legacy. I need to get her back.

Juni knew where she was. His dreams had told him as much. He always knew that's where he needed to go, back to where he first met the creature as a child. And now it had his kid. He knew what it wanted. It wanted to force his hand. Force him to kill for it just like Dad did. To offer human lives.

No, it *won't end like this.*

I'm going to kill it.

THIRTY ONE

Shota lifted the frame of what used to be a roof and set it on his thighs. Mrs. Sato scrambled under the edifice, sifting through the waterlogged items of her home. After a minute, Shota's arms buckled under the weight.

"Got it," Mrs. Sato yelled out. She came crawling under the frame holding a photo album. When she was clear, Shota let the beam fall.

"You're a lifesaver, dearie. I know they're just a few photographs, but they're all I have left of him. And don't worry, they're in a waterproof album, so they should be okay."

"No problem," he said.

"Now run along and help somebody else who needs it more than me."

Shota gave her a quick bow and left her to ruminate over the devastation of her home. Everyone had come down from the school to sort through their belongings and maybe find a survivor. Not to mention that someone had to bury the bodies strewn about before the rot overtook them.

There were none that they could see.

They had been at it for hours. Water was the priority and thankfully, Mr. Ando was a bit of a prepper and had twelve jugs of it under his porch.

And better luck for the village was that he was missing, since never in his lucid mind would he have given it away freely.

Nearly every other home had water stored somewhere as well. At least one need wouldn't be a problem for a few days until rescue workers arrived.

The task at hand was something that would take years to undo. If anyone wanted to still live here, that was. The immediate priority was water, perhaps some food, blankets, supplies to make a fire, and dry clothes if possible. There was talk of marching up to the Table Top and demanding to be let in. Shota recovered his welding torch from his shack and stuffed it into a backpack. He put aside the metal siding of his home in a pile. If he could get his hands on some more, he could make a better barrier for the doors at the school in case the monster came back.

The gym had collapsed, leaving behind a mess of blackened, soggy wood. Aside from the three who were lost inside, everyone else had made it out just fine. Physically, at least. Shota helped the elderly across the dark puddles while those younger made it across by themselves.

The only structure left standing that could provide even a modicum of safety was the school proper. The remaining residents of Tanosawa scurried like sand fleas across their neighborhoods, which now resembled a swamp. They needed to be in and out. Grab what they needed and head back up to the school. Shota counted fifteen people. If that was all that was left, it meant hundreds had died.

He could weld the metal to the doors that lead to the main hall, and if that thing came back, the welded metal could at least slow it down for the others to escape. Escape for how long? He didn't want to think about it.

Everyone monitored the coastline as they worked. Like a lion stalking its prey, the creature had not left them alone. Shota could see the white spines darting back and forth in the water. A strange red light washed over the ruined village.

The thing that disturbed Shota the most was the black pools all over the village. Over trees and cars and even the ground itself. If last night proved anything to him, it was that now the creature had full access to any point in the village. Even the school grounds were covered in mold.

Sakagawa Shota was the kid no one counted on to make anything out of his life while he was in school. Teachers said he was dumber than the fish that sustained the village. Parents never bothered to say anything one way or another. Even his friends, Juni and Keisuke, never thought much of him. Told him he'd probably end up stuck in this village for the rest of his life fishing just like his father did, and his father did before him, and so on.

The one thing Shota had been good at growing up was hunting with his uncle. Guns were near impossible to get for the average guy, but his uncle Seiya had gotten his license decades ago for hunting boar and the occasional bear. He never renewed said license, and whenever the police came by to check on his rifle, he said he had thrown it away years ago. His license was revoked, but his gun and the stockpiled ammo, like a thing out of legend, remained hidden, out of sight, but nearby. And he knew where it was.

Shota spent every weekend he could, especially after Juni left town, with Uncle Seiya. The man was a living embodiment of grit. Wild, frizzy white beard. A gut that probably blocked his view of his feet. Forearms like pistons. Shota and Seiya would spend days in his hut up in the mountains, never saying a word to one another, just waiting for a deer or something worthwhile to cross their paths.

Shota never cared for the killing. It was the moments of silence that stood out as beacons of light in his dreary life. The moments spent with Seiya, right before the cancer ate out his insides, the moments of not being judged that spoke volumes to him. He had hoped to one day bring his own son to the mountains and teach him the ways of solemn contentment.

He thought about the rifle now. Last he saw it, it was in Seiya's shack, hanging above a set of antlers. There was maybe a single box of shells left for it. They needed a weapon for the thing in the water, and that seemed to be the only option. Shota wasn't going to let another massacre happen. After seeing Shun torn in half, his blood forming a wet trail from the gym's entrance to the parking lot, and Katsumi disappearing into an abyss and never returning, Shota swore not to let anyone else get hurt.

Not like his boy. Shota tried never to think of little Kentaro—Ken-chan, he would call him. Seven years of not knowing where he was and what happened to him. He would have blown his brains out with Seiya's rifle years ago, but he didn't have the courage.

Never again. Gotta live for him.

And fuck Juni. It was his fault this was happening, and the guy just walks away from it all? Not me. At least I can try to do something.

As if drawn by the mere thought of him, Juni's voice came in, "Shota, it's good to see you made it."

He didn't turn around. He didn't trust himself not to lay another one right into that prick's nose. He closed his eyes and breathed deeply. "What you want? Gave up already?"

He turned around and saw Juni standing there, eyes red, tears spilling out, completely covered in mud, completely soaked. His hair might have been black at one point; now it was brown and gray, caked in both wet and dry mud. For a split second, he felt sorry for him. Then he remembered how Juni had just walked away from the mess that he caused, and the empathy died out.

"It has my daughter."

It was as if he was speaking a foreign language.

"What? Isn't she in Tokyo?"

"Don't ask me how I know, but I saw her on Tajima. My wife called me, too, and said she was missing. I just know it; she's there right now. I need help."

"Shit. I'm sorry, but what can we do?"

"I'm sorry for what happened too, for what I said to you, and for what I did. I should never have messed with this thing. But I want to go there, to Tajima, now. I want to go there and kill this thing. Can you help me?"

Shota's rage smoldered down into annoyance. But still, regardless of how he felt about Juni right now, there was a child involved.

Never again.

"Juni, look at the people here. That thing can come back at any time and kill us all."

"If it comes back, none of you will survive. It doesn't matter what you're preparing; you can't live through it. It can go wherever it wants to. Our only chance to save my girl, and to save the people here, is to go out there and kill it. Soon. Like right fucking now. I have an idea of what might hurt it. Last night, it pulled away from the candle you threw at it, like it was afraid of the fire. I'm not sure, but that might be something that can hurt it. I need your help to find kerosene or gasoline, and we need to get out to Tajima."

He was speaking fast, stumbling over his words, like a man drunk on the fumes of his sorrow and out of touch with this world.

"I can get some kerosene; almost every house has some for the winter, shouldn't be hard to find some still around. But the harbor's been destroyed; we can't get out to the island."

Juni fumbled his fingers together. "It wants me to come. It wants me to go there, my dreams, ever since I came here, they end at Tajima, at the void, the blackness beneath the surface, the thing that writhes in the dark."

Shota became worried about his friend. He seemed on the verge of a mental breakdown. Talking nonsense. "I can get the fuel, we can try fire. The boat is a lost cause. But I'll go look with you. I need to go get something at my uncle's old shack before we head out."

"Okay." Juni's response was quick, but his eyes spoke of a mind that was in another world.

"Holy shit, I can't believe it."

Shota stood at the edge of the shattered dock, hunting rifle slung over his shoulders, hands holding two canisters of kerosene. Two boats were washed up on the beach. One of them was upside down and broken in two. All the other boats were missing, washed out to sea. The dock was nothing more than a collection of wooden poles sticking out of the dirty waves like splintered wooden teeth emerging from a swirling mouth of sea.

Amidst the chaos, one object stood out, defying all reason.

Shota's boat. In all of its gaudy glory. Imperial flag flapping in the hot wind.

It was untouched by the storm and the tsunami. Not even a scratch on its hull. It floated near the shoreline. No anchor holding it in place. It was just there.

"I told you, it wants me to go to Tajima. It's not going to let me just walk away from this."

Juni waded out into the water a few feet and threw his two kerosene canisters into the boat. Shota followed and did the same. They pulled themselves over the side and onto the deck.

"Is it still following us?" Shota asked, looking out at the water. The sun was nearly gone, swallowed into the ebony nothingness of the night. The sea was a pale and dead gray that was quickly rolling into an infinite world of the unknown. Shota refused to go with Juni unless he had his gun. But it was a weapon. It was something they could use to put some distance between the creature and them if fire didn't work. Shota didn't have time to strip, oil, and test the rifle. A fool's hope. Juni was against this. He felt deep inside that fire alone was the answer. But he needed Shota to be on board for this. He couldn't go out there alone. Shota humored Juni by bringing along his welding torch in his backpack.

"No, I don't see it anymore."

The creature had tracked their steps as they walked towards the ruined dock. Swimming parallel to them, always there. The remaining villagers whispered as they left, and Juni could detect the faintest chatter of joy in their gossip. The bad man was leaving, and with him, so would the monster.

"Wait, there it is. See it?"

Juni squinted his eyes. But even in the growing dark, the white of its dorsal spines was obvious. It was now swimming away from the coast, swimming out towards Tajima.

A personal escort.

Juni knew this is what it wanted. It wanted—no; it *needed* him to be here. To see something. Juni couldn't bear to tell Shota more of his dreams, couldn't bear to think about the thing that dwelt on the sea's floor. Something worse than the Sea Priest. Worse than the malformed freak that had brought so much death to the village already. There was something out there, something that it served, the Slithering God.

The Writhing One. Where did that name come from? No one told me that.

He knew things he shouldn't, saw things no one should see.

Shota revved up the engine, and it roared to life. He turned the boat to face Tajima, turned on the floodlights, and piloted forward.

"I can't believe there's even gas left in this thing or that it works. I mean, what the fuck?"

"I told you, it wants me."

"Why you?"

Juni laughed. Something both inappropriate but somehow fitting to his situation. "I'm the Son of the Wave, didn't you know?"

Shota didn't answer. He gave his friend a stern and hard look.

"It means I belong to the Wave. And we're going to find out exactly what all that means before the night is done."

"Juni, shut the fuck up. You're losing it. We need you to be on your game for what comes next. Your daughter is counting on you."

For a change, Juni did shut all the fucks up.

The boat sped out into the infinite blackness of the sea. Dark clouds covered the night sky. No stars above. No moon to light their path. Only the floodlights of Shota's boat. The area directly in front of the boat lit up as they flew by; the outer limits of their vision were nothing but pure blackness. It felt like they were voyaging out into the depths of space, never to return.

Juni unscrewed the caps of the kerosene, tipped the containers over onto the rags and old clothing Mrs. Sato lent them, and soaked it all. He lined the fuel-soaked cloth near the side of the boat, tying them off on the cleats. A preemptive barrier, just in case. Juni didn't want to think about lighting the boat on fire and what that meant about their chances of returning to shore. But what else could he do?

When he was finished, he sat down on the bench near Shota at the steering wheel.

"I've been an idiot. I came out here for money. Plain and simple. I found a way to get it easy. And now, it's my fault that Tanosawa is gone. All those people. I've screwed you over. And Mai-Mai..." Juni trailed off and stared into the dark, lighter gripped tightly in hand. "If I had just stayed home. Who knows? Maybe I'd be dead. I owed money to some bad people. But my wife and kid would have been okay. I had life insurance, they would have gotten a payout."

"But your little girl would be without her dad. No amount of money would make her feel good about that."

"True. But it'd be better than being here. Out there, alone."

"We'll get her. I hate your guts right now. You're an asshole, but I'll help you get her back."

"Thanks, man. Hate you too. But thanks."

The two men laughed as the boat sped into the dark. A welcome levity on the lonely journey.

Neither man spoke for the remaining half an hour to the island. The only sounds were the motor of the boat and the hull crashing into the surf. Darkness all around. The sky an immutable presence of unfeeling space.

The sea beneath the flimsy boat, an open mouth of eternity.

THIRTY TWO

"D o you see that?" Juni called back to Shota.

"I do, but I don't know what I'm looking at."

Tajima had appeared. Barren and inhospitable as ever. But something was different tonight. A faint red glow emanated from the land. It wasn't bright. It was a muted, almost imperceptible spectrum, buried under the floodlights of the boat.

"Kill the lights for a sec," Juni asked.

Shota shut them off as he brought the boat to a stop. It floated in the empty space of the sea, surrounded by darkness on all sides save one. The island was giving off a color. A dark red. Like dirty blood spilling out into a barrel of oil and staining the night.

"The fuck is doing that?" Shota asked.

"Nothing we want to see. Let's move closer."

Shota moved the boat towards the island and stopped it right off its shore. He hit the anchor lever and dropped the heavy load off the side of the boat. They unscrewed the caps on all the kerosene containers and set them aside. Then they wrapped some more clothing—Mrs. Sato had given them an entire garbage bag of her husband's things—around two fishing rods already in the boat and spread the gas over them. Shota readied the hunting rifle. He shifted it from shoulder to shoulder, nervous and agitated. "So, what next? We just wait for it to come?"

"Yes. Or until it forces us to move." He stood up on the bow's gunwale and shouted, "I'm here! You want me? Then get me."

In response, dozens of white lights appeared on the rock face of the island, hundreds of feet up.

Shota raised the gun. Juni put his hand on the barrel and lowered the weapon. "Don't waste your bullets. They're already dead. That thing just uses them like puppets. I think it takes their voices, the last things they say, and can twist that into its own speech. I've never seen any of them actually do anything, like move objects or hurt people."

"Well, aren't I just fucking relieved at that."

Amid the shadows, the dozens if not hundreds of eyes forming a castle wall above the rocks, a new form emerged in front of them, that of a man holding a small child in the air. The smaller shadow kicked and screamed.

"Mayu!" He knew it was her. If for no other reason than that she was holding a stuffed dragon at her side. The man—his father, no doubt—dangled her over the cliff. Her screams rang down the rocky side of the island and pummeled his heart.

In an instant, the eyes went out, and the shadows were gone, as was any trace of Mayu. The faint glow of the island deepened in color. Crimson lined the rocks, almost as if volcanic energy was bursting forth. The red light revealed the water between the boat and the shore in its bloody shade.

"Shit, Juni, look out!"

Completely silent in its movements and covered in darkness until the island grew brighter, the umibozu was swimming towards them, its head and eyes just above the surface. With force, it rammed its head into the hull. The boat tilted, and the men fell down, their bodies piling up against the railing that was now almost level with the sea itself. The boat came crashing back down and stopped its leeway. Juni flew to the other side of the boat, smashing his right shoulder into something hard. The pain shot through him as he heard a crunch tearing through his arm. Shota got to his feet first and scrambled for the rifle he had dropped. The pungent smell of gas invaded Juni's nostrils. The kerosene had spilled out over the deck.

Just as he got to his feet, the boat spun violently around and he fell back down. Shota gripped the steering wheel and somehow stayed on his feet. When the boat stopped moving, he fired a shot into the water. Juni clawed his way up the deck to a railing and pulled himself up. The center of the deck split as a webbed claw burst through it. Shota reloaded the rifle and fired another round into the whitish-pink flesh. Blood splattered from the wound, but otherwise the creature made no sound of pain, nor did it retract its hand. With purpose, methodically, one of its arms reached out from the hole and swiped in Shota's direction. He fired off another round, this one also hitting its mark just above one of its many joints. This one was also useless.

Juni fumbled for the lighter in his pocket, found it, brought it out, and lit it.

The monster's arm came back, striking out in a circular pattern, nearly covering the entirety of the deck's space. It hit the captain's chair and steering wheel. Both were ripped off the deck and flung off the side of the boat. Juni ducked under the attack. Shota leaned back against the railing, missing the claws by inches.

A fuel-soaked fishing rod had rolled towards the center of the boat. The other was nowhere to be seen. Juni got on his knees and crawled forward. Shota fired two more rounds into the arm as it came back swinging around. Juni felt the air swish above him as the arm passed. He smelled the rotten-fish stench of its flesh. He grabbed the rod. Struck the lighter and lit the cloth. It went up in an instant. He kept it away from his own fuel-swamped arm and thrust it out at the creature's. As if sensing the heat, the arm fell back into the hole and into the sea.

"Shota, the gun isn't doing shit. Grab something to light!"

Juni heard the rifle clank to the deck, followed by the sound of Shota rustling through the garbage bag. He kept his eyes on the hole and the water bubbling up, filling the boat.

"We're sinking fast. We need to swim for shore," Juni commanded.

"With that thing out there?!"

Juni held the burning fishing rod in one hand and grabbed the nearest kerosene container. He shook it. Halfway full. He dumped the contents into the water off the side nearest the shore. Shota followed suit with another canister. In seconds, they emptied what they had in a rough semicircle around the boat.

The port side exploded into splinters and fury. Two arms shot out of the water and gripped the deck. The creature's head came next. Its weight tipped the boat, what was left of it, towards its unhinged jaws. Its eyes were wild with hate. No longer pale and dead, they burned and shone white like hot metal.

Shota fell down, and his body slid towards the creature as his limbs flailed out, failing to find a grip. Juni gripped the burning fishing rod and threw it at the monster. It didn't sail straight as he had hoped. It flopped and spun sideways. But it struck the creature's right hand, nonetheless. A howl that popped his ears. Maybe even rupturing his eardrums. The fire spread up that arm in seconds, as if the creature itself were made of dry newspapers, despite being covered in water. With its entire right arm engulfed in flames, it let go of the boat and fell backward into the water. The boat tipped back level, though without the quarter that was destroyed, it started sinking even more quickly.

The spot where the creature fell erupted in steam. The fire from its arm must have hit some of the kerosene in the water, because a ring of fire soon encircled the remnants of the boat. There was no way they'd be jumping over the raging flames.

"Now or never!" Juni shouted. He dove through the hole in the middle of the boat. The water filled his lungs as soon as he dove in. Never did learn to keep his mouth shut. He swam under the orange glow at the surface and emerged on the other side. As his head rose out of the water, he gagged and puked out what he had swallowed. Not much had changed since he was last here as a child. He shook his head and started swimming towards Tajima. He heard Shota break the surface feet behind him. The shore was as far away as a city block. May as well have been a mile. He pushed himself forward. His clothes weighed him down. He dared not look back, but now heard a fire roaring where the boat was.

No sign of the creature. Didn't matter; what did matter was pushing forward. Shota soon overtook him and made it to the shore first. Juni followed. Flopping his body onto the small strip of rocky shore that lay before a steep rock cliff. He gasped and inhaled furiously. Shota helped him to his feet. He could now see the last bits of the boat falling into the sea, burning bright, like some Viking funeral pyre. Shota, still wearing his backpack, looked like he could cry. It was his livelihood, his hobby, his whole life that was sinking.

"We're not alone."

The men looked to their left and saw an expensive-looking speedboat run aground, half in the water, half on land, the frontmost part smashed into a rock.

"Who could that—"

A massive figure leaped out of the black surf. The men split, each running to either side of the monster as it made landfall. Its right arm was gone. No bone or burnt flesh: it was entirely missing. A charred and ragged bit of skin remained where the arm should have connected to the body. The fire must have reached its face before it was extinguished. Half of the thing's skull was exposed. Its right eye was nothing more than a bloody pool, leaking out over the ground. That smile, that world of teeth, was even bigger now without the curtain of flesh to hide its utmost extremities. Smoke poured from the skin nearest the wounds.

Shota ran down the beach to a section of rock sticking out, providing a natural climbing wall of sorts. He frantically pulled himself up as far as he could, only a few feet off the ground.

The creature couldn't care less about him. It turned and focused on Juni. He could feel the absolute hatred in the thing's face as it stared him down. Juni ran down the brief stretch of beach until a wall of rock stopped him. Escape completely closed off, unless he wanted to try his hand at swimming again in the open sea. The umibozu crawled towards him across the rocks. No rain struck the island, which must have been why the creature pursued him slowly. Juni climbed the only boulder at the base of the wall and dropped on the other side.

To his right, there was a pool formed between the rocks, most likely filled when a high tide came in. In the red glow coming off the rocks, he could see a dark hole under the water. A space just wide enough for a man to squeeze into.

The thought of forcing his body through that opening stole his breath away. The only other fear that was heavier was what awaited him if he did nothing.

As he stood there contemplating what to do, a sizzle came from the rocks behind him. The deep and guttural breathing, the heat of the rotten breath on the back of his neck: without looking back he knew the thing was just above him.

Juni dove into the pool. He swam, grabbed the sides of the rock tunnel, and pulled himself inside, head above the water. A heavy splash followed him. Juni dove his head under the water and swam blindly into the tunnel. He smacked his head against a rock. Scraped his already bruised shoulder against a surface less pleasant than a cheese grater. His head came out of the water and took in gasps of air. In the tiny crawl space, the creature roared. Its echo made his ears ring.

The tunnel became narrower. Juni still had room to breathe above water, but his shoulders could barely squeeze through the space. Furious splashing behind him. Juni forced himself even deeper inside until he couldn't move forward anymore. He couldn't turn around. Panic seized him as he started swallowing in the sparse air of the tunnel. The only saving grace was that the creature's roars were not getting closer.

The thing was too big to fit through.

Juni could have laughed until he felt a talon slice the area above his tailbone, catching only his shirt. The monster couldn't fit, but its one arm could.

He could feel the water swish back and forth as the thing must have been waving its hand about to grab hold of him.

There was only one way to go.

Down.

Without knowing if there was even a way to go, Juni took a deep breath and submerged his body. He swung his arms up and propelled his body downwards. Something large swung above his head, catching his hair for a moment. Further down he went.

Total darkness. But there was space enough to fling his arms more widely now.

Space enough now for him to flip his body over and swim downwards.

Breath tightening in his lungs like a straightjacket.

Heart racing.

He noticed a faint glimmer farther down and further into the tunnel. He struggled and fought his way to the light. Growing into a red haze.

His mouth opened a crack, unconsciously seeking air.

The light felt like it was getting further away no matter how hard he swam. The pressure of the water felt like it was crushing him into the floor.

Push. Fucking push.

The red light grew stronger, illuminating the tunnel. He couldn't hold his breath any longer.

Please let there be a "there" to go to.

Juni launched himself towards the surface. He burst into an empty cavern. The sound of his gasping echoed off the chamber. The light was gone. But at least there was air. After catching his breath, he paddled forward and bumped into a hard surface. He reached forward and pulled himself in. Land of some kind. Mostly rock and wet soil. He rose carefully so as not to bang his head on the cavern's roof. Standing up straight, he reached up and touched nothing but the cool air. Behind him in the pool, the water remained undisturbed. As far as he could tell, nothing splashed in it. Still, the further away he was from it, the better.

He inched forward with his hands outstretched. He walked for minutes like this, touching no wall, meeting no obstacles. Slowly, he made his way in the dark. Soon, red fissures in the rocks became visible. Like the surface of the island, the red seethed and pulsed from within the rocks. Not enough to fully light his way, but enough for him to get a general sense of where the walls were. The sound of water dripping in a large chamber. Soon, the drips became a pour, became a torrent. The soothing rush of a waterfall or a whitewater river came to him.

Juni rounded a corner and faced a wall. No way forward. At the bottom of the wall, another pool dimly glowed crimson. Juni could hear the racing water on the other side of the barrier. The red lines carried on down into the rocks that formed the tunnel below, providing some light. Behind him, he heard a heavy thrashing in the water.

Did it find a way through?

Juni dove into the water again.

THIRTY THREE

Smothering water rushed into his face. His lungs quaked and threatened to let in the black water. The red light in the stone guided his path. It felt like forever, but Juni swam until his lungs and then his muscles burned. His cuts, bruises, and possible broken bones all faded into the background. One goal. Reach the surface.

Above him, the red haze thickened into a blood-red cloud. He placed his feet on the floor of the tunnel and launched himself upwards. The surface. Like a fish flung from its home and onto a dirty wooden floor, he gasped and sucked in the air. He crawled onto the nearby solid ground and flopped his body onto his back. This chamber wasn't dark. The ruby light filled the space. Bright enough to see all the details about him. The stalactites descending from the roof-like twisted spires ending just out of his reach, several small pools of water sunk in the ground reflecting the red air, the clear manmade path leading out from the water and towards an opening that led to some larger area.

Juni got up and followed the trail and soon came out of the caverns.

Great walls of stone on all sides, an open crevice above to the naked sky. A canyon. Innumerable stars glowed red, perhaps because of the unnatural hue of the landscape. Juni felt watched by them. A thousand lidless eyes staring down at him.

A waterfall spilled its bounty from high above the canyon floor. The water crashed into an unseen opening near the center. The entire area glowed with a vermilion light. As bright as midday, but bathed in blood. Lights from the rocks on the surface rimmed the edge of the sky red.

The gorge itself was the size of a soccer field. Filled with stone columns and statues. In the center, near the end of the waterfall, was a Shinto shrine made of rock.

Three figures dressed in black lay on their backs before it, with a figure in white next to them lying on a stone table. The surroundings and the primitive shrine looked just like the photograph in his father's journal. At first, Juni thought the people were taking part in some bizarre ritual. As he drew near, he saw they were motionless. One of them was lying in a pool of blood. Long hair spilled out of the black hood. Black and gray strands splayed out wildly.

He walked over to them.

The one in their own blood was Sakura. Eyes opened wide in terror, hands gripping a knife she clutched to her chest. Her intestines were strewn across her body and wrapped around the shrine's gate. One man looked like he was asleep, but his chest didn't move. The other, a man with a shaggy goatee, had his mouth open, blood streaked across his face. Moments later, Juni found a tongue a few feet away from him, as if the man bit it off and it rolled away.

Under the shrine's gates was a girl. At first, Juni's heart nearly burst out of his chest. But it wasn't Mayu. She looked around sixteen and was in a white nightgown. Pink ribbon in her hair. Sheep-faced slippers on her feet. A pool of red coalesced over her heart. A knife wound.

There was blood on the sides of the torii gate of the shrine. The blood was almost invisible in the red light, but hand marks could be seen from whoever smeared it over the stone. Like a child's finger painting gone wrong. He wondered if they did this to themselves. Was this Sakura's attempt to undo what had been set in motion? Offer their own sacrifice to get on the good side of their god?

"What the fuck happened to you, guys?"

"What the fuck... happened... guys?" came a croaking voice from somewhere above him.

It was the umibozu, forcing its way through one of its stained mold doorways in the rock's side. It emerged and slithered down the side of the chamber. Wrapped itself around a pillar-like stone and wound down to the ground. A half-skeletal nightmare, it squirmed its way to the shrine area.

Juni pried the knife from Sakura's hand. He had to break a few fingers to release it, but she wouldn't mind. He held the knife out in front of him.

The creature rose from behind the shrine, gripping it with one hand and sitting atop it. The black acid poured from its mouth, shrouding the altar in steam and brown smoke.

But it didn't move. It stood there, watching him.

Had it led him—herded him — here?

A grinding sound of stone on stone. The floor before the shrine opened like a camera lens. The man without a tongue fell into it. The waterfall flowed into it. Stairs pushed themselves out of the wall beneath the sudden opening, descending into the dark.

Smiling, skull half-exposed, the creature nodded its head down into the hole.

From the abyss, he could hear Mayu crying.

Step by step, he went down into the depths of the earth. The spray from the waterfall splashed against his face. The same light from above shone down below as well.

The rocks, the very earth, were alive.

The weeping pulled further away. Juni knew this was a trap. But if it had wanted to kill him, it could have easily done so at the shrine. It was still up there, watching him descend. Soon he couldn't see it; the opening above was growing smaller and smaller. The stairs ended. In front of him was a tunnel, shining red. He could hear Mayu at the end.

What was he going to do when he got to her? He didn't want to think about it. There was no way out. No way to kill the creature now. At least he could be by her side at the end. Go down fighting. End her suffering before things got too bad.

He still had the knife. Resting in his pocket.

The thought made him shudder with shame. But imagining the same scene above at the shrine happening to Mai-Mai was also too much to bear.

He yelled out her name with no response.

The path descended as he went. Further and further into the womb of the world. A sound filled the passage.

BA-THUMP. BA-THUMP.

Rhythmic. Unchanging. It shook the walls slightly.

BA-THUMP. BA-THUMP.

Like a heartbeat.

The red lights grew brighter with each beat and faded with the in-between silence. The sound. The pulsing lights. They grew in intensity the further in he walked.

The color of the light changed. First red, then it took on an orange hue. Soon, a touch of gold and pink bled into it. It was almost beautiful.

At the end of the tunnel, what looked like a great fire pulsed in tune with the heartbeat sound. The tunnel grew wider. Juni could make out what looked like murals on the walls. The paint was too faded to make sense of them. He passed shrines and altars built into the rock wall. Each was the size of a common grave, but they were many. With each pulse of amber light, he could see more and more of the things. He looked into a few of them as he walked.

One was painted red. Inside the altar he saw a statue of a human-like figure, hands stretched out to the sky. What looked like flames etched into the stone around the figure. A scene of a red starry sky painted on the roof of the altar box.

Another had a statue of a hideous bear sitting inside the holy place. It held a child in its mouth as its worshippers lay prostrate before it. Juni winced at the image.

The last one he dared look inside had a painting of an emaciated woman holding onto what looked like a dead infant. Her unhinged mouth was swallowing the sun.

Juni left the shrines behind him and came to the end of the tunnel.

He called out Mayu's name.

Her weeping was barely audible below the sound of the pulse. Juni was in a large chamber with a pool of water at its center. The amber light was pouring out of the pool.

BA-THUMP. BA-THUMP.

He called out, "Mayu! Tell me where you are, baby."

He heard a tiny scream. A call for daddy. Tears welled up in his eyes.

"Mayu!"

He ran around the room. There were no other tunnels. No other exit points. Save for one. The pool. Black water cut through by a pulsing light.

She can't be down there; that's not possible.

Juni bent down near the water's edge and looked into the abyss. As the light radiated out, he could see the silhouette of a little girl as if laying on her back, staring up at him. Maybe ten feet down into the water. Her hair snaked around and floated in the water.

Juni dove in and swam towards her.

The light went out. Darkness swallowed him. No way of knowing which way was up or down. He blindly kept on swimming, trying not to open his mouth and scream. No matter how hard he paddled forward, he touched nothing. He needed air. Go back up, breathe, and try again. Juni pulled himself toward what he believed was the way out. He reached nothing. Frantic now, bubbles exploded out of his mouth as he yelled. He clawed at the water, looking for something solid to grasp.

He swam harder. His lungs began shaking.

Panic.

Then came the peace. The acceptance that there was no way out. The fear drained out of him, and he felt warm. He floated there.

In the Void.

Moments passed. He closed his eyes. Feeling the sleep of death take him, he snapped his eyes open.

No, not like this.

Then a thought came to him: *Why am I still alive?*

He calmed himself. His lungs no longer hurt. He should have drowned by now, but here he was. Testing the situation, he waited. Nothing happened. He dared to open his mouth, and the water rushed in. But he didn't choke on it. It felt... freeing.

Juni could breathe underwater.

THIRTY FOUR

Floating in the nothingness, Juni swam around. All his life he had feared the water, but now here he was, moving in it freely; it had no power over him.

Two white lights sparked to life in the nothingness. They drew near him. The eyes bounced up and down as if their owner was walking, not swimming, towards him. The screaming baby, the shrill cries of desperation, echoed all around him. The formless thing took form and revealed its pregnant belly and long flowing hair.

"Mom?" Juni's voice came out clearly and not distorted by the effect of being underwater.

Mako's spirit lifted a shadowy hand and placed it on his face. The black curtain around him was pulled away, and he found himself in the air, looking down at a speeding boat off Tajima's coast. Mako—Mom—was there. Holding a metal rod above her head. She struck out at someone. Dad. A golden light erupted from the sea, and a giant wave swelled up near the boat, towering over it but not falling over. A wave frozen in place.

He saw Dad strangle Mom when her back was turned. He lifted her body and tossed her overboard.

That scene was ripped away, and Juni was now in the water, enveloped in the amber light. He saw his mother's corpse sink down. The umibozu was there. Waiting for her. It took her body in its hands and slit open her stomach with its teeth. It took the child from her womb and let the mother float down into the dark.

The creature breathed into the child's face. The baby came alive. The creature lifted the child up to the surface, to the father's surprised and terrified face. Dad fell on his knees before the sight.

Darkness filled everything, and Juni was back in the Void.

Too much. This is too much.

A current, cold as ice, stirred beneath his legs. The tide of its movement pulled him along with it. He could have been moving down, or up; nothing made sense anymore. There was no light in the water, but he saw... something.

Darkness moved beneath him. The Dark within the dark.

The pulsing of the heartbeat returned. With it came the amber light. In its brilliance, for brief moments before the light blinded him, he could see what emanated the light. A writhing thing on the ocean floor. Black tentacles the size of cruise liners. It moved, it stirred, it watched him.

The light washed out all sight before dimming again. Flashes of images. Each more horrid than the next. He thought he saw the thing, the Writhing God's body, extend for what must have been miles along the sea's floor.

The sea was alive with its movement. He saw other things attending to it. Things that looked like men but were far too large, darted around the behemoth and disappeared.

Eyes, teeth, spines, what looked like a malformed ribcage, a titanic heart, jutted out from the colossal body of mangled flesh. A melody of madness spanning mountain ranges. Whatever this thing was, it was beyond comprehension.

Despite the searing light, Juni couldn't close his eyes. If they could close, tears would streak his face. The light was cold as it enveloped his body.

A single pale eye opened amidst the mass of dark flesh. It was far away, but looked massive, maybe larger than a skyscraper. The milky white eyeball rotated around. There was no pupil, no other distinguishing color in it. But Juni could feel that it rested on him. Out of all the expanse of the sea it could have turned on, it focused on him alone.

Never had he known such fear. The bottom of the world fell out beneath him. He was stranded in the Void, wishing he were alone. He feared that the spliced image of the Writhing God would never leave his mind, no matter how many years passed.

Then, his body was ejected upwards. He came crashing through the surface of the pool, flew up in the air, and crashed down on the stone floor of the chamber.

He lay there for minutes, unblinking. He was right about what he saw; the images seared themselves into his eyes. The shadows in the room became tentacles. His body tensed with the consistent flashing of the light that still pulsed from the pool, afraid of what the darkness would reveal.

"Mayu," escaped from his lips. The sound of his own voice was withered, like that of an elderly man. He rose to a sitting position and looked over at the pool. No more crying. No sounds at all.

"I'm so sorry."

Juni rose to his feet and left the room.

He climbed the stairs back out of the pit. Pain filled every inch of his soul. Mayu wasn't there. There was nothing in the water but pure horror. He had no tears left to cry. He could barely breathe.

He came to the last step and walked into the canyon. The umibozu was still there, perched atop the shrine, glaring at him. Beneath it, lying on a stone table, was Mayu. It had flung the girl's body to the side like trash.

Juni sprinted towards the shrine. He knew it might be another illusion, but his heart leaped at the sight of his daughter. When he got close enough, he could see her chest rising and falling. Before he could run to her, the creature fell off the gates and landed between them.

Juni felt for the knife he had put in his pocket, assuming it had already fallen out in the water, but his hands gripped the blade. He pulled out the weapon and held it above his head.

"Back off, fucker. I've had enough of this shit."

Giving off a look that was disappointed despite its permanent grin, the monster flicked out a black serpentine tongue and lashed Juni's arm. He let go of the knife with a yell of pain. Steam rose from his left forearm, and he watched in horror as the black mold ate through his flesh. It dissolved the elbow and ate through to the bone. Soon, the entire forearm fell off and landed sickly on the ground.

Pain seared his nerve endings like fire traveling up his veins. He clenched his teeth and wanted to escape out of his skin. The creature picked up the knife with its tongue and dropped it in front of Juni's feet. It nodded towards Mayu, and Juni knew what it wanted. It wanted blood. Needed a sacrifice, and Juni was the one to do it. The thing that writhed on the ocean floor demanded it. For this reason, Juni was spared as a child in his mother's womb. For this reason, he was called the son of the Wave. It was all so clear now.

All of this. All the death and the gifts, everything designed to bring him here and make him sacrifice his daughter.

"Kill," came the woman's voice from somewhere and nowhere all at once.

Juni may have been a shit dad and a bad person, but even a god couldn't make him do this.

Fuck destiny.

Juni grabbed the knife in his right hand and lunged at the creature.

A second lash of its tongue. This one sliced at his right kneecap. This strike didn't dissolve fully through his leg. But he felt the liquid fire slice through his kneecap, and he screamed in pain. He fell to the ground. The leg was still attached, but he saw the bone. There he lay, knife in hand, slashing at the creature, making no contact, dying.

The thing lurched over his head. At any moment, he expected the acid to drop on his face and end him then and there.

The suspended silence was shattered by its high-pitched scream. This one was different from all the others that came before. The former was predatory and threatening. This one was a cry of pain.

Juni looked up and saw blue flames bursting out of the creature's chest. The fire ripped across its pale body, consuming every inch. It flung itself to the ground and thrashed. The fire consumed the tail entirely, leaving behind a trail of ash. The skin of its torso melted away, revealing bone. Skull. Ribs. Its steel smile was the last to go until the creature was only smoldering embers.

Amid the smoke it gave off, Shota appeared. He was holding a welding torch, the flame still burning. He shut it off, dropped it, and ran over to Juni.

"Holy shit. Don't worry, I'll get you out of this."

Juni propped himself up on his one good arm. "How did you?"

"After the monster went down that tunnel after you, I stayed on the beach trying to figure out what to do. I saw a way to climb up the cliff, took me forever."

"Fucking amazing."

Shota helped him into a sitting position against a rock.

"Is that your girl?"

Juni looked over at Mayu, still unconscious, on the table. She was clutching Keke to her chest. Despite the pain, a smile spread across his face. "Yeah, isn't she the most beautiful thing?"

Shota had tears in his eyes. "Yeah." He wiped them away. "Okay, we need to get off this rock."

"Sakura," Juni nodded towards the bloody mess of the woman nearby. "That was her boat we saw at the beach; check her body for the keys."

Shota left him, flipped the body over, and found the keys in the back pocket of her jeans under the robe.

Shota furrowed his brow and came back. "What about you? You're, uh, missing a few parts."

Juni couldn't bring himself to look at his wounds. "I don't know; maybe that acid stuff cauterized it. They'll get infected, but that's tomorrow's problem. Hurts like a bitch though."

Shota was a beast of a man. He picked up Mayu from the table and draped her across his shoulders, holding onto her with one hand. Then he let Juni lean on him as he had to hop his way up the path that led out of the canyon.

They reached the summit and sat down on a flat space above a sharp drop. Shota laid Mayu down gently. From their vantage point, they could see the entire island, the abrupt edges of the cliff face that formed the shoreline, and the water beyond. The rocks still faintly glowed red. The sea was dark, but the first glimmers of sunrise were teasing the shadows with their cold blue light.

Juni brushed a lock of hair out of Mayu's eyes. "I'll get you home soon, baby. Then you can see Mommy, and everything is going to be alright."

Screams in the distance. The cries of foxes in the night.

A multitude of white eyes in the water. Surrounding the island on all sides. They disappeared as they moved forward, obscured by the cliffs. Shota grabbed the welding torch he had tucked into his pants and lit it.

Soon, dark forms crawled over the edge of the cliffs. They drifted as if not used to dry land. But their shape was unmistakable. Bulbous heads. No neck. Long arms. Long tails. And the smiles flashing out of over a hundred different mouths.

They made their way to the mount, where the three humans remained isolated, trapped on a rock in a sea of monsters. Their bodies fell into the canyon behind them; they covered the paths ahead; they were everywhere.

Shota stood tall, torch in one hand, the other acting as a useless shield over Juni and Mayu. Juni brought himself up on his one good leg, slightly balanced on the other, and looked out at the sea of death.

Off in the distance, the water churned. Something darker than the night was rising out of the waves, on all sides of the island.

"It's useless, Shota. We barely survived one of them. We won't make it. And you haven't seen what I've seen, the Thing that they serve."

Shota said nothing but kept his face on the oncoming hoard that would be upon them in seconds.

Juni knew what he had to do. There was no fighting this. The Wave demanded a sacrifice. He looked down at his daughter and placed his hand on her cheek, caressing her face. "I'm so sorry, baby."

Shota asked, "What are you ta—"

Then, Shota was flying.

Juni fell on his face, throwing himself at the Shota.

The torch fell near Juni's feet.

Shota fell thirty feet down.

Before his body struck the jagged rocks below, Juni glimpsed his face. Eyebrows arched in surprise. Confusion and betrayal in his eyes.

Then he hit the ground.

Juni could see that he was still alive. Trying to crawl forward on broken arms. Blood sputtered out of Shota's mouth. A faint moan of entreaty escaped his lips. The creatures stopped their onslaught. Hundreds of demonic faces stared on in silence.

Shota didn't die. This was going to be hard. Juni left Mayu on the rock and tried hopping down the rock-covered slope to where Shota lay. He made it halfway before the pain in his leg proved too much. He, like his near-death friend, crawled the rest of the way.

Shota was almost gone now. But Juni had to be sure he did this the right way. This was one offering that wouldn't be rejected.

With one hand he grabbed a stone the size of a grapefruit, propped up his body on his left nub of an arm, and brought the rock down on Shota's face.

His feet twitched. But still alive. Juni raised the rock and brought it down two more times.

No more twitching.

Looking at the unholy spectators, he said, "From what is mine to you, so that what is yours will be mine."

One creature came forward and grabbed Shota's broken body with its teeth. It carried him away, back to the sea. The rest followed suit, leaving Juni alone.

As they reached the water, Juni saw a light. The most beautiful light. No sunrise could compare to it. Amber rays of glory shot out of the sea. He saw a wave rise above the cliffs. A mountain of light rising to the heavens.

He wept with joy.

THIRTY FIVE

Two years later.

The warmth of the sun greeted Juni's face as he peered out his bedroom window over Tanosawa. Little patches of snow on the tree branches gave off a light steam in the golden light before melting. A few birds chirped here and there, perhaps too eager to return home for spring before their time.

The roofs of the village below reflected the light, causing him to wince as he looked out. But he smiled with pride at what he had done. The entire disaster zone cleaned up, homes rebuilt, new families brought in on government subsidies to repopulate the countryside. It was a fucking miracle. And he did that.

He opened the sliding glass door with both hands and stepped out onto the deck. He sat down on a chair he liked to call his throne. A massive seat made of a hollowed oak tree. A fitting place from which to observe his little kingdom.

Dad's home was gone. Nothing left to salvage. So he set about building something new, something better. Isn't that what sons are supposed to do? Take their father's legacy and do more with it?

Juni cracked his back on the seat and stretched out his hands. Two hands. He flexed them both in the morning light and smiled. The right one looked much the same as he'd expect it to. Maybe the skin was a little looser than two years ago but not worse for wear. His left hand was smooth and gave off a gleam. Like new skin healing after a burn. His right knee, too.

The Wave was truly good to him. Haruka eyed the new-looking skin with suspicion when he reunited with her days after the incident. She was fairly forgiving of his lack of contact because of the disaster. On the surface, at least.

He told her he had gotten burned and that his skin was healing. In a way, that wasn't a lie at all. The only odd thing was that it never went back to normal; it was always "new."

Juni got up and entered the house. Before he closed the door, a wave of excitement hit him. Or was is fear? He wasn't sure anymore. But today was a big day. Two years had passed since he last did his duty, since the Wave so thoroughly blessed his life, since he last made an offering.

Dishes clanged downstairs. The smell of freshly brewed coffee thickened the air.

"Well, isn't it my two favorite girls in the world?"

Haruka looked up from the stove and smiled. Mayu was coloring something at the kitchen table and looked up. "Morning, Daddy." Keke rested on her lap as always. A little worse for wear, but intact, mostly. If anything, her attachment to the toy had only increased since Tajima. Mayu didn't remember a thing, or at least that's what she said. But she nevertheless seemed affected by the experience. She was eight now, but in many ways acted the same as she did when she was six.

Juni feared that her mind would always be that of a little child.

Haruka was driven nearly insane during the whole thing. But Juni got their daughter back, didn't he? Why did it matter, the unimportant details like "why" and "how" Mayu got to Aomori?

Why couldn't she just be grateful for what I did?

She threatened divorce and refused to see him for weeks afterwards. It was only Mayu's hysterical grief that brought her back. The nightly terrors that she saw in the dark without her dad around.

And then the money came in. So much money. Forget the debts. Things like that didn't matter anymore. Juni received an unlimited supply of wealth. Of course, Haruka was suspicious, as always, but she shut up quickly when she saw the future her daughter could have if she stayed.

Juni looked over at his wife.

Good girl. You finally learned, didn't you?

He bent down and kissed Mayu on the cheek.

"Gross, Daddy. You just woke up, stinky breath."

"Mai-Mai, I'm offended. Keke doesn't mind my kisses."

He grabbed the dragon and pretended to eat it.

Mayu shrieked with joy, jumped up, and ripped the doll from him.

Juni sat down, his smile faded, and he adopted a more serious tone. "Mayu, are you ready for today? All packed for Grandma's?"

She put her face back into her drawing and furiously colored outside of the lines. "I like it here better. Why do I have to go?"

"Because Mommy and I are going on a special date night tonight. And Grandma is in Tokyo. She'll take you to DisneySea tomorrow, and we'll be there afterward to meet you and go wherever you want to for dinner."

Mayu's frown morphed into a smile. "Even pancakes?"

"Especially pancakes. All the pancakes in Japan. Even jelly bean ones."

Mayu seemed satisfied with the state of things and left to grab her bag.

Smoke rose from the stove. Haruka was so focused on their conversation that she burnt the eggs.

END AT THE BEGINNING

Haruka wiped the tears from her eyes as they put Mayu on the ferry that would take her to the train station. She was a big girl now; the ferry was owned by her husband, and the staff on hand would escort her personally. Mayu was going to be just fine.

It wasn't her daughter's safety that pained her heart, though. She had a deep, sinking feeling in her chest that she would never see her again. It was something that Juni had said two days ago—that he wanted to show her something, show her how he turned everything around for them and got to where he is now.

Haruka had stomached the obvious lies for two years now. All for the sake of Mayu, as she had done many times before. She tried to tell herself that at least now money wasn't a problem.

But Juni was not the same man he had been before he left for Tano-sawa. Sure, he was a screw-up, and she thought about leaving him even then. But there was a sliver of love, a fraction of kindness in his heart for her then. These past two years showed her this was no longer the case. Juni loved Mayu, maybe even more than ever before. But to his wife, she felt like he barely tolerated her existence. Like he was keeping her around for something that she couldn't fathom the reason for.

Then there were the nights when Juni left the house and didn't return until morning. He would return with his hair slightly damp, his clothes slightly moist. At first she thought he was showering at some other woman's house, so she followed him one night. If she could prove infidelity, she could get sole custody of Mayu and be owed half of his assets.

She could be free.

But what she saw that night transformed her dislike of her husband into fear of him. Until that moment, she had tried telling herself that the man with white eyes and even that night when she saw the thing rising out of the sea were products of delusion. A psychotic break. This one night told her she wasn't insane. And that nearly made her so.

Juni drove the car down to the harbor, and she followed on her bicycle. She rode until she saw his land cruiser in the parking lot of the harbor, left her bike leaned up against a streetlight, and crept up to the dock. There were no lights out on the water. He couldn't have gotten a boat out that far that quickly.

She was about to give up and go home when she heard a splash. Haruka ducked down behind a wooden post and saw someone out in the water, near the docks. She couldn't believe that her husband, the man who had been afraid of deep water his entire life, would dare swim in the ocean, let alone at night.

But she recognized the man's outline. The instinctual knowing that comes with being with someone for so long. It was him. In the water. And he wasn't alone. She saw a large pale shape swimming next to him. A shark? A whale? Then they both sank under the waves and did not come back out. Haruka waited for five minutes and then raced back home. She thought about calling an ambulance, but fear froze her, and she waited under her covers like she was Mayu's age, hoping that Mom would come save her and make the bad things go away.

Juni came home hours later. Nothing wrong with him at all.

Then came the mold stains. She could no longer sleep in the same bed with Juni because above the headrest, a deep black vortex of mold grew. Juni refused to do anything about it. Haruka felt like it was watching her, so she moved into the guestroom down the hall.

"You ready, babe?" Juni asked. The question snapped Haruka back to the present moment.

Sunglasses hid his expression. He smiled, but she had learned not to put much stock in that.

They got back into the car and drove away from the harbor.

"Juni, why did you ask me to send Mai-Mai to my mom's place? I think we're both past date nights, aren't we?"

Juni's smile faded. He took off his sunglasses and set them on the dashboard. Looking over at her, she saw a faint glimmer of sincerity, a rarity. "I know things have been hard between us recently. Everything has changed so quickly. I want to come clean with you. I've been lying about where the money's been coming from. It's not from Dad's estate."

Haruka tried to swallow saliva despite her throat being desert dry. "I know, Juni. It's pretty obvious even your dad wasn't this rich."

He looked back at the road. "So, where do you think it's been coming from?"

"I don't know. I don't think I want to know."

"Well, I'm not doing anything illegal, okay? I'm just carrying on what my dad would've wanted me to do. And I have to show you today. I can't live with myself if I wait any longer."

The melodramatic words sickened her. Something was off about all of this. But he wouldn't hurt her; she believed that. Why not humor him?

"Okay, show me."

The speedboat cut through the waves effortlessly. Like a hot knife through butter. Haruka held onto her seatbelt as if she'd go flying off to nowhere if she didn't. The water sprayed up and into her face each time the boat went flying and landed back down on the water.

Juni was beside her driving. His smile was wide, youthful—manic, even.

Before them, an island came into view. She had never seen an uglier rock formation in her life. Sure, the dramatic cliffs were cool and all. But there was a sheen to the thing that seemed unnatural. A black shine to the rocks that were wholly alien to anything she had seen before, like this was an island that fell from the sky and burned up on the way down.

It shouldn't be here, she thought without knowing exactly why.

Juni slowed down and killed the engine right off the island's shore.

"This is it, my love. The secret behind my success."

Haruka was worried now. Maybe Juni had finally snapped. Maybe he was into some dirty gang business or crooked land deals now, and the stress of that life was finally breaking him. Looking out over the sea, she became acutely aware of how alone they were. Nothing but miles of empty sea and that horrible monstrosity of rock.

"Juni, I think I want to go home now."

He walked over to the edge of the bow and raised his hands to the sky. He threw his sunglasses into the water and took off his shirt.

"What are you doing?" Haruka's voice now rose in pitch. She unbuckled her seatbelt as if preparing to escape.

Juni undid his belt and took off his jeans. Then his shoes and socks and even underwear. Fully naked, he cast his clothes into the water.

"After today, none of this is going to matter, babe." He waved his arms wildly. Tears poured out of his eyes. "It's all going away today. That's why I sent Mayu away, so she wouldn't be here for what happens next."

"What are you talking about?" She looked around for something to grab and defend herself with.

"I don't want to do this, babe, you have to know that. I need you to know that. But... He's coming. Soon, you will see. He will be here. Just one more sacrifice is all He needs. But it has to be a big one. Something that costs me. And I can't give him *that*! Do you understand? I can't give him my daughter. Not after all I've given up to be here. So he has to be mollified, sedated with someone else, at least for a little until I figure something out. But time is running out. Do you get what I'm trying to say? It has to be you."

Haruka found a toolbox under one of the passenger seats. She tried to open the lid, but her fingers tripped over the padlock. When she looked back up, Juni was right in front of her. Haruka stood quickly and struck his jaw with her palm. He stepped back and leaned against the railing. Blood trickled out of his mouth.

With fury spilling out of his gaze, Juni rushed her. She tried to strike him again, but he caught her wrist, spun her around, and bear-hugged her from behind. She kicked and screamed and bit his hand. He didn't react to the pain. Juni pulled her over to the bow of the boat. He hung her off the side, feet dangling over the water. He let go, and she fell.

The water hit her face, and she breathed in too much, too fast. Struggling, she surfaced and gasped for air. Juni was nowhere to be seen.

Light blinded her as she emerged from the water. Golden and orange. Calm and terrifying. It was coming from down below. Soon, the radiance enveloped her. The water churned, and she bobbed up and down, cast about like a piece of wood.

Then came the wave. The water in front of her swelled and curled up. A golden wave. It came crashing down on itself. Again and again, it repeated this pattern in place.

Her mind was frantic.

What is going on?

She sobbed as she tried to paddle back to the boat. Get back and leave him here. Something tugged at her feet and pulled her down.

Wading in the water, Juni watched as Haruka's body floated down into the depths. Her eyes wide open, staring at him not so much in accusation as in deep sadness. Tajima quaked. It rose out of the sea like a tumor being extracted from a patient's body. The stones broke apart, revealing writhing things. Eyes. Teeth. Bones. Tentacles.

Juni laughed hysterically as the god awoke. The golden wave was getting bigger now. Towering above what he'd once thought was an island. The wave reached towards the sky. A titanic tidal wave. It broke free of its frozen motion and rushed forward.

Juni watched in abject horror as the wave raced towards Tanosawa's shore.

He looked back down into the water and saw Haruka's face just before it disappeared.

And with her, the last of his humanity buried.

All love, now under the sea.

All of it.

All of him.

Under the Amber Wave.

Get a Free Book In My Newsletter.

Sign up for my newsletter below and get my Japanese cannibal ghost novella, "Devoured."

For ebook readers, click this link: https://dl.bookfunnel.com/hlaez dpu8g

For print readers, go to my website here, and the sign-up form is the first thing you'll see: https://www.shawnbrookswrites.com/

Get Book Three in the Black Sun series: Iomante

Find it at: shawnbrookswrites.com

About This Horror

Thank you for reading the second book in the "Black Sun" series; a set of five books connected thematically within the same universe. Characters from one book may or may not make other appearances as I would like each story to stand on its own.

However, I have a plan to tie everything together in the end. All five novels will take place in Japan and be based on actual folklore and myth. Of course, with my twist on things. One element that will prominently feature in each story is the horror that comes from the wild places of the world, the unknown and secret haunts of nature.

The region of Japan this horror takes place in is northern Aomori, in an area called Shimokita. The town of Tanosawa doesn't exist (well, it does, but in a very different location). I based the village on the real Sai-Village, a beautiful and wild area of the world. I lived near there for three years, teaching English starting back in 2014. The population is sparse, and the wild forests and mountains and untamed ocean are everywhere. In winter, winds from Siberia encase the peninsula in relentless snow. Bears, monkeys, and raccoon dogs can be seen with regular frequency.

The myth at the center of this tale revolves around the umibozu. Their name means "Sea Monk" in Japanese as their heads resemble the shaven head of a Buddhist monk. I call them "Sea Priests" in my story because I like that better. I reshaped some "facts" about this creature to fit my story, such as the acidic mold it spits out. In actual legend, this spirit would rise out of the sea to destroy any vessel that would dare enter its territory. The spirit would ask sailors for an offering out of their cargo, and even if they gave it, they would be killed anyway. The version of this creature near Aomori has the added lore involving sacrifice. Usually of fish, but that was enough for me to run wild with the concept.

Other aspects of Shimokita's folklore that make a brief introduction here are the itako, the blind mediums who commune with the dead. These are real people. If you visit Oser-zan (Mt. Osore) near Mutsu city, you might see and speak with them.

Some things that might bother a reader well-versed in all things Japan is that I use inches, miles, and pounds in the book. Japan uses centimeters, kilometers and kilograms. Yet, most of my readers hail from the USA, so I adhere to those conventions for comprehensibility. One last non-Japanese aspect regards the name of the main character. Junichiro's shortened name in the novel is Juni. But in Japan, it would be shortened to Jun instead. Since this is fiction, and Juni suited my feeling for the character better, I went with that.

I thank you sincerely for your support in reading my work. Hope to see you at the next one!

Leave a Review for Under the Amber Wave

If you enjoyed this book, please leave a review wherever you like to!

IOMANTE: BLACK SUN BOOK 3

C hapter One

December 1915, Hokkaido, Japan

Yayo Inoue sliced the radish with a butcher knife in her shaking hand. If she wasn't careful, she could cut her knuckles. Snow raged outside the small home. The wind battered against the walls and even shook the log rafters overhead.

But it wasn't the cold that made her shiver. It was the sound of gunshots and screaming from somewhere just outside her front door. A door that was locked with a sliding iron bar and built of heavy oak. Her home was one of the better-off ones in the village of Kamuy-Kotan. Not too hard when there were only ten families who had tamed this forested wilderness together.

What did that soldier say right before he left her here?

They were devil's eyes.

That's what the young man said, with bloodshot eyes of his own and a tremor on his lips. Right before he ran off into the night to chase down that bear.

That accursed bear.

The one who injured the Otani family, all seven of them, killing three of the children. The one who slaughtered poor Miyako-san as she was drying her linen on the line in broad daylight! To add salt to that wound, she was pregnant.

Was.

Yayo shivered even more and had to put down the knife.

The bear assaulted the tiny community for an entire week. If it didn't stop, there would be no one left. That's why her husband was out there now. Out in the dark storm. Hunting it along with the rest of the men. There was even a nearby detachment of imperial soldiers that Mayor Tetsuya—*ha! what a title for this hamlet*—had convinced to come and assist.

So now, there were over forty men in those woods. With guns. Even dynamite. Hunting the bear. She should have felt safe in her home—*my home*—kneeling by the hearth. The light of the fire mixed with the overhead whale lantern's orange radiance. But instead of filling her home—*my damn home, not that animal's*—with that special kind of comfort you get sitting by a fire when the outside world is nothing but dark and cold, instead of that, the lights cast shadows in the corners of the room. Long and erratic things danced on the walls. She could have sworn she saw something, something large and hairy, moving just out of sight, crouching in the kitchen. But when she looked, nothing but shadows and light.

Her baby boy, strapped to her back in a straw harness, gurgled and wriggled, bringing her mind back to reality.

Yes, reality. Keep your mind away from these delusions.

Her daughter sat in the room's corner, under a writhing shadow, playing with a doll made from corn husk. The three of them were safe. They were sound. Sealed away from the snowstorm. Warm and dry and about to eat dinner.

But those shouts? The gunfire? So many of them rang out. How many did it take to bring down one bear?

Yayo shook her head free of those thoughts. Picked up the knife. And began cutting the radish into thin slices. Grabbed them. Tossed them into a pot of boiling water hung over the hearth.

Her baby fussed and let out a brief cry. Yayo took a leftover slice of raw radish from the cutting board, crushed it in her palm, and reached back to give it to him. She heard him munch away as he settled.

A shiver of frost danced down her spine. She fidgeted on her knees and rubbed her lower back. She was safe, safe, damn it. The men were taking care of things. Armed as they were, how could they fail?

She looked at her daughter, a girl of six, as she fiddled with her makeshift doll. An overwhelming wave of feelings welled up in Yayo's chest. It was the need to protect. The need to hold. The need to keep those she loved safe. The need to run and hide. She gripped the knife tightly in her left hand. She didn't know why she did this. They were safe. It was perhaps the shadow off to her left, near the front door. A flicker of flame caused the darkness at the top of the door to dance. Looking just for a moment, like the head of a bear.

Gunfire. Several shots. Far away. Further away than last time.

She exhaled the stored-up breath she hadn't been aware she was holding. She relaxed her shoulders. Of course she feared for her husband, and the further out that they went, the more dangerous it could be out there in the forest. But it also meant that danger was moving away from her home.

"My home," she said under her breath.

Her daughter perked her head up and looked at her mother. Yayo saw her open her mouth to say something, maybe to make fun of her for talking to herself, when the girl's face went white as bone.

She was looking at the kitchen window.

Yayo turned quickly. So fast that her baby laughed, enjoying the ride. The kitchen itself was empty of anything aside from onions hanging from the rafters, crates full of potatoes and rice, and a steel washbasin. Snow beat against the window, almost like rain. Splattering itself against the glass and leaving behind streaks of ice. Beyond that was the void of night.

Yayo put her hands on the floor and pushed herself to her feet, balancing the baby on her back.

She was still holding the knife. Now held out in front of her.

She walked over to the kitchen window.

Looked out.

At first, she could see nothing but the white whirlwind of the snow and the vague dark shapes of trees beyond. If it hadn't moved, she would never have noticed it. The large black mass, just outside the reach of the light from the window. Yayo peered closer, fogging up the window with her breath.

And recoiled when she saw them.

Animal eyes reflecting the minimal kitchen light. A brief glint, a momentary shine, before night swallowed them.

The mass rushed forward.

Breaking glass.

Window frame splitting.

Screaming.

Running.

Water pot upturned.

Hearth flames doused.

Steam rising.

Lantern knocked to the floor and shattering.

Darkness.

Yayo slashing the knife out into the darkness. Yelling for her daughter to follow her voice.

And more screaming.

AUTHOR BIO

S hawn Brooks is a horror and fantasy author living in Japan with his wife and Siberian husky. He teaches history for his day job, enjoys hiking and paddle boarding, and loves winter storms while lying comatose next to a fire with a good sake and a better book.

Other books by Shawn Brooks

Endless is the Night (Black Sun Book 1)

Under the Amber Wave (Black Sun Book 2)

Iomante (Black Sun Book 3)

Dead Roots of the Earth (Black Sun Book 4)

Above the Ashen Sky (Black Sun Book 5)

What Dances in the Dark (Short Stories)

Pine Haven (Short Stories)